CU01498306

BLURB

My father is Boston's **Pakhan.**

Powerful. Merciless. Unforgiving.

And he just arranged my marriage—

to his most dangerous enforcer.

Dmitri Volkov.

Cold. Controlled. *Sin wrapped in devotion.*

He kills for my father.

But on Christmas Eve... he'll vow himself to me.

A **sacred Bratva wedding.**

Blood vows. Candlelight. *No escape.*

He swears his promises are holy.

That once spoken, they can't be broken.

But I'm already keeping a secret.

A heartbeat he doesn't know about.

A truth that could *damn us both.*

Because when vows are lies,

love becomes a battlefield.

And when the cathedral erupts in gunfire,

my father dies in my arms—

while my groom bleeds at the altar.

Now blood stains the marble,

and the vows meant to save us...

might destroy everything we love.

This Christmas, when the echoes fade—

will our baby ever know the love of its parents...

or be swallowed by the war that made us?

Author's Note: A dark, emotional **Bratva Christmas romance** where vows are sacred, love is dangerous, and one secret changes everything.

Arranged marriage • Age gap • Secret pregnancy • Mafia power • Holiday passion

BOUND BY THE CHRISTMAS VOWS

AVA GRAY

Copyright © 2025 by Ava Gray

All rights reserved.

No part of this book may be reproduced in any form or by any electronic or mechanical means, including information storage and retrieval systems, without written permission from the author, except for the use of brief quotations in a book review.

❀ Formatted with Vellum

1

VALYA

I'm not supposed to drip pizza grease on an illuminated manuscript, but here we are, me and mushroom slices and a leather-bound book of Russian fairy tales, and the page with the firebird has taken a shine in the corner that I will never be able to explain to a conservator. The gargoyles on the exterior cornice do their usual performance of judgment, faces set in the kind of long-suffering disdain that looks very convincing through snow.

Wind throws lace across the windowpanes and the whole of Beacon Hill holds its breath. Inside, the estate glitters the way a cathedral does when someone rich has confused reverence with chandeliers. There are gold trims where there should be plain moldings and antique crosses that have known more gossip than prayer, and a neat little lens in the smoke detector that is not a smoke detector at all.

I lick my thumb, dab at the glittering grease spot, and make it worse. The saints on the icon above my bookshelf look down with beautifully painted patience. I raise my slice toward them like a toast.

"Don't judge me. It is mushroom and not even pepperoni. This is practically fasting."

I'm twenty-five, and this room has been mine since I was old enough to understand that doors can be locked from both sides. My suite is at the top of my father's estate, two rooms and a private balcony that collects snow like sugar on a tart, a bathroom tiled in green stone that always looks like it is wet even when it is not, and an adjoining dressing room where fur coats hang beside thrifted sweaters I pretend no one sees. The guards stationed at my door downstairs are selected for their loyalty and their convenient blindness. My driver is a professional who respects schedules. He is also a man who believes that if a young woman ducks out of a moving car near the corner of Columbus Avenue and vanishes into the night, it is probably because she spotted a sale on winter boots.

On the carpet near the door, four labeled cardboard boxes wait in a tidy row like obedient children. One says *Coats* in my neat handwriting and another says *Toys* and another says *Pantry*. The last one is *Books*. I have sorted them the way only a person who has alphabetized her spices does, and the tape is squared and uncompromising. I keep the ledger for the community program under a stack of *Vogue* magazines because no one in this house has ever willingly moved a *Vogue*. This is the part of my life that doesn't fit here, the South End Christmas program that Reza and I run for families who don't attend charity galas because they are too busy holding down two jobs. We are not a registered nonprofit with gala invitations and embossed thank-you notes. We are people who want kids to open something that feels like love on Christmas morning. I keep our lists in a small black notebook and in my phone under a code name that would make my grandmother sigh with pride and my father summon three men with guns.

The pizza box is not near the charity boxes. It lives on my coffee table because I'm a responsible adult who cannot be trusted with tomato sauce near wool coats.

I wipe my hands, close the fairy tale book on its silk ribbon, and stand up on the couch to reach the icon shelf, because I'm not tall and I refuse a step stool on principle. The room smells like snow and oregano and the faint lemon of furniture polish. I light a small beeswax taper and whisper the kind of prayer my grandmother taught me when I was six and convinced that God listened most closely to small girls with sincere intentions. *Bless the work of our hands. Keep my father safe. Keep me invisible. Forgive the grease.*

My wardrobe is a battle that I rarely win. I pull a fur-lined cape over a hoodie and consider myself both designer and disgrace. Sneakers or boots? Boots. Boots say I don't intend to run, although the truth is that I have been running in place for years. I tug my braid over my shoulder, check my mouth for sauce, and practice a smile that reads as harmless. I'm very good at harmless. People assume harmless will not overthrow their plans.

I carry the flat of books to the door, their weight significant. There is something beautiful about hardback spines, the way they declare themselves with a straight line, as if they are sure of what they contain. I press the elevator call button with my elbow and hum a line of a carol under my breath because all the streaming services have insisted it is already

Christmas even though it is only advent, which is the season for thinking instead of celebrating.

The elevator doors open with their usual sigh.

The man inside is not a guard and not a servant and not a guest. He is not anyone who belongs here. The first thing that happens is not thought. It is recognition, the body knowing danger the way a deer does when the forest goes quiet.

Dmitri Volkov stands with his hands loose at his sides, a black coat open to a dark suit that looks like it understands violence. He is taller than the threshold wants him to be, lean in the precise way of someone who can move without sound, and his eyes are iron pale under lashes that would be pretty on a woman and are alarming on a man who doesn't smile. His hair is close cut and not soft. A thin white scar bisects his eyebrow. There is a shadow of ink near the open collar of his shirt, the suggestion of a cross or a line of words that disappears under fabric, and my mind does a very impractical thing. It wonders how far the ink goes.

The elevator thinks we are both entering and chimes again in confusion.

"Good evening," he says, in Russian first and then in English, and both versions are low and exact. There is no attempt at charm. His voice sounds like it could be kind if it ever had permission. It doesn't have permission now.

I could step back. I don't. I step in, and the box in my arms tilts, a paperback slides, and *Anna Karenina* in an unfortunate translation drops to the elevator floor with a slap. He bends before I can, quick as a hawk, and his fingers close around the book. They are steady. There is a faint scrape of dark ink on his wrist when his cuff rides up. It is something that is not a bracelet and not a watch and tells a story I don't know with characters that look like old church script. He hands the book back to me and our fingers don't touch, which *should* be a relief and is not.

"Thank you," I say, English because I'm less likely to blush in English, and then my mouth betrays me. "The old woman throws herself under the train because men are cowards."

He looks at the cover for a heartbeat and then at me. "Some men," he says with an infuriating shrug that makes him look goddamned sexy.

There is a pause in which every neuron in my brain opens small curtains to look out. I could be polite and silent. Instead, I decide to lean into the part of me that is not polished. I tip the box up against my hip and offer him a wobbly smile.

"You are here for my father," I say.

He studies me the way people study paintings when they are trying to decide whether they are looking at a master-piece or a forgery. "Yes. There is business I must discuss with him."

Everyone in this house knows what business Dmitri has with Father. The men who shadow me in hallways know his footsteps by sound. He is my father's right hand, which is a quaint way of describing a weapon. He has the reputation of the most powerful and underrated sword in battle.

I should say *it is nice to see you this evening, Mr. Volkov*, and then stare at the elevator numbers. I shouldn't look at the line of his throat or the place where the ink disappears under his shirt. I shouldn't be a person who is curious.

"Well, I suppose I'm in a bit of trouble with him," I say, because I'm also a woman who understands titles and their use. "You know that."

Something almost like humor touches his mouth. "I know that."

I cannot stop my eyes from flicking to his wrist again. The ink is a small confession. He follows my glance because he is a hunter, and then he lifts his cuff just a fraction in the way a man might adjust his sleeve. The edge of something dark and ancient curves along the bone. I try to keep my voice even and fail.

"Is that Old Church Slavonic?" I ask, which is the most embarrassing sentence I have ever offered a stranger in an elevator. "On your wrist."

He could choose threat. He chooses truth. "Yes."

"What does it say?" I ask, and then I realize what I have done and heat rushes into my face. "You don't have to tell me. It is not my business. You don't know me. I could be very untrustworthy."

He looks at the book box with its tidy label and the ink on the floor where Anna left a smudge and the bookmark sticking out of my fairy tale volume. He looks at my boots and the one salt stain I forgot to clean. He looks at the small smear of pizza sauce near my wrist that I had not noticed. The corner of his mouth turns the minute amount that counts as a smile in a man who doesn't offer them cheaply.

"It says *By Honor and Pain*," he says. "My choice. No one else's."

The elevator opens on the ground floor. He steps out, and I follow with my books, which are now heavier than they were because the air has changed weight. The corridor smells like wax and old wood and the smoke of candles that have been out for hours. Two of the house guards stand by the staircase pretending they are not listening. Dmitri moves with the unremarkable grace of someone who has had to build a body he can trust. His coat falls back, and there is the outline of a holster that would make any reasonable woman run. I don't. I angle the box on the console table to check the labels before I send them with the driver. I don't mean to glance again at his hands. I do.

"Thank you for returning Anna to me," I say, because I'm strange and I cover it with formality. "She is good company on nights like these."

"Your father will not like the pizza," he says almost gently. "He will pretend it is the most offensive thing you have done this week."

I make a small face. "It is not."

He doesn't ask for the list. It is for the best. I clear my throat. "It was nice to meet you."

"You too," he says, and he doesn't move until I turn back to the elevator and press the button with my elbow. When the doors close, I watch him for a second longer than is appropriate because I'm an idiot who has read more novels than is healthy.

Inside my suite again, I set the books back near the door and fold my hands against my mouth the way a small child does when she knows she has misbehaved. My heart is doing its own carol and my cheeks are warm and my brain is trying to write a poem about the angle of his wrists that I will never admit to anyone. He is older, he is ruthless, he is the definition of not safe. He is also not my problem. I belong to fairy tales and schoolwork and small acts of rebellion that smell like cinnamon and laundry soap. I don't belong to any of this. The part of me that is my grandmother's voice whispers that vows are holy things. The part of me that is my father's daughter catalogs the way Dmitri stood between me and the guards without thinking about it. I refuse to let either part rule the night.

I open the ledger to the next page and cross-check the wish lists for the Nelson family and for Mrs. S, who doesn't want her name in any book because she is hiding from a man who married her and forgot the meaning of the word. I text Reza a photo of the boxes and the little smile I make in the corner of my mouth when something is finished. He replies with a string of celebratory mugs. I look at the time and sigh. If I run down the back stair and avoid the hallway camera that has a dead spot near the Cullinan landscape, I can get the pantry box into the service corridor without any of the older men who think I'm a relic noticing. There is something satisfying about the choreography of mischief.

The snow deepens its quiet. Somewhere downstairs, a radio murmurs in Russian about a soccer match from last week and the clink of glass sounds like an argument being shaken. I put on a different sweater because the old one smells like pizza, and I'm not giving my father the pleasure of that joke. I slide my phone into my pocket, slip my grandmother's tiny crucifix on a chain under my hoodie where it can rest against my skin, and carry the pantry box back to the elevator. The doors open and the car is empty. My reflection looks like a woman who knows better. I decide to forgive her.

The service corridor is narrow and practical. It smells like starch and black tea and the secrets of linen closets. I set the box by the door we use for deliveries and tape the little note on top that says *For Reza*. The ink smudges because the cold sneaks under the weather strip, and I dust it dry with my sleeve and wonder if anyone else in this house knows what it feels like to put your name on something that is not yours and be proud anyway.

On the way back, my phone buzzes. I look without thinking and see a name that makes the back of my neck ice. I don't open the message. I delete it. I'm annoyed to discover that a man can still upset me with a digital vibration two years after he took himself to New York and sealed himself behind a glass wall of his own ambition after promising me he would be different from the rest. I'm a scientist of my own heart. I refuse to let a subject contaminate the study surface. I return to my room and slam the bathroom cabinet a little too hard because this is the kind of emotional maturity I'm working with tonight.

When I open the door to the sitting room again, my father is standing beneath the arch like a statue that has learned disappointment as a first language.

He doesn't knock. He never does. He fills the doorway with winter, a broad man in a black coat cut to hide a body that still remembers youth even if the lungs have begun to forget. His hair has gone silver in a way that makes strangers trust him. He smells faintly of myrrh and tobacco and the whisper of cold air from the chapel downstairs. He looks at me, at my boots, at the fairy tale on the coffee table, at the pizza box with a face like he has had to sit through every bad opera in Moscow.

"Valentina," he says, and the name is an entire history. He sees the charity boxes near the door and his mouth tightens as if cardboard can insult him. He sees the pizza, and his eyes move very slightly toward heaven as if to ask for strength.

"Hi, Papa," I say, because I'm still his girl even when I want to throttle every patriarch in a five-mile radius. "Do you want a slice? It is mushroom. It is basically salad."

He says nothing. He crosses the room with deliberate grace and picks up the pizza box like it might explode. He opens it, regards the humble survivors of my dinner like they are a chemical experiment gone wrong, and closes the lid. He sets it down like one sets down a small animal that has died.

"Our kitchens are staffed by people who can cook," he says in the voice that would make a lesser person fold their lungs into origami. "You choose to offend them."

"I choose to save them the trouble," I say. "I'm adapting to modern times. Convenience food is a sign of a historical era. Think of me as an anthropological study."

"This," he says, and gestures in a circle that includes my hoodie and the fairy tales and the boxes that hold other people's Christmas, "is not an era. It is a performance."

"It is also a pantry drive," I say. "Please don't confuse pizza with beans. The one is for my stomach. The other is for people who need actual food."

"You slip away," he says, ignoring my distinction with the skill of a politician. "You evade protection. You invite eyes we don't want. There are men in this city with nothing to do but look for a weakness in my house, and you walk around offering them choreographed opportunities."

I sit on the arm of the couch because he hates it when I do and because I need a little height. "I walk to a church basement and sort donated coats by size," I say. "If this brings down the Kirov empire, perhaps the empire is not as stable as you think."

He lifts his gaze to the icon and then back to me. "You make jokes in order to avoid the seriousness of the world."

"I make jokes in order to survive the seriousness of this family," I say, and then I regret the steel in it because he and I have a rule about verbal knives. He doesn't flinch. He sets his hands behind his back in the stance that says he is either about to bless me or sentence me to a very polite prison.

"Your driver reports that you left his car on Tremont Street last week and vanished for ten minutes."

"He is a liar. It was eleven."

"Do you think you are clever?" he asks, and his eyes are not angry and not sad, which frightens me more than either. "Do you think you are the first Kirov to pretend the world will wait while she has a good time?"

"I don't have a good time," I say, and the heat in my voice gains words before I can stop it. "I carry crates. I make lists. I tape boxes. I listen to other people talk about rent. I stay alive by pretending I'm not drowning in chandeliers."

His mouth softens for a fraction. It vanishes almost at once. "You are my daughter," he says quietly. "You are not a social worker. You are not a ghost. You are not a symbol for common people to project fantasies upon. You don't understand how quickly kindness can turn to leverage."

"I do," I say. "I understand the cost of everything in this house." My thumb rubs the crucifix, a reflex whenever my father presses me with his plans.

He studies me. The room stays suspended. He looks at the boxes again and the way I have written in block letters like a schoolteacher. He looks at my braid and the crucifix that is hiding under my sweater but never hides from him. He looks past me as if he can see the chapel as he always does when he needs strength. When he speaks again, his voice has changed, thinner in a way that makes the back of my own throat hurt. "Enough, Valya. You are going to do what I say. No more choices, no more questions. There's a man I've chosen for you."

2

DMITRI

I leave the elevator, and the last of her clings to the air, cool and light, and then dies before it reaches my face. The doors close behind me with a sound like a decision made. My mind is not where my feet are. It is still in the car with her, measuring the tilt of her chin and the way she asked about the ink on my wrist as if language were something you could touch. Pleasant. Not the kind of rich that forgets how to say thank you. I shake my head. She is still too wild for my taste, the sort of wild that leaves doors ajar and windows unlatched. I prefer bolts that seat cleanly and keys that turn only in my hand.

Order is how I breathe. Knives oiled, laces tied the same way every morning, sheets pulled tight enough to teach the body honesty. I write the day in rows in my head and move through them one at a time—check the cameras, walk the perimeter, and count which men look at the floor when I pass and how many look up. Every room is a problem with an answer if you refuse to let noise pretend to be music.

My phone buzzes in my pocket. I glance and keep moving. A contact sends a time and a street that don't belong together. I file it where it goes and don't miss the shadow by the chapel wall. The lamp throws it long and thin across the stone, feet set in like a winter bear ready to turn space into readiness. That silhouette is as familiar as my coat.

Misha, my second-in-command, his coat turned up against the ache of the wind, his beard dusted with gray that comes from staying alive. He doesn't waste words when I step under the arch and let the cold take my face.

"Southie is moving," he says, syllables set like bricks. "L Street and the projects. Vetrov's boys. Likely Grekov's money." I smell it in the cold. His money stinks, perfume for men without honor.

"He is the new breed that wants the underworld run like a corporation," I say through my teeth.

"Appearances fill coffers faster than incense." Misha scratches his beard.

I look at his knuckles. Old Slavonic runes caught in candle-light. "We keep vows, Misha."

"Old ways keep bones straight but slow our feet." Misha grunts. He says our men were pushed off the pier fingers. An unauthorized crate landed on our turf.

"Sasha took a graze and laughed. He will live until I find use for his courage." He wipes snow from his beard, shoulders set like a wall, waiting.

"Sergei picked L Street for a reason," I say. "He likes to make a point in old places." If Sergei wants to drag the city by my ankle and call it strategy, that is the kind of insult I answer not with volume but with accuracy.

Sergei Vetrov comes into my mind with the clarity of a problem I have no intention of admiring, a mouth that pronounces tradition as if it were a childhood disease. He mistakes novelty for evolution and calls vows a tourist story to be sold with the souvenirs. He insists that order can be replaced by leverage and fear is a permanent currency.

"Who are the hands?" I ask, because names set the shape of a night.

"Soft-palmed drivers and a Chelsea face I don't enjoy," Misha answers, and he keeps the rest in his eyes, the small reckoning that the docks always demand. The docks tell me Grekov is laundering confidence along with the rifles because this is a song I have heard in three languages.

"We don't like many men from Chelsea," I say. "Bring the car."

We take the covered path into the service hall, let the estate's heat wrap our bones, and move on without tasting it. I prefer stairs that echo less and corridors that have been scrubbed so often they confess lye and salt and the old taste of blood.

The car is a mean black one that squats at the curb like a threat on four wheels, paint so deep it drinks the street-lights. The driver keeps his eyes pinned to the windshield, hands at ten and two, jaw locked, mirror never drifting toward the rear seat where I sit breathing order back into my bones. The city slides under us in a slick ribbon, tires whispering, chassis steady, the whole machine moving like a sled over winter glass.

I think, because I'm obliged to be honest with myself when I wear a cross, that Sergei's timing is not chance. He smells winter in Anatoly's lungs and calculates how many candles remain on the altar of a man who taught me to read a room before I mastered the alphabet.

The club in Dorchester sits behind a tired shutter that pretends to sell used speakers, a lie that must be told loudly to be believed. The back corridor smells of bleach and brine and the clean twang of metal. Its underground vaults keep the accounts no banker will admit exist. I walk into the locked room with the tiled floor that I don't enter unless I must.

I earned more than hallways a long time ago. Anatoly keeps me close and gives me war but not a seat. The young soldiers fear me and tolerate the old man because they still know the color of his hands. Power is a weight I already carry. I don't need a crown to feel it. Still, when the talk dies in a room because I have entered and the map of Southie waits under my palms with pins like small red prayers, something in my chest remembers that I was thirteen when a fixer told me I could be more than a number in a ledger. He was right. He did not say the price would be my voice.

"Here," Misha says, tapping the parish block where the mural of saints watches the wrong kind of worship on summer nights. "He set the line at St. Monica's block and paraded a young soldier under the saint's mural so the mothers would see. Sergei wants tongues to carry his name over breakfast."

"Then he wants them to remember mine when they put children to bed," I answer, because we keep order not to be loved but to be predictable. "We keep it clean," I add. It means no broken windows at the school, no stray rounds disturbing old men who play cards under a heat lamp, no theatrics that make the sinners look like saints.

Sasha comes in with his shoulder taped and a face like a stubborn animal. He is quick to laugh and quicker to bleed. I will have to keep him alive. He is the kind who will not keep himself. He nods at me with the reverence young men save for the idea of a father.

"Vetrov has three cars and a truck," he says. "Black SUV with borrowed plates. Conlon's boys in the kitchens already took pictures. Someone had the bright idea to carry some suspicious crates through the alley. Sergei means to deliver a surprise tonight."

"Surprises belong to children and holidays," I tell him, not smiling. Sasha is learning. Vetrov plans a handoff tonight. "Call the driver. He will take the long way."

The street swallows us. South Boston holds the worn beauty of an old fighter, still able to pivot when unwatched. The air holds that thin knife-cold that finds the seam in every coat, and the snow has not yet committed to a full confession. The driver loops the long way into Southie and idles two blocks off L Street. We go in on foot, cutting the alleys, past metal stairs that complain and windows that watch.

The SUV idles without lights, the driver pulling on a cigarette with the lazy mouth of a man who has never had to run for a bus. Sergei is hiring men who don't know how to hold a life. The truck sits with its breath held because it knows in its mechanical bones that this corner belongs to someone else and that absence is a lie. Two men by the tailgate perform the posture of criminals who learned their craft by watching television. Their feet confess what their hands cannot.

"On my count," I say. Sasha's breath clouds the air in small bursts. The boy loves his counts. Time is a weapon.

On three, we open them like a lock that never fits the door. The driver turns toward the glow of his cigarette. I pull the door open and my hand closes on his collar before he remembers the word gun. I take the gun out of his hand after I have introduced his face to the frame. He sighs like men who thought they could buy a night and got a lesson instead.

Two men by the truck turn as if they heard a song they cannot place. Sasha brings one against the bumper and teaches his shoulder a new shape. The other reaches for his waistband, and I put his face on the hood before his fingers learn courage.

Misha appears with a man tucked under his arm like a disobedient child. The crate sits in the back, slats pried just loose enough to flash plastic and grease, the sickly shine that never belongs to anything good. I lift one corner and see what I expected—the familiar AK pattern in oiled steel. Sergei thrives on the old comforts.

Sasha jerks his chin at the truck bed. Under the crate sits a heavy square box, not ours. Greek letters scrawl the lid. I lift it. Foam, hard plastic cases, triggers that end nights fast. Sergei wants insurance and modernity. Some idiot thought that he could hide it like a priest can hide a knife under a cassock.

I close it with two fingers and give Misha the look that

means he will carry it to the basement safely. He nods because we have spoken this language for fifteen years.

Sergei's reinforcements arrive late and loud in a car, young men who wear the night the way children wear capes. When they see us, they form a circle of predators who have never had to finish anything they started. I don't let them taste the mistake because I prefer to teach in rooms without an audience. Two are enough for conversation. I send the driver back to his boss with a face that is not what his mother gave him. I just tell him to say my name correctly because names have teeth when spoken with attention.

We load two into the back and ride silently to Dorchester. They sit like stone. We walk the same dim corridor to a windowless anteroom. A single bare bulb glows without impatience. Except for a few chairs and a calendar from a hardware store with a woman dressed for a climate that is not ours, the only other feature is a drain placed where it needs to be.

I set my coat on the back of a chair and roll my sleeves with care. I cross myself because judgment without prayer is vanity, and then I do the work, not as a butcher, but as a man who has learned that patience breaks bone without leaving a mark you can photograph.

I have learned how to carve fear away from truth with a knife I keep hidden in the quiet edge of my tone. The younger one looks at his buddy for courage and finds none. He wears the badge of silence as if it will buy him a reputation. He is wrong. This is the sort of room that hears a hundred small lies and cannot be surprised anymore.

He breaks the way they all do when you let them feel safe for one minute and then take it away. He gives me the name of the man who received the crate on L Street. He gives me a time that smells like midnight. He gives me a place that doesn't matter. He gives me a sentence I don't like. "Christmas is good for business."

The second man tries to bargain. He tells me Sergei thinks Anatoly is an old saint with a tired heart and that the city wants a younger god. He calls power a stage and says Sergei will not clap from the seats. He strings together words he thinks make him sound like a man with vision.

I take control with a piano wire and my silence. When I stop, both men have learned that pain without purpose is noise. I don't make noise and end the lesson. They breathe. There is no need to decorate rooms with bodies. Sasha cleans the floor the way I showed him when he was eighteen and warming his hands on the engines of stolen cars. He hums to himself. I tell him to stop, and he stops.

The dock wind follows us back to Beacon Hill. The case in the trunk feels like an accusation. Misha drives with his mouth set and his eyes steady. The adrenaline has stepped off his bones. Snow comes hard now. On Dorchester Avenue, a man in a Santa hat sells hot dogs and salvation in the same shout. Sometimes, fools tell a kind of truth.

Beacon Hill looms black against the snow. We roll through the iron gates. Two watchmen lift the bar, check the plates, and wave us into the hush. Misha will log the case in the basement under my name because the chain of command is the spine of order. He will warn the guard on duty to sleep with both eyes open.

I don't seek my Pakhan. I take the back stairs to my room and let the hall grow quiet around me. My room is modest. The dark wooden bed remembers the hands that carved it. The rug on the floorboards is from a man near Tula who never wrote down a price because he wanted me to owe him. I put my things on the small table and stand for a moment before an icon corner where the Mother of God meets my eyes with a tenderness that breaks me if I let it.

I turn away, undress, and stand for a minute without the weight of cloth on my shoulders. The mirror throws back a body that was built to do work. Scars where history signed its name. The black ink of the Bratva insignia across my left chest, where loyalty anchors itself. I touch the bleeding cross over my heart with the old words that kept me alive when I was thirteen and starving and angry. *By honor and pain*, a vow marked in Old Church Slavonic shimmers along my ribs. They don't yet form a complete sentence because I have not finished earning it.

I wash the salt from my face, shave, and pour strong tea without sugar from my samovar. Setting the cup to the side of the icon shelf, I dress again, cloth over the cross, the weight of the holster settling where it always does, the ink cooling under the shirt.

In the quiet of the room, the thoughts I don't permit easily come back again. A girl at the top of a house that is too rich to be useful, sitting cross-legged and pretending the world cannot see her. Valentina Kirov with her braid and her sharp mouth and the way she looks at men like she has read the book that tells the truth about them. She moves through rooms like light that has decided to avoid glass.

Her name stays unspoken before God, a test withheld. I say nothing and feel everything. No boy sets a heart on a table to beg mercy. Love is not a word kept close. Protection is the choice, the only confession worth making.

The latch clicks. The door opens without a knock. Only one person would risk that. My half-sister Katya slips in with a red knit cap in her hand, her dyed hair cut blunt at the jaw, her boots loud against the floor. She tosses the cap onto the chair, seasoning the room.

"You look like a funeral," she says.

She frowns, touches the icon, and then says, "Tradition keeps you standing. But loneliness eats iron."

"I don't rust."

"You are thirty-nine," she shoots back. Then her voice thins, betraying something she hates. "You are tired."

"I'm working."

"You need a wife," she says softly. "Someone who knows your kind of holy."

I pour her tea because I don't know how to hold that sentence any other way. She watches me like she wants to see if there is still gentleness under my ribs. I let the steam fog the air between us.

She drains the cup, sets it down with a clink. "Fine. Ignore the sister who fixes your servers and your suspects." She leaves. The door shuts with a small sound that feels like a period at the end of a line. I stand for a moment with my hands on the back of the chair and let the muscles in my shoulders remind me that they still exist.

Katya's boots are hardly gone before the walls press close again. I must say my prayers. The estate chapel waits at the edge of the estate, its lamps dim, its air dry with incense and old wood. I cross myself, step inside, and let the hush take me. Icons watch from the walls, saints with eyes that know too much. I kneel before them, the stone cold beneath me. My words come easily.

My mother taught me prayers when fever burned her thin and luminous. Then she was gone, and the orphanage gave me rooms that stank of boiled potatoes and chlorine, beds too small for sleep, and fists that came quicker than food. Boston taught me that structure is the only boat a child can build when the sea comes in. That tradition is a spine strong enough to hold your head when nothing else will. That control is not cruelty. It is survival.

Lord have mercy. Christ have mercy. I don't come with petitions, only with the weight I carry and cannot name aloud. When I rise, the house is already shifting. It stirs with preparation for tomorrow's gala. Laughter climbs from the main stair, a piano threads through the rooms, chandeliers catch every polished surface. In my world, an enemy's enemy can be a friend. Tonight, the house whispers it in that language.

The room tightens to a single point. Valentina stands at the window, snow scoring lines against the glass. Her black silk makes her a silhouette of light, a crucifix gleaming at her throat. She doesn't move, doesn't need to, her stillness a dare. I count the distance between us, and in my mind, I erase it. She is beautiful and dangerous, untamed in a house built to break the wild.

God help me, I already choose her.

3

VALYA

Morning is the only hour that doesn't argue with me. The house still sleeps like a great animal with a jeweled collar. Cameras blink in a slow rhythm, and marble floors hold their breath as I walk the rug edges and practice vanishing. I carry the last box for the South End program against my hip, *PANTRY* written in neat block letters, and the elevator mirror returns my face—one girl who belongs to a house like this and one who might run, both of us sharing one mouth and an inconveniently honest pair of eyes.

Reza once said every escape is easier when it looks like an errand, and Baba Yaga in my head cackles while I turn it into a small art. I text my driver that I must stop at the library annex to return books, which is true because I'm carrying Tolstoy on top of beans. He replies with the exact thumbs up he sends when he doesn't want to know more. The service door breathes me into the courtyard, where the snow lies in delicate sheets on the boxwood. The gargoyles look pleased today to be dusted with sugar. I breathe the clean winter and feel the weight on my shoulders slip half an inch to the left, not freedom yet, but still a miracle.

In the car, I tuck my braid into my collar and pull the thrifted camel coat close. I hold the box on my lap like a sleeping cat, possessive and careful. Beacon Hill tilts its chin at the morning like a dowager who has earned her arrogance. The city below her stretches and mutters to itself like a clerk ticking through a list under their breath. Bus brakes sigh, storefronts yawn open as we take the long way to the South End. The short way passes a patrol car that has grown too friendly lately. The driver asks whether I will wait at the curb while he loops the block. I say yes in the voice reserved for doing the opposite.

The community center stands as a brick cube more forgiven than funded by City Hall, paint scuffed at the handrail, a bulletin board crowded with flyers for ESL classes, plus a notice about a lost calico cat. Inside, it smells like coffee, floor wax, and the kind of stubborn hope that dresses itself in tinsel. Reza lifts his head from behind the card table we pretend is an office and gives me his tired, patient smile, the one that includes every late-night email and every delivery of store-brand cereal I have ever bullied out of a wholesaler.

"You are early," he says, which is code for *I'm grateful you are here, and please avoid your driver seeing you.*

"I'm hiding, avoiding a breakfast with my father," I say, which is the kind of truth we trade like contraband.

We move like dancers on a floor. Reza peels tape, I stack cans by category because I believe beans should marry beans and never hide beneath peaches. We take inventory with the mutual pleasure of people who like lists for their clean edges. Mrs. S arrives with a pan of pastries and pretends she baked them, which means she went to the good bakery and asked for yesterday's tray at a discount. She presses a warm paper bag into my hands and tells me I look thin in a tone that is ninety percent affection and ten percent command.

The boxes I brought from the house sit like obedient children at the foot of the stage, *PANTRY, TOYS, BOOKS* stacked as straight as I could make them, and the hum in my chest eases. I cut another length of ribbon. I fuss. I write down Mrs. Liu's pledge because she forgot her glasses, not because I doubt her. Two more step up and ask for quiet credit. On the clipboard, I put *Anonymous A.L. and R.H.*. In my notebook, I write the names small and the words *no recognition* even smaller. This is the part of my life that makes sense. It is the same reason I memorize my grandmother's prayers— because tasks are the opposite of drowning.

I step out for ten stolen minutes into the pale winter light and walk to the corner cafe. The girl knows me as the woman who orders tea and tips like someone who never counts, which is half wrong. I slide into a table near the window and open my small black notebook full of schedules, sizes, lists, and the names I will never say upstairs. I sip my tea and taste cloves.

For a blessed ten minutes, I'm no one. A woman reads the paper, a man in paint-speckled jeans stirs his coffee and hums along to a song the radio almost remembers. Nobody here calls me princess. Nobody watches my mouth for moments I overrule my father's edicts. I finish, buy a sack of oranges, carry them like I'm bringing the sun home in segments. Reza teases that I'm bossy when I stack the oranges in a pyramid. We load his van. I put my hand flat on the door and promise it will not betray us, which is ridiculous and still feels like a binding. I check my watch and see the day pulling me back by the hem.

Toma waits by the loading ramp. Most afternoons, I find him there, knit cap tugged low, palms cupped around a paper star he folded from a donation flyer. He taps it twice against his chest, then points to me, his language made of eyes and small rituals.

Beacon Hill is a different planet by noon. The house has woken up into an orchestra of logistics. Florists in black carry in winter like a choreographed storm, white roses and pearled branches and garlands of cedar that perfume the hall with a memory of the forest my grandmother always said was God's first chapel. Men on ladders test the lights that will make the marble shine like ice. Someone in the kitchen laughs in Russian at a joke, and the laugh comes out tired and real.

Yelena meets me at the service entrance like a general on a mission, skirt in black, braid coiled at the nape of her neck, hands already reaching for my coat and for the oranges. She smells of cedar and soap and can do six things with two hands and makes them look like grace. I loved her before I knew what love was. She once hid me in a laundry cart during an argument laced with gunfire and hummed a lullaby that filled the hallway. She fusses over me in the careful way that mothers do. Her grief for the daughter the Bratva raid took from her has turned each gentle touch into a second chance she will not name.

"You look like the wind," she says, her way of saying I'm underdressed and smug.

"I brought oranges," I say, useless and proud.

"Good," she says and lifts the sack as if it weighs nothing, then tucks a stray piece of hair behind my ear with fingers that have set bones and kneaded bread with the same firm tenderness.

"Upstairs. Bath. Then we choose which face to wear."

I want to say the face I wear is always mine, but I kiss her cheek, smell flour and beeswax, and carry myself up the back stairs with a quickness I will deny later.

Hot water and eucalyptus pull the city out of my muscles. I let my hair down, and it falls halfway to my waist, rich chestnut, heavy with shine, carrying a faint veil of chapel smoke. I think of my grandmother's hands working a lifeline of braid, her voice telling me that a woman should know how to hold her crown. I smooth oil onto my skin. The mirror gives me a body I know too well, the scars I can count and the softness I guard, the crucifix shining with tiny stubborn light. I press it to my lips and ask for patience, the only thing I never owned outright.

Yelena arrives with a garment bag and a basket of cosmetics that looks like a painting of opulence. She lays everything out with a ritual that turns a dressing room into a sanctuary —a comb, pins, the velvet roll of Grandmother's rosary, a small jar of kohl mixed with rosewater that grandmothers bring out only when the city wants to believe in fairy tales. She parts my hair with diamond-cut precision and braids it low, then ties the end with a narrow carmine silk ribbon. She sets the braid into a shape that would catch any candle within ten meters. I pretend I don't want to wear the gown she chooses, pale silver with a slit for legs that know stairs. When she unzips the bag, the fabric unfurls with the hush of expensive secrets.

"You are not a picture," she says, easing the gown up and settling it on my shoulders like snow. "You are a reminder. Tradition is not a cage, Valya. It can be a handrail on black ice."

"My grandmother said a necklace can be a prayer," I answer. I touch the little crucifix where it rests at the hollow between my breasts, somehow both heavy and weightless, and think of her kneeling in a winter chapel with candles turning the air to honey, her voice as steady as a bell, while my father and his men argued about legacies and debts. Heat ghosts my palm. The tiny burn scar from vigil candles pricks like a remembered lesson, a white seed of pain I rub when I need courage.

Yelena paints my mouth with a color that could be a bruise or a blessing depending on the light, and she uses kohl on my eyes to make the brown look like burnished gold, then dusts my shoulders with a powder that smells like violets. By the time the gown settles and the red-and-silver ribbon glints and the slit proves its usefulness, I look like the kind of woman men write about and the kind of girl a grandmother can still recognize.

"You will be kind," Yelena says, smoothing the line of fabric over my hip, "and you will be ice when you need to be."

"I prefer snow," I say.

"I know," she answers and tucks a tiny sprig of pine into the braid as if to claim me for the season.

The house blooms hour by hour. Candles stand in ranks along the staircase like a procession of small saints. Musicians warm up in the gallery, their scales spilling like champagne bubbles. The first guests arrive with a murmur of expensive wool and good perfume, and the coat check becomes a theater of shrugged shoulders and practiced laughter. I stand at the top of the main staircase and pretend I'm a painting, then I descend because a painting cannot offer its hand to the mayor's wife and ask how her mother's hip is mending.

The Kirov winter gala dresses tradition for modern cameras. Place cards bear the family crest beside a discreet QR pledge to the Foundation, gilt icons printed on thick stock, a glass votive glowing electric where beeswax once burned. Everyone here knows the performance, and everyone is practiced at pretending the stage is a church.

I move through it like a queen exiled in her palace, smiling with a mouth that can bite, making small talk with politicians whose hands are too soft and with Bratva sons whose hands are too eager. From the service corridor, the kitchen breathes dill and lemon, the steam of fish and warm bread, a quiet signal of family beneath the din. I let that scent anchor me. I deflect a compliment about my gown by praising a woman's earrings. I soothe a councilman who wants reassurance that my father will never retire. I pat the hand of a judge who looks tired enough to be honest. I gather pledges with charm and a careful ledger memory, and when one young heir tells me he would like to make a private donation, I tell him we accept checks with signatures and not promises with winks.

Anatoly appears at my shoulder like a portrait that learned to move and tells the ambassador from somewhere cold that he is honored by his presence. I incline my head and let the men talk about stability as if it were a thing that can be loaded into a cruciform glass and sipped. I catch sight of Dmitri across the room, not moving. He wears black, which has everything to do with intent, shoulders built to teach a doorway respect, a stillness that reads as a threat until the passage feels earned. He speaks seldom, nods even less. Elders watch warily. The younger men do their best not to imitate him in front of witnesses.

When the Moscow import arrives, he is the exact kind of handsome that looks better reflected in a spoon, hair just long enough to be described with a sigh, cologne that would be expensive if it were not so eager. He introduces himself as Daniil Reznik. His vowels have a Moscow gloss that always makes me want to check my pockets for protection. He is one of Sergei Vetrov's recent acquisitions, a man who believes a fresh passport is a personality.

"Miss Kirov," he says, taking my hand in a grip that is polite for men who think possession is manners, "I have long wanted to meet the crown of Boston."

"I prefer citizen," I say, retrieving my fingers and the sensation in them. "Crowns bend the neck."

He laughs as if I told him a dirty story. His eyes slide to the slit in my gown and back up in a way that makes my grandmother's rosary cold against my skin.

"Your father has created quite an evening," he says. "You must allow me the honor of the next dance."

The waltz begins as if choreographed by my karmic enemy. He leads me to the floor with confidence. I step in because it is easier to step than to make a scene, and because I'm good at turning time into leverage. His hand at my waist lingers past politeness. His breath tries to lean on my ear. I keep my smile as diplomatic as a treaty that knows it will be broken, so I ask whether he is enjoying Boston. He says the architecture pleases him and the women are soft, and I say the weather is less forgiving than it looks. He twirls me with more force than necessary. I take my balance back without letting him see me flex for it.

"Sergei speaks of you," he says, and that is meant to be a threat, or a compliment, or foreplay. "He says you are the most valuable ornament in the Kirov collection."

"I'm not an ornament," I say gently. "I'm a knife that remembers where it came from."

He smiles in a way that says he doesn't hear words, only tones, and his hand slides a fraction lower, a fraction closer. I lift my chin and let the music end. I thank him with genuine relief disguised as courtliness. He bows and steals a look at my leg, then moves into the crowd with the swagger of a man who believes he has planted a flag.

I need air. I slip out the side door to the stone terrace that overlooks the courtyard, the snow clean as linen, the night calm in a city way that reminds me that silence is a sound. The cold strikes my bare shoulders with a sweetness that almost hurts. I stand with my hands on the stone and think of my grandmother lighting vigil candles, of my mother's perfumes lined like soldiers on her dressing table, of the way this house catches me in its palm every time I try to jump.

Footsteps scrape. I turn my head and see Daniil in the doorway, that smile again, the open collar of his tuxedo showing a chain that doesn't look like it knows any saints.

"You are difficult to catch," he says, crossing the stones with the easy arrogance of men who have never been told no by anyone they respect. "I prefer conversations away from the noise."

"I prefer conversations with content," I say. I don't step back because I never do.

He steps in close, closer than manners, closer than tolerance, and lifts his hand to the wall beside my shoulder. His fingers press near my waist with the confidence of a man who has always been punished too late for the wrong things. I bare my teeth behind a smile because I have been trained for diplomacy since I had knees. I turn my face away so that my crucifix is what he sees.

"Don't," I say, softly enough that the words are silk over steel.

He leans anyway. He puts his other hand on my hip. I catch his wrist in a grip that would make my father proud, but he is heavier than his manners, and I'm boxed by stone and by my refusal to scream for a room I will have to reenter. For a long breath, I consider breaking his finger, and I probably would if the door behind him did not open with a noise I feel in my spine.

Dmitri is there. The room rearranges itself around a man who doesn't have to announce to be believed. He crosses the terrace in one swift step, and his hand closes on Daniil's shoulder with a control that makes the body beneath it obey like a knee to a prayer. He doesn't look at me, not yet, because he is busy deciding how to remove a stain without getting it on the stone.

"Pakhan's dog," I mutter under my breath, because I'm cruel in very small ways when I'm afraid, and because I want to see if he will flinch.

He doesn't. He takes Daniil's face in one hand with a precision that wouldn't spill a drop if he were holding a chalice, and then he introduces it to the wall in a single fluid correction that is so efficient, it feels like hygiene. Daniil makes a noise that is mostly indignation with a little blood in it. Dmitri speaks low, Russian in his mouth like a blade he has polished, and I catch only the shape of the warning.

It is over fast. Daniil slumps with more insult than injury, which is probably worse for him. Dmitri releases him without theatrics and finally looks at me. It reads heat and location and safety before it reads anything else. I stand very straight. "don't fight me here," he says, and then his fingers close around my wrist.

4

VALYA

His grip on my wrist is like iron, pulling me down the back hallway of my father's estate, away from the glitter of the gala, away from the prying eyes that would never forgive this. My heels skid on the marble as he drags me through a side door, then shoves it shut behind us. The music from the ballroom muffles to a distant hum. It's just us now—me pressed against the cold wood, him looming like a storm cloud that has finally broken.

"Do you know what you looked like tonight?" Dmitri's voice is low, dangerous, the accent curling sharp around every word. "Parading in that silver dress, slit to your hip, showing every man in that room what belongs to me."

I want to argue, to bite back with something cruel. But his hand is already on my thigh, dragging the silk higher, his other palm braced above my head, caging me in. His eyes burn down into mine, ice-gray and merciless, and my mouth betrays me.

"Maybe I wanted you to notice."

His jaw flexes. Then his mouth is on mine—brutal, claiming, devouring. He tastes of vodka and smoke, his tongue thrusting past my lips like he owns the right to take. My gasp feeds him. He growls into me, grinding his hips against mine, and I feel the thick, hard press of him through his trousers.

He breaks the kiss only to drag his mouth down my throat, sucking hard until the bruise blooms, sharp and stinging. "I'm going to mark you everywhere," he murmurs against my skin. "So no man forgets who you belong to. Not your father. Not Sergei. Not anyone."

His hand finds my breast through the silk, palming me roughly, thumb circling the nipple until it stiffens against the fabric. I arch helplessly into his touch. He chuckles, low and cruel. "Such a spoiled little princess. But this body was made for me."

I gasp as he yanks the straps of my gown down, baring me. The cold air hits my nipples before his mouth does, hot and wet, sucking one deep, teeth scraping. My cry echoes in the small room. He switches, tugging the other with his teeth while his hand pinches the first. The pain makes me moan.

"Dmitri."

He pulls back just enough to snarl, "Say my name again. Say it when you scream."

I can't think. His hand slides lower, under my skirt, fingers finding me wet and ready. He groans, a sound so filthy it makes my thighs shake. "Look at you. Drenched already. Tell me, Valentina—did you touch yourself before this party, knowing I'd be watching you?"

I bite my lip, defiant, but his finger circles my clit and I break with a whimper. His laugh is dark, victorious.

"You'll learn," he growls, pressing two thick fingers inside me without warning, stretching me until I cry out. "You'll learn what it means to be taken by a man, not some boy who whispered lies in your ear."

His other hand fists in my hair, tugging my head back so he can mouth over my throat again, sucking hickeys into every inch of skin he can reach. My body writhes against him, torn between fighting and giving in.

He drags his fingers out of me, slick with my arousal, and shoves them into my mouth. "Suck."

I obey, sucking hard, my tongue curling around his fingers, tasting myself. His cock twitches against my hip and he groans, eyes closing for half a second. When he looks at me again, it's feral.

"You'll take my cock the way you're sucking my fingers. Deep. Hungry. No complaints."

He pulls his hand free, then grabs my waist, turning me toward the long oak desk in the corner. Papers scatter as he shoves me forward, pressing my chest against the polished surface, my ass raised high. His palm smacks down hard, the sound echoing, the sting making me cry out.

"You think you can mock me? Call me your father's dog?" His voice is rougher now, lower, his hand spanking me again, harder, until the burn spreads. "I'll show you what I am. I'll fuck you until you can't walk back into that ballroom without everyone knowing you've been ruined by me."

My thighs tremble, wetness slicking down them, humiliated by how much his filthy threats make me ache.

He leans over me, his breath hot at my ear. "Open your mouth, princess. Beg me to give you what you need."

The smack of his palm still burns across my ass when he shifts behind me. I hear the rasp of his breath, the low scrape of his belt buckle, and for a moment I think he's going to take me now—rough, merciless, like he promised. But instead, the weight of him disappears.

I glance back over my shoulder, chest pressed to the cold desk, and my breath catches. Dmitri is on his knees.

"Don't move," he growls, hands gripping my thighs hard enough to bruise. He spreads me open, baring me shamelessly. "You want to mock me like a dog? Then I'll eat like one."

The first drag of his tongue is brutal, a flat, wet stroke from my entrance up over my clit, slow and deliberate. My cry echoes sharp against the paneled walls. He groans low in his chest, like the taste of me is something he's been denied for too long.

"Sweet little cunt," he mutters into me, lips and tongue working like he's devouring a feast. "I knew you'd be dripping for me. Do you even realize how wet you are?"

I can't answer. My fingers claw at the polished desk, my body arching back against his mouth. He licks me again, slower, circling my clit with the tip of his tongue until my thighs shake. Then he plunges in deep, tongue fucking me hard, groaning like a man starving, each growl vibrating straight through me.

I bite my lip so hard I taste blood, trying to keep the sound down. His response is immediate—he smacks my ass, hard, making me cry out.

"Don't you dare hide those sounds from me," he growls, licking me again, rougher. "I want every scream, every moan, every filthy little whimper. Give them to me."

He buries his face deeper, tongue stabbing into me, his nose grinding against my clit until I'm thrashing against the desk. His grip on my thighs tightens, keeping me spread wide, open for his mouth. His groans grow louder, wetter, spit dripping down his chin as he eats me like he's gone feral.

I can't breathe. I can't think. My body is vibrating, every nerve raw, every muscle trembling as I ride his tongue without meaning to, grinding down like I need it more than air.

"Dmitri—" My voice breaks, sharp and desperate.

He pulls back just enough to growl, his mouth slick with me. "Say it properly."

"Please. Please don't stop."

He chuckles, low and dark, before diving back in, tongue circling my clit now in slow, punishing laps. His pace is deliberate, cruel, drawing me up higher and higher but never letting me fall. He switches, sucking my clit hard into his mouth, then dragging it between his teeth until I scream.

"Good girl," he groans, his voice muffled against me. "Shake for me. I want to feel you break on my tongue before I even put my cock in you."

My body obeys him before my mind can resist. I'm trembling, thighs quaking, the edge so sharp it's almost unbearable. Every stroke of his tongue drags me closer until I'm practically vibrating, nails clawing at the desk, my cries spilling shamelessly and brokenly.

His mouth is merciless. Every flick of his tongue, every hard pull of his lips on my clit, has me spiraling tighter, body clenching against him like I'll shatter. The edge comes rushing, sharp and brutal, but just as I begin to fall, Dmitri pulls back with a growl, his mouth glistening with me.

"No," he rasps, standing in one fluid motion. His hands grab my waist and drag me back off the desk, shoving me against it again, face pressed down, ass arched high. "You don't get to come yet. Not until I fuck it out of you."

I'm trembling already, slick and aching, when I feel the thick head of his cock pressing against my soaked entrance. He slides in with one brutal thrust, burying himself deep to the hilt. The stretch is overwhelming, tearing another cry from me, my body jerking against the desk.

"Christ," he snarls, voice breaking. "You're so fucking tight, I can feel you trying to strangle me."

My legs shake as he withdraws and slams back in, setting a punishing rhythm that leaves me gasping. His hips drive hard against mine, each thrust pushing me flat against the polished wood, the slap of skin echoing sharp and filthy in the quiet room. His hands grip me, one tangled in my hair, the other pinning my hip, forcing me to take every inch.

The overstimulation is unbearable. His tongue had me raw, trembling, so close I thought I'd die—and now his cock is pounding into me, grinding deep, each stroke threatening to snap me in half.

I can't stop the way I clench around him, can't stop the broken sobs spilling from my lips. "Dmitri, please..."

"Please what?" he growls, yanking my head back so I'm forced to see us in the mirror. His cock spears into me again, deep and brutal. "Look at yourself. Look at how you tremble on my cock. You think you can run from me when this is what you do? When your body begs me to keep going?"

The mirror shows it all—my flushed face, tears streaking down my cheeks, breasts bouncing with each thrust, and his cock disappearing into me, slick and brutal. My body jerks helplessly, caught in his grip, trembling as he fucks me harder, deeper, grinding every nerve raw.

"You're mine," he snarls into my ear, hips snapping against me with vicious precision. "Every clench, every cry—it all belongs to me. You'll come when I say. Not before."

My vision blurs. My body is vibrating, shaking uncontrollably, every thrust dragging me closer but never letting me fall. His hand slips between my thighs, fingers stroking my swollen clit as his cock drives into me from behind.

The combination is unbearable. I sob into the desk, my whole body racked with tremors, every muscle taut, every nerve burning with the desperate need to let go.

His fingers circle my clit in ruthless rhythm, every stroke timed to the deep drag of his cock pounding into me from behind. I'm already trembling, already wound so tight it feels like my skin can't contain me. His pace is relentless, punishing, like he wants to carve me open and brand me with every thrust.

"Dmitri—oh God—" My voice is broken, torn between pleading and surrender.

"Say my name when you fall," he growls against my ear, his teeth scraping my skin. His hips slam into me again, harder, sharper. "I want the whole fucking house to know who makes you come."

The overstimulation is unbearable—his cock wrecking me deep, his fingers stroking me raw, his voice in my ear, dark and commanding. My body jerks violently, my legs giving out, but he doesn't let me fall. His arm locks around my waist, holding me upright, forcing me to take every brutal thrust.

And then it breaks.

The orgasm crashes over me like a violent wave, ripping through my body with sharp, uncontrollable tremors. My scream is muffled against my own arm, my cunt clamping down around his cock so hard, it drags a guttural groan from his chest.

"Christ—yes," he snarls, pounding into me faster, riding out the spasms of my body as if he's trying to fuck the orgasm deeper into me. "That's it. That's it. Squeeze me, Aoife. Milk my cock."

I can't stop shaking, my body convulsing with aftershocks while he keeps thrusting, using my spasms like a grip, fucking me harder and harder through the pleasure that borders on pain. My vision blurs, my mouth open on silent cries, my nails raking the desk as he drives me past any point I thought I could survive.

"Look in the mirror," he growls, dragging my head back, forcing my dazed eyes to focus on our reflection. "Look at yourself trembling while I fuck you. Look at what you are when you're mine."

The sight is obscene—my body quaking, breasts bouncing, his cock buried inside me slick and raw, stretching me wide as he pounds deeper. I sob, another shudder tearing through me, my body clenching helplessly around him as another wave threatens.

"Don't stop," I choke out, desperate, wrecked. "Please—don't stop."

He bites down on my shoulder, growling against my skin as his hips keep driving, merciless, grinding me into the desk, fucking me like he'll never let me go.

He grinds deeper, faster, dragging every last tremor from my body until I'm limp against the desk, my cheek pressed to the cool surface, breath shattered and broken. My cunt still flutters around him, sensitive, overused, pulling his cock tighter with every aftershock.

"Enough," he rasps, his voice wrecked, guttural. His thrusts grow rougher, uneven, every stroke a battle between restraint and the hunger he's been holding back. His grip on my waist turns bruising, hauling me back to meet his thrusts.

"Dmitri—" My voice is hoarse, a plea and a warning all at once.

"Can't hold it—fuck." He snarls against my skin, teeth gritted as he rams into me one last time before dragging out, his cock glistening, swollen, slick with me.

The next moment is fire.

Hot, thick spurts spill across the curve of my ass, streaking my back, dripping down my thighs. His release hits me in hard ropes, messy, marking me, his hand still stroking himself as he groans through it, head thrown back, chest heaving.

I watch in the mirror—watch him spill every last drop on my body, the look of ruin and reverence on his face, the sight of his cum glistening on my skin obscene and beautiful all at once.

When he's finally wrung dry, he collapses against me, his weight heavy, his breath hot and ragged against my neck. His hands are still on me, sliding down my hips, claiming even in the aftermath. "You belong with me, Valentina. And God help me, I will show you what it is like to be loved by a man, a real man."

A shiver runs up my spine as the words register deep in my gut. His words are terrifying, yet, they are all that I want to hear. And they stay with me long, long after he puts his clothes back on and leaves.

5

DMITRI

After leaving Valentina, I head back to the party, although it is the last thing I want to do. Valentina will likely return shortly as well. There is enough work to keep me busy the next day, but no matter what I do, I cannot shake the image of Valentina's mouth, her moans, her body arching beneath mine.

The last I saw of Daniil Reznik in the corridor is a thin line of red and a curse, still upright on pride and luck. I send Misha three words, *make it tidy*. He can do the math—walk Reznik out through the service hall, ice his mug, scrub the phone, and sell the fall on the terrace. His reply lands before the buzz dies, *on my way*. The terrace must vanish from the night, and Sergei's dog must return to rumor with nothing worth repeating.

The ballroom meets me with noise I can read. Laughter is high and thin on the stairs, which is a sign of nerves, not joy. Glasses kiss and don't ring, so deals remain unsettled. Cutlery keeps a steady march where hired muscle is eating. Russian syllables lengthen by the balcony, which means a late arrival of rank. At the coatroom, fur collars lean close, voices dip, pockets settle heavier. Money moves. I move through it as through an incident cordon, hands quiet, face neutral, permission and warning in one.

I take the service passage toward the chapel. The little side door is open. The chapel is dark except for the faithful flame of two vigil candles that are not meant to go out until morning. Someone has left the lavabo filled. The water is cool and clean. I rinse the scrape, and the sting is sharp enough to help. My reflection in the brass is warped. My mouth is a line.

I make the sign of the cross without thinking, fingers moving—brow, chest, shoulder, shoulder. My mother's voice rises from the old room inside me. The words find air even as the music down the hall shifts tempo. *Lord, have mercy. Christ, have mercy. Lord, have mercy.* I don't pray for enemies. I pray that order doesn't forsake me and that my hands don't fail. The cadence puts my pieces back where they belong. I don't smell blood anymore, while candlelight goes on forgiving whatever it touches, and that makes me grateful.

Then I step into the light and let the room fall into its proper grid. Men and their wives when they think no one is watching. Young soldiers trying not to look at the doors. The room remembers who is in charge, so I enforce it. I make one clean circuit, not prowling, correcting. A glance puts a guard on the east exit. Two fingers rest on the balcony rail where a lens might try for courage. A nod sends a busboy to wipe the camera halo and keep moving.

From the corner of my eye I catch Reznik's exit, between hydrangeas and a smile, as Misha ghosts him past the garden statues, ice pack intact. The house handler, solicitous by design, whispers *slipped on the terrace* like liturgy, and I watch it spread because the city loves humiliation when it comes with a napkin. I nod to the guard at the back gate, and he nods back. The night has returned to its cruelty within acceptable limits.

I take a drink because a man should know what he looks like with a glass in his hand. *Vodka*. It slides like clean fire. I hold it until the chill leaves the crystal, and then I swallow. I let it burn discipline into me exactly where it threatens to soften. She is everywhere in this room, even when I don't look at her. Cedar and violet threaded through her hair move on the air like a winter dream that refuses to end, leading out of the dark and asking to be believed. The high, clean line of her neck shows when she turns to listen to a man she intends to disarm, and something in my chest answers. The deeper thing from earlier still rides my mouth and hands, heat that doesn't belong in a public room and refuses to obey simply because I'm good at rooms.

She holds back even when her body tells the truth. She wants to be soft, and she wants to be safe, and she believes those two things have never lived in the same bed. I'm not a poet. I know in my bones there is a wound in her that belongs to a ghost with a smooth voice and a pretty jaw, and it makes me want to pull brick from the wall with my hands just to prove a point about permanence. I'm a man who can carry both if she asks. I don't say it. I never will. It is not my place, and the room is watching.

Anatoly holds the head table the way a cathedral holds its altar, standing just off his own chair, breathing like a man who measures the room and himself with the same ruler. He softly speaks of *zoning, sanitation, a fundraiser in spring* to the city officials he permits to believe they understand pavement and blood. His smile is slow, all patience. I watch the angle of his shoulders and know his breath is shorter than it should be. I count three seconds between laughs. I count the hand that goes to the back of the chair twice in a minute. I don't step in. Tonight, I keep the performance intact and take notes on the truths it leaks.

Around us, the room works in its own way, yet it is curated. Champagne climbs in thin columns. A waiter pours a Bordeaux that smells of old wood and iron. A spoon rings once on marble before a busboy catches it with his palm. A councilman murmurs about permits and pretends the word means mercy. A donor's wife laughs too loudly at a joke about snow and forgets she is holding her glass. One too many. A single nod shifts the tray path so nothing sloshes near her or a dignitary and keeps the press sightline blocked so no messy candid gets framed.

Valentina moves with that odd grace that is half queen, half girl. Pale silver gown, low braid, red ribbon flaunting as a rule. Effortless is the hardest work in this room. She poses by the west wall, light on her, a dignitary angling into the frame with a public smile and a hand that settles too easily on her shoulder. The flash pops. I take the space beside the photographer and lift my chin. The next shot reads correctly —Anatoly's daughter, the donor, the house. The press handler nods. The picture that will run tomorrow is the one we can live with. Valentina scowls. I let it pass.

A woman with mascara gone wrong clutches at sleeves, saying, *purse, blue, I left it here.* I nod. My man moves, quiet as a priest. In one turn of the floor, he has the clutch from under a chair, and the woman is crying "thank you" into his sleeve. He smiles like a doorman and steers her back to her table. Anatoly doesn't look over. He doesn't need to.

My phone lifts into my palm without thinking. Katya is sending just two screenshots, no text. A warehouse camera at the port shows a timestamp that tries to lie and fails when you look at the pixels. The second image is a ledger line, a sender's name I recognize with disgust. I text one word. *When.* She replies with a number. *Forty minutes.* I send her the prayer hands because she hates it. It makes her swear, and swearing keeps her awake. I send Misha the timestamp. He sends back a thumb and then a location. He will put our plainclothes spotters on the corner, and when the truck passes, those eyes will melt. East Boston will not become a mirror of L Street. One rupture per night is enough.

I'm back again at my post. Vetrov's satellites move like moths that have learned to pretend they are birds. I mark Grekov stays off-camera. His cufflinks ride other wrists. I mark the two men who don't track the dancers. They track the doors. I mark the woman in rubies who watches the vice director like a wolf in silk. Three reporters who discuss canapés while they negotiate how not to anger a man they cannot name on camera.

A woman from the philanthropy board takes my arm. She wants to tell me a donor is very concerned about the optics of distributing toys in neighborhoods where the police budget is already maxed. I listen with a face I rent for this purpose. I give three sentences that sound like a promise and are in fact a schedule. She leaves satisfied. I check the balcony rail again for the curve of a lens.

I ask for a second drink and don't drink it. I hold it because it gives my hands a reason to be in the open. I'm thinking of the way her mouth opened against mine when she forgot to fight me, the way her eyes went flat when she remembered she is not a woman with liberty, and the sound she made when I put her back against the wall and told her with my hands who she is to me. I shouldn't be thinking of any of this with a room full of judges and criminals twenty steps away. The problem with vows is that they begin before a man is ready to admit he made one.

I took a private oath on the terrace when I touched her wrist and felt her pulse. Protect her without spectacle. Protect her without permission. Protect her in ways that look like common sense. It unsettles me because it is the opposite of the distance I have used to remain useful. I file the oath where I keep the other dangerous things. I don't lock it. I'm not that foolish.

Calls try to thread the night. Two go to voicemail because I'm standing within sight of six men who could decide a small war if they had the courage to. One I take. The number rings only when water is already in the room. A salt-streaked shed on the pier, a door that never answers the first knock. I ask three questions. Hear three truths. I tell the man not to touch anything that is under canvas until I count to six with him on the line. I count. He is a fast counter. I slow him down with my voice, and his pulse steadies. We are none of us saints. We are all of us boys handing each other the tools we did not have when we needed them.

A press photographer with a good tie but bad timing tries to catch Anatoly with the judge in the frame. I take one smooth step and put my shoulder in the way as if it were a mistake. Not the judge. He needs daylight between his robe and our table. The frame becomes a chandelier and the donor wives. The photographer swallows a curse. I give him a smile that belongs in the museum of almost sincere. He nods because the rules are the rules. He will still get paid. He will still come back next year.

A quiet buzz at my hip. Misha again. He writes one word. *Clear.* Meaning Reznik is someone else's problem and will be back in his hotel with an ice pack and a story about stairs. The house breathes easier. I let myself breathe with it.

There are tells you learn in a room like this. The way mouths thin when they lie about charity. The way shoulders settle when deals conclude without signatures. The air changes when a knife walks in wearing a suit. I mark three men who touched their right cuffs within two minutes of each other and one woman who arrived unaccompanied and is never unaccompanied. Patterns are how you stay alive. Order is not a preference. It is a spine.

I feel the old weight like a hand between my shoulder blades. The orphanage taught me that no one will make a place for a child where he is allowed to set both feet. You carve it with the bone in your teeth if you have to. Anatoly opened a door when I was thirteen and said *come in and pay me for the meal with your life,* and I walked in because hunger makes saints of cowards. He taught me that oaths are more than a man's mouth. He stood me in a room with a chair under a bulb and told me to keep my voice outside the door unless I had to bring it in. He gave me war with no promise of making me the hero. I understand, although I don't forgive him for everything. I don't forgive myself for wanting the seat.

I'm circling back toward the west door when I feel it. The center of gravity has moved, like a hand on a glass settling the liquid without asking permission. Everyone here learns to feel it. The servants feel it first. Then the wives. Then the men who think they are kings. I turn and see Anatoly watching me. He lifts his chin a fraction. It is not a summons anyone else can see. I set my glass on a passing tray. I allow myself one glance at Valentina, because a weakness in me still believes it is strength, and then I cross the room.

It is past one, the dance floor already bare, the gardens still lit for the last stragglers. Anatoly's office at the back of the house is where real conversations happen. The door is heavy and old and has been opened only for the men allowed to pick up the city and examine it. I stand on the threshold and wait because that is discipline. Anatoly nods me in. The desk is a slab of wood that could be a monastery table if God had different ideas. There are two chairs, and they are for men who don't need more than wood and fabric.

Anatoly closes the door himself. The click is small and absolute. He pours two vodkas with the care a priest uses when he pours wine. He hands me one. He doesn't sit. He studies me the way he did when I was twenty and still angry at the wrong things. He considers, sets his glass on the edge of the desk, and says, "I want you to marry my daughter."

6

VALYA

Morning breaks like glass that almost decided to be kind. Light presses through the tall windows in clean squares and climbs the wall toward the ceiling medallion, where cherubs have been judging me since childhood. I lie very still in the center of the bed and let my body speak the truth before the mind begins its arguments. It always does when faced with happiness, hammering a list of reasons not to trust it. Yet, my mouth is tender. My pulse remembers hands it shouldn't.

The gala swims up in pieces—pearled branches glinting along the stairs, the room tasting like cedar, butter, and expensive promises. Memory pauses on Daniil's cologne arriving two seconds before his mouth, my own smile weaponized into diplomacy. And he, Dmitri, walking into the night as if it were a river he commands, the current bending to his stride, speaking in a voice that sets things back in their places.

My skin shivers under the duvet. I close my eyes to press back an unwelcome visitor from the past. Sometimes, memory taps like a polite stranger, asking if it may come in. I let it stand in the hall. Every time, my jaw locks until my teeth ache and my tongue tastes like old pennies.

Aleksandr and I talked as if we believed weather could be negotiated. It could not. He apologized, not late but strategic, busy with women and with a bride whose name bought him streets. Truth stood ankle-deep even as his mouth shaped promises while he measured me as a crest on a letterhead. I did what I could. I bought clove tea and walked home counting saints. He went to New York to be seen through glass and alliances. I stayed and learned to vanish on purpose.

A soft knock breaks my spell. Yelena slips in without waiting because she raised me. Privacy, in her theology, is something mothers grant, not obey. She sets down a tray with tea, orange juice, and a small bowl of honey cut with lemon. On her other hand is a folded linen napkin, the corner embroidered in blue thread by my grandmother, truth and the Mother's color, stitches neat as a prayer I only remember in honest light.

"Valya," she says, setting the tray on the little table by the window where the glass magnifies the world into something simple, "you sleep like you wrestled the wind."

"I did," I say into the pillow. She draws the curtains back with a practiced flick, and winter pours into the room without the cold. Bright sky, the kind of blue that believes in itself. No fresh snow, just yesterday's clean sheet untouched except for the small track of a cat who belongs to no one. A red bird, a cardinal, my grandmother would say, a messenger, hops on the bare branch and tilts its head at me like we have an agreement. The world is glitter and gold without permission from any chandelier. For a moment, I can drink it.

"Tea," Yelena says. "And this juice will make you remember you like being alive."

"Later," I mumble and turn onto my back and stare at the ceiling and try to solve the equation of the night. *He will not come back*, I think, so my thoughts cannot break me. *It meant nothing*, I try, and the way my body answers that sentence makes me bite my lip. I'm too old to be naive and too young to be cynical, and somehow, I'm both. My mother's ghost chooses the moment to remind me that vows are iron fetters dressed as gold. I tell her, in my head, that I have made no vows. *Not yet*, she whispers back.

Yelena goes on with her usual inventory without looking like she is taking stock. She adjusts the throw at the bottom of the bed and notes, without comment, that my gown is draped over the chaise. She touches the crucifix at my throat like she is checking a clasp and not checking my soul, and her fingers smell like cedar and soap.

"You are quiet," she says. "That makes me nervous."

"I'm thinking about resurrections and how much the city likes them," I say. She lifts one eyebrow. "Fine. I'm thinking about last night." I scowl.

"The gala," she says, steady as an altar rail, her way of letting me borrow dignity until I can stand on my own. "It was successful. Your father did not frown. He was pleased."

"Mm."

"And your own night?" she asks, her tone light enough to float or sink depending on how I breathe.

"Frighteningly educational," I say. "don't ask for a syllabus."

"I wouldn't dare," she says, and then more gently, "I remember what it is to be young and strong and confused."

She leaves the tray and straightens a stack of books just to assert that order is available if I want it, and at the door, she pauses. "A bath would be good. I have spruce oil. It smells like a good winter."

"I will," I say, lying.

When she leaves, the room is mine again. I sit up and set my feet on the cold rug. It feels like punishment, then like a blessing. I pick up the juice because Yelena's faith is sacrosanct. I sip, wince, and smile despite myself. The world settles another inch.

My phone lies face down where I left it. I flip it over. Reza's name crowds the screen with a string of texts I should answer. I hold the phone, then set it down again. The silence is an indulgence, and I'm not yet ready to end it.

I stand at the window and rest my forehead against the cold pane, then pull back and pretend I did not. My grandmother would scold me about marks on the glass. The cardinal hops closer as if to say *listen*. The branch wobbles under his red righteousness, then he steadies, a small king with a sense of humor.

I try to see only what is in front of me—blue sky, brick warmed by light. The tiny white line along the parapet where the sun scours snow to glass. I decide to be exactly here for thirty full seconds. I make it to eighteen and smile because that is, by my standards, very good.

The smile lingers, and my body remembers faster than my mind permits. I breathe in cedar and winter light and the ghost of his cologne on my wrist. The room tilts by a degree only I can feel. My heart goes quick, an honest drum. I press my fingers to my mouth and find it smiling again.

Last night unfurls in small flashes, not a parade but a constellation—his hand closing over mine and guiding, his voice roughened by restraint, the way he read my breath and answered it, the certainty in his touch when I curled toward him and asked without speaking. Warmth gathers low and sweet, a tender ache like the bloom of a new bruise where pleasure has left its signature. My knees feel untrustworthy in the nicest way. Heat climbs my throat and settles under my skin, and I'm suddenly aware of every place he held me steady, of how easily I opened when he set the pace and waited for my yes. I have never trusted steel to be gentle. I did, and it was.

Yet I know this is not love, only sweetness that tempts me toward more. I think of my mother moving through mornings like a house of silk, perfume a soft wound. She made rooms feel seen until walls built by men tightened as she grew. She was left with good China while silence ate her voice. I don't believe she forgave my father, but she forgave me for not knowing how to help. I set my palm to the glass and vow not to repeat it, even if the world prefers lineage to choice.

The knock comes with the particular rhythm of men who are trained not to announce themselves. For a ridiculous second, I lift my chin like an empress and then drop it because I'm a woman in a sweater with a braid that has decided to be ungovernable. I open the door a hand's width.

The guard on the other side looks at my shoulder instead of my face in the respectful way they learn if they want to avoid broken bones.

"Miss Kirov," he says. "Your father requests you in the chapel."

Of course he does. Of course the summons comes when my hair looks like I wrestled the wind. The little bones around my heart clack against each other like tiny cups, then stack themselves neatly. I'm practiced at putting on a self that will pass where it needs to pass. I pull on a soft black dress and a cardigan that looks innocent and is armor in the language of grandmothers, tighten my braid with a ribbon so red it is almost ridiculous, and slide my feet into flats because I prefer to stand my ground without worrying about my ankles. I touch the crucifix at my throat. It is where it always is, like a hand.

The path to the chapel drops out of the bright hall into the cool, polished hush of the older wing with dark mahogany paneling. The staircase turns with quiet grace, a thick runner swallowing sound. A porcelain vase holds winter branches on a marble console. Above this, oil portraits in gilt follow me, unsmiling, to the chapel door. It is carved and heavy, a piece of Russia an artisan once smuggled into Boston plank by plank. It opens with the smallest groan, the polite complaint of age.

Inside, the air is thick with incense and old wood polish, scents that carry prayers like beads on a string. Oil lamps throw soft halos across faces that look down with patient, gold-leaf mercy, a quiet piety that feels more like light than rule. Candles stand where my grandmother taught me to set them for birthdays, for saints' days, and for the small sorrows kept unspoken so breathing stays simple. My father stands at the rail as if the chapel grew him, long black coat, hands clasped behind his back in that priestly posture that can be humility or control depending on the day.

He turns when the door clicks shut. He doesn't smile or scowl. He takes me in with one slow pass of the eyes that would insult me if I did not love him, and then he nods once.

"Valya," he says. "Come."

I walk up the aisle and take the place opposite him. My gaze falls on the little lavabo at the back that glints like a shallow spring, as if a bird might come at any moment to dip its beak and be satisfied.

"You sent for me," I say, pretending this is theater, not life. We are two people and a dynasty, with arguments postponed because guests listened and icons seemed to blink.

"I did," he answers, voice measured. "There is no need for ceremony between us. You will marry Dmitri Volkov."

I hear the wick spit as his words strike. The chapel holds its breath. A sound I did not intend escapes, closer to a laugh than sense. "Excuse me?"

"You will marry Dmitri," he repeats, as if repetition could make it into something other than audacity. "It will be a sacred Bratva wedding on Christmas Eve. You will exchange blood vows by candlelight, before a priest, with God as witness."

"You brought me to church to tell me I'm a contract," I say, and the humor leaks from my mouth before I can sharpen it. "Father, you cannot be serious."

He sets two fingers on the rail. "I'm serious," he says. "The matter is settled."

"It is my life," I say, calm for someone reconsidering silence in favor of arson. "We don't barter women. Not in my century."

"No, we don't barter," he answers. "We bind."

I snort. "Beautiful word for a leash."

"Don't be foolish," he says. "This is legacy and protection, the old ways that kept us alive when men like Vetrov sharpened knives on stones. Enemies circle. The new breed would break us and sell the crumbs as innovation."

"Marry me to your soldier, and the crumbs become a loaf," I say, clever mouth unlatched. "We will be a bakery."

He exhales, a man who has carried weight so long, he forgets air. "Dmitri is not merely a soldier. He believes as we do. He understands vows, words before God that don't bend."

"And how will he protect me?"

"When I no longer can, he will."

The sentence slips under my ribs. I straighten. *No. Not like this.*

"I don't need a bodyguard," I say, and I hear how thin the sentence is the moment it leaves me. The memory of a hand on my hip last night is not the one that answers. The memory that answers is a different hand from years ago, taking something I did not understand I could refuse. I lift my chin. "I need my life." My thumb finds the edge of the crucifix, as it always does when my father corners me with his decrees.

He looks at me. For a moment, he looks old, eyes gone opaque like river ice, mouth loosening at the corners, the polish thin enough to show the grain. "This marriage is not about love," he says. "This is about salvation."

"For whom?" I ask. "Me, or your name?"

"Both," he says without apology. "I will not lie to you."

A dozen arguments line up on my tongue. I'm not an ornament. I have work that matters beyond these walls. Even Dmitri deserves a choice. Behind them come quieter truths, candlelit. I respect vows. I believe in a God who sees. I'm my grandmother's blood, and I wear tradition like a necklace because it feels like protection. I remember my mother sitting with folded hands and a polite mouth while men engineered safety out of her house. I swore never to sit like that. I also remember when Dmitri corrected the night and met my eyes. He did not save me. He set the ground so I could stand on my own.

"This is not a cage," my father says, more softly than I expect, which is how I know he is afraid. "It is a roof. When the snow comes hard, you will be glad for it."

"I'm not cold," I say, which is pointless. Heat stings my eyes. Fury keeps it from falling.

He steps past me to the little side table where the candles rest between tubs of beeswax and boxes of matches that have seen more winter than I have. There is a worn leather prayer book there, the one my grandmother used. The spine is cracked, the corners rounded by the pressure of a thumb that knew how to insist and how to praise. He picks it up, and for a second, I remember being small and watching those hands lift me out of a pew.

"Valya," he says, and when he uses the endearment in this room, I want to leave. He places the book in my hands like it is heavy and I'm strong. The leather is warm from his palms. I open to the page he has already marked with a bit of red ribbon that looks enough like blood to count as symbolism. The line waits there in a script that is not mine and will be if I consent.

I read it. The words lay themselves across my tongue like a dare and a promise, and they are very simple and very impossible.

I come to you with no secrets between us.

7

DMITRI

I want you to marry my daughter. My Pakhan's sentence settles in the room like ash after a fire. I refuse the comfort of looking away and let the silence press on the walls. Then, I place my palms flat on the desk, empty, so he knows the decision is not something I'm gripping to win a fight.

"Does she know?"

His mouth barely moves. "She will." He keeps his eyes on the window as if the winter could answer for him. Then he looks straight at me. "You will marry my daughter on Christmas Eve," he says, his voice flat. "The Vigil. A sacred rite with blood vows. Father Gavril will stand. The council will attend."

The quiet after that is not empty. It is a ledger where we both write.

"Did you ask her or inform her?" The room listens. Grammar is a kind of law.

"Inform her, then persuade. She will comply."

I draw the breath that lives in my spine and let it out without heat. "I will not force her. If she doesn't consent, there is no sacrament to speak of. I will not put my mouth to a vow and turn it into leverage." He takes his glass and sips. Once.

Lamplight draws a low ember out of the oiled grain. The muted polish of the wood keeps still as judgment. Anatoly doesn't answer for a count of four, which is how I know he is irritated, not surprised. He takes another small sip, sets the glass back with the same care, and looks at me fully.

"You are romantic," he says, making the word sound like praise he doesn't intend.

"I'm orderly." I let the truth sit bare. "I will take the engagement if she agrees. If she doesn't, I will still hold the roof and keep her name clean and settle the lines that need settling. My work doesn't change."

He tilts his head so slightly, most men would miss it. "She is my daughter. The house needs this."

"The house needs truth spoken in a church," I say, and my voice stays level. "If she comes to the altar, she must walk to it because she has decided to keep what she says there."

"You will discover I'm not wrong about her," he says, and now the corner of his mouth offers a thin version of what other men would call humor. "She is her grandmother's blood. She knows what a vow is."

"So do I," I say, and my hands are still and open. I'm not here to win an argument. I'm here to choose the terms under which I can keep breathing without lying.

He leans forward the width of two fingers on the desk, and I see the moment his body remembers its edges. "*You want the seat.* Everyone with eyes knows this." His eyes narrow. "You think you have earned more than I have given. Perhaps that is true. Perhaps it is not. If you marry her..." He leans back. "You will be closer to it than any man alive. Are you prepared to choose her when the seat demands a pledge? She is the vow."

I feel a private vow stir the way a river stirs under winter skin. "The seat can learn to live with being second." I deny him an answer.

He watches me with the evaluation of a craftsman tapping a blade.

"If she agrees, I will keep her name clean," I say. "I will close the routes that bleed and open the ones that feed. I will end the threats that matter and ignore the noise that doesn't. I will not parade her. But I will not let this house trade her patience for optics. If she refuses, I will still do every part of this."

The lines at the corners of his mouth deepen in something like relief that doesn't want applause. He picks up the glass, touches the rim to mine, and doesn't smile. "Then you will go ask the priest for God, and you will ask my daughter for consent. Bring me a yes, and I will bring you the rest."

"I will bring you the truth," I say, and I drink the measure he poured.

He turns away to the window and pretends to be interested in the snow that has decided not to fall. I leave him there because kings deserve privacy for their small acts of mercy. The hall outside is cool. The last of the staff are clearing the wreckage of the party. I walk the back way that keeps me in the shadow of the walls.

The house is a body, and I'm its nervous system. I send two messages as I move without appearing to move. One to Misha with a time and a corner in East Boston, *low presence, eyes only, no phones out, no heroics, let the second truck roll so we can see who follows the noise.* One to Katya. *Pull the camera that spoofed the timestamp, install a replacement before noon, and send the invoice so I can scold the vendor with precision, not volume.* I step through the east doorway into the ballroom, now empty, and look up once to catch the reflection of the balcony in the chandelier.

By the time I reach the courtyard, the last car has gone. The snow from the afternoon sits in patches across the night street. I take out my phone and write six words to the only person in this house I'm allowed to ask without making a scene. *Are you in the church this hour?* The reply arrives before the question finishes ringing in my bones. *Always, when the day ends.*

I write back. *I'm coming.* I need a church that doesn't answer to Anatoly.

The Orthodox church that will hold our marriage opens its heavy doors to me even at this hour. I step onto the marble. The vaults lift on painted saints, chandeliers dripping small suns. The nave receives me, tall candles standing in ranks, each flame a warm bead bracing the winter. Gold leaf returns the light in halos. I pass the pews and reach the solea. At the altar rail, Father Gavril, our priest and keeper of the house chapel, waits for me as if he had known the exact second I would come. Men like Father Gavril keep time with God.

"Dmitri." His voice is deep and melodic, like cathedral bells. "You have the face of a man who has agreed to carry a heavy thing as if it weighed nothing."

"I have been offered a crown that comes with a bride," I say, letting the humor make the sentence polite without softening the metal in it. "I came to ask for a different thing."

"You came to ask for permission to make a promise you already made." He nods with a little smile.

"I will not force her into a wedding." I have already scraped the words on the stone of my discipline until they have no decoration left. "I will not let a vow be turned into a knife."

He reaches for the small brass lamp and adjusts the wick until the light stops shivering. "The old vows don't work when spoken for show." He intones, "If she comes to you by choice, you will be bound until death and after. If she comes to you by command, you will be bound until resentment rots the floor under your feet. Your insistence is correct."

"She is already inside the line I draw when I move men and money."

He gives me the kind of smile that has earned wrinkles. When he speaks, each word is set down with measured care. "You kneel to God. That is no small thing in the business you run. You have learned to keep your anger in the pocket where other men keep mercy. I will stand for you. I will stand for her, but never for a lie."

"Nor will I," I say.

Gavril winks, the wrinkles lifting his smile, a priest's way of admitting romance is no stranger to God. "Ask her in daylight, in a place with windows and ordinary plates.

Order tea. Put your hands open on the table and ask the clean question. Don't negotiate with her answer."

"At a cafe?" I ask.

His eyes crinkle again. "Leave your men outside, let the room be small. God is not louder in palaces."

"Don't rehearse," Gavril says, a note of caution in it. "She will hear the script before you speak and punish you for thinking she is ordinary."

"I can do that," I say, though my chest feels too tight for space. "The words will be plain. My promise will be work."

"Work is a prayer," he says. "Keep them as clean as you can answer for. God knows the rest." I kiss the icon of the Mother before I go out into the dark.

Morning is already lifting a thin blue at the windows when I step back into the street. I walk home through a city that has not yet chosen to wake. Brick holds the cold and gives it back along the sidewalk. I keep an even pace, hands visible, letting the blocks fall behind me.

The house is quiet after the party. I shave, change into a charcoal wool coat that drinks the light, black merino under it instead of a collar and tie. My trousers are pressed clean, and my boots are polished but quiet. The bleeding cross sits on my chest under the knit where only God can see it. I take coffee and no sugar, because sugar makes hands shake. I get back to the office to set smaller gears turning. Then, I text Katya. *I need a place with windows and ordinary plates. Tea and something like honey cake if there is mercy.* Her reply lands before the coffee cools. *Cambridge, Mass Ave. A bell that sounds like a coin in a bowl.* She adds the address and nothing else for a long breath, then, *Who?* I write back, *A citizen.* She sends a single dot that could be suspicion or restraint.

A call to the garage toggles the rotation. The mean black car goes to the Back Bay, the quiet sedan comes forward with its plates cleaned by rain and time. The driver asks for the destination, his eyes on the glass.

"Cambridge, Mass Ave. at the river," I reply. I tell him to slow through the square and then leave me a block away from the cafe. It is exactly what Katya promised. Old green enamel on the walls. Sheer curtains that make the winter honest without pretending to warm it. A bell that rings like a coin in a bowl. The glass samovar steams behind the counter. The case holds honey cakes and poppy rolls and black bread that smells like the hunger I remember from days when I was small and somebody else's God had forgotten me.

I take the corner table that lets me watch the door without making the watching feel like an accusation. I sit with my back to a wall that has seen worse men than I sit and make better decisions than the ones I will be offered. The girl behind the counter wears a kerchief. I order tea, for my hands need a cup. The tea arrives in a chipped white pot that has boiled itself into usefulness.

I write her a message that uses fewer words than I want and more truth than I like. There is no order in the sentence and no command. There is a request and a place and a promise to leave if she says no. I send it. I set the phone down face down, choosing to leave space for her to answer or refuse the dare of the answer. The tea is almost too hot to drink, and the heat teaches my mouth to be patient.

The radiator ticks. The city declares morning in its own small measures. A barista clacks the grinder, milk hisses, someone unlocks a newsstand, a bus exhales its fumes. I think of the way she held herself against me and the way she pulled back because the past is a dog that doesn't stop barking just because you feed it once. I think of the house and the routes and the men who will test my name against their knives. I think of Anatoly and the way his breath shortened between his laughs. I let the work idle. No routing notes, no quiet orders that move men like commas. I don't text Katya, I don't call Misha. I let the city run on its own long enough to hear my own.

I order another pot. Patience is not a gift I trust to last. The bell makes its myriad soft coin sounds. The door opens to a slice of blue winter, and she steps in, her face composed in a politeness that looks like a weapon if you have ever been on the wrong end of a woman's intelligence. My heart miscounts once.

She came.

8

VALYA

I'm without makeup, in my honest secondhand wool coat, the sleeves a little too long, the collar softened by other winters. I keep the red ribbon in my hair to show a small loyalty to the women who raised me.

The bell over the cafe door makes a small coin sound that feels like a blessing spilled into a saucer. Inside, roasted tea hangs in the air like a thin veil, warm with clove and dark honey and a faint pine smoke. The enamel walls are the good green, scrubbed into virtue.

Dmitri is already there. He sits in the corner chair that lets him see the room and the door and his own reflection if he chooses. His coat is folded across the back of the chair with a neatness that belongs to ritual. His hands are still on the table, fingers resting near a chipped white cup. The stillness in his face is attention rationed like warmth when the wood-pile is low.

I stop by the counter and choose tea with cloves and honey. I choose a plate with honey cakes that shine as if they remember the sun. I carry both to him and sit facing the window. For a minute, we don't talk or greet. Somewhere behind the counter, a kettle sighs, and a tray of pastry gives off the warm smells of ginger and honey.

I make a little tent with my hands around the cup and let the steam find my face.

"I have not made up my mind," I say to the cup.

He doesn't rush his answer. "I know."

"Comforting. You are trusting your future to someone still arguing with her tea."

"I trust the women who taught you to argue well," he says softly.

"She would be the girl who carries her own light into the forest," I say, meaning my grandmother.

"Like *Vasilisa*," he answers, the corners of his mouth softening into lines drawn the way a river carves its banks.

I ask if he has read *Vasilisa*, catching my voice before it tips into delight. He says she feeds the little doll, says her prayer, keeps the old rules even in the witch's house, and survives by honoring a mother's blessing. He speaks without forcing the room to listen.

He reaches for the cup, and the collar of his black knit pulls a fraction lower. A narrow lick of ink climbs toward the bone at his shoulder. I remember the dark line where the shirt did not hide it. I look at his throat and then at his face.

"Tell me a story," I say. "Not work. A story."

"I don't carry many stories," he answers. "I carry a sound."

"Whose sound?"

"A woman with a fever. Her voice made the walls hold." He looks at the cup, not at me. "*Gospodi pomiluy.*"

"Lord, have mercy," I translate, because my grandmother taught me that one before she taught me to braid. "She lit candles when she said it. The room changed shape."

"My room did too," he says. "I don't remember her face. I remember that line."

He places the cup where the light falls, handle straight, saucer still. He says quietly that his mother left a prayer, told him to keep it, to feed it with breath. He says that winter was already in the house by then, that the window wore frost inside as well as out, and her voice thinned to a thread that still held. He says that in the dormitory later, when the lights went out and the bleach smell climbed the stairs ahead of the cold, he would say the words once and the hunger would sit down and behave.

He looks at me. The ice gray of his eyes, ringed darker at the edges, doesn't change so much as sharpen. What lives there reads as unspoken resolve rather than warmth.

"That is quite a fairy tale," I say, not quite smiling. The steam rises between us like a page turning.

Dmitri falls quiet, letting his thumb rest against the saucer as if remembering a different rim. He turns the cup a quarter-inch so the handle points toward me. His gaze drops to the small cross at my throat and lifts to the ribbon in my hair.

"Your cross sits like it knows the place," he says, voice clear as water. "You touch it before you answer hard questions. The ribbon today. Is that for her?"

"For my grandmother," I say. "She tied a red thread when the season turned. She said it kept the old promises from wandering."

He inclines his head, as if the answer fits a pattern he respects. "She taught you the rules with her hands," he says. "Candles, braids, small prayers. You kept them. Like Vasilisa."

Something warm opens behind my ribs. My shoulders loosen a fraction. "Yes. Like Vasilisa," I say. The agreement tastes sweet in a way that has nothing to do with honey.

He slides the plate a finger closer, an invitation shaped like manners. I cut the cake with the edge of my fork and set a small piece on his saucer before taking one for myself, because sharing makes the table honest.

"She said hair remembers how it was held in a ribbon," I murmur. "A clean part makes a clean mind."

His eyes listen the way good rooms do. "My mother crossed thresholds with two fingers on the lintel," he says. "Kept salt by the door and a match in the samovar lid. A house should be ready to forgive and ready to light."

We don't speak of altars or men who carry guns under good suits. We let the tea set the pace, and we talk about older things. He asks what song my grandmother liked for washing days, and I hum the first bar without thinking. He answers with the last bar in a voice so low the China seems to hear it before I do, and a small, steady happiness rises.

He asks which fairy tales my grandmother loved, and I tell him about the boy who forgets his name and learns it again in front of a door not meant for him. He nods as if he expected that, then shares a fisherman's prayer for hard weather. Words like "rope" when the sea reminds you you're small. I hum the first line of the lullaby my grandmother crooned. He finishes it, voice low.

The room holds us like a well-loved book. Porcelain meets porcelain. Outside, the light tilts slateward as the first flakes test the street. My cup warms both hands.

"My grandmother used to make honey cake," I say, touching the glazed edge with my fork. "She cut it with a string because she said knives tell too much truth."

"Your grandmother was a wise woman," he says.

"She was a collection of sharp corners dressed as a tea cozy," I say, and he lets himself smile, a small one that wouldn't survive the cold outside. A warmth surges in my chest, something I fold like linen.

He is careful with his words. I watch the care because it tells me more than the words do. He doesn't touch the honey cake until I lift my fork. He doesn't reach toward my cup, but he inches the little pot of more honey into my line of sight in case I want sweetness on my own terms.

"You said your mother left you a prayer," I say, letting the question settle where the warmth has already made room. "Do you still say it?"

His eyes go quiet without going far. He rubs the cup's edge with his thumb, speaking like each syllable costs something.

"She taught me, 'Brow, so you remember to think. Chest so you remember to love. Shoulder and shoulder so you remember you are held.'"

Heat rises behind my eyes, gentle and known like a hearth lit long before I walked in, waiting only for someone to sit beside it. I lower my gaze to the steam curling between us, soft as a thread pulled through time. His hands are steady on the porcelain, the scar at his thumb pale with age. It looks like something once mended.

His phone lights once against the wood, a small square of winter. And then again when he picks it up. He doesn't apologize. He writes a single line with his thumb, places the phone face down so the glow disappears, and lifts his cup.

"What was that?" I ask, because I'm trying to be honest with the room I'm in.

"Nothing that belongs to this table," he says, and his mouth tilts a fraction.

So we go back to old stories and old prayers, and for a moment, I see past the suits and the guards and the reputation that moves down hallways ahead of his boots. I see a boy who learned to keep time with prayer. I see a man who would like to build a room where promises are not threatened by drafts.

He asks about my scar, his eyes dropping to the tiny burn in my palm. His fingertip hovers, not touching.

"Here," I say, turning my hand to show the tiny burn in my palm, a pearl of old fire. "From vigil candles when I was a girl. I held the match too long and wouldn't blow it out.

Babushka pinched the wick and said, "Learn the heat." He nods.

I choose a second pot of tea. I choose to stay for it. He leans a little back, not retreat, permission. Steam writes a pale script on the glass. Outside, the snow has become more insistent, flurries deciding to be a fall. The bell tells the street every time the door opens, and still the heat holds.

We step out together without making an announcement. The cold finds our faces, and the snow patterns the wool of my sleeves. The city is almost empty. The low winter sun pours its small gold onto the falling white. We turn east because neither of us is in a hurry to hand the day back to its schedules.

Our steps fall in time without any effort. Our breaths make clouds that meet and drift apart and meet again. A bicycle glides by, the chain keeping a clean, steady music, the kind that pretends it has forgotten how to slip.

We talk mostly about things that don't require choosing. The best translation of a line from Pasternak. He asks me how many languages I speak. I say four. He talks about the way Boston pretends to be small when it wants to hide. Whether honey is better in tea or on bread. He says tea. I say bread. He considers this as if it reveals character. I touch the crucifix at my throat just once and feel the small, familiar weight find the notch above my heart. He sees the gesture and doesn't comment. I decide I like his style of silence.

At the corner, the wind turns and lifts a little of my hair. I reach up to smooth it. His hand moves and stops. There is a part of me that wants the touch. It rises fast and clean as the arc of a bird changing direction midair. Another part, older and stubborn, sets its feet. Our hands hover for a second, then both drop. The moment folds itself and tucks into my pocket like a note I will reread later.

We keep walking. The world is blue and gold and white. We don't speak for two blocks. It is not awkward. It is honest. My boots squeak on the clean parts of the snow and thud on the parts where people have gone before me. His steps are almost silent. He is that man.

At the square where we usually turn toward the river, he asks, without making it a question, if I would like the long way back. I say yes because the long way is a choice that belongs to me, and because I'm beginning to understand that he will walk as far as I ask and no farther.

By the time we reach Beacon Hill, the snowfall has softened into a steady curtain. The gas lamps wear small white hats. The iron fence around our steps holds beads of ice like a necklace that belongs to nobody. I stop outside the door because I want a second to keep this and once I go in, the house will put its hands back on my shoulders. He doesn't say anything that would ruin the quiet by naming it gratitude. I tilt my face up, let a single flake melt on my lip, and then I go inside.

The marble in the foyer holds the chill the way marble always does. A faint trace of incense lingers from the chapel. The house guard nods, eyes on my shoulder instead of my face. My heart hums a song, one it refused to sing so long, I forgot it lived inside me.

The day moves easily. I meet Reza, trade lists and smiles, and leave with jokes. I buy bread, oranges, a small fist of white flowers. I make a note to check mittens and caps. I sleep lightly and a sound wakes me.

It is a scrape and a grunt and then a silence that gathers itself around something that has just fallen. I step through the arch. The room offers the picture without commentary. A man lies stretched on the carpet near the hearth. His face is broken at the temple, one eye sealed shut by swelling, mouth slack in benediction. His hands are bound with wire, tight and deliberate, blood drying at the knots.

My father stands by the mantel, holding a glass untouched and never meant to be. The slow turn of his head is both a greeting and a command. Dmitri is nowhere, but his absence presses on the room like a thumbprint.

"What happened?" I ask, voice calm by long habit.

"A traitor," he says, almost gently. "Not your concern."

The man on the carpet exhales, low and wet, a thread of froth and blood catching at his mouth like a secret trying to leave. Iron cuts through polish and candle smoke. My father's jaw tightens once. He holds my eyes until I read what he wants me to understand. I set both palms on the chair back so my hands will not shake. The house calls this order. I call it a wound we dress in linen.

Every time the room turns violent, I see my mother in her bright, separate rooms, safe and aside, while men praise a code that chooses where and when to punish. When my father finally looks away, the air loosens, but the fact remains. I count the stains and the seconds, and I don't forgive the room for learning to watch.

I go upstairs because there is nowhere else to put my body that feels true. My hand finds the banister's curve, worn smooth by a hundred ghosts. A door sighs. Somewhere, a lock clicks softly, like comfort pretending.

My room is too warm. I set down my coat, unbraid my hair, slide the ribbon into the dish where memory sleeps beside earrings. Nothing in this house is ever plain. I stand at the window but don't lean my head. Snow keeps falling steadily. The street tries to stay blank. I touch the cross at my throat. I don't ask for anything. I don't know what to ask for.

I make tea from the tray Yelena left and take it to the chair by the window. Honey and clove rise with the heat. I try to inventory my heart, and it refuses to be itemized. There is warmth from the cafe and the walk. There is caution that pulls the warmth into order before it can spill. There is a thread of anger for the man on the carpet and for the way my father made him a lesson and called it housekeeping. There is a small, foolish happiness because Dmitri listened to fairy tales as if they mattered.

I set the cup down, and it leaves a ring because I forgot the saucer. I wipe it with my thumb. I tell myself I will sleep because sleep is a discipline. The house listens the way a cat does before it is ready to pounce. I close my eyes. I open them again.

My phone lights the room and then settles into a dim glow that still looks louder than the dark. I pick it up because I'm weak and because sometimes, the worst thing to read is better than not reading at all.

A message. Aleksandr.

Are you really marrying him? Tell me it's not true.

9

DMITRI

The cafe's steam is still in my throat when I walk her home through a white, unhurried morning. At her gate, the day is flat and bright, a clean page, but I know too much to trust it. The message sits on my screen like a cut. I see her to the hall anyway, let the porter close the outer door, watch the red of her scarf disappear around the turn, and only then look down again at the line Misha sent from a ghost account. *Aleksandr Morozov. Back in Boston. Seen twice near Tremont and once outside the parish that keeps our feast days.* A second ping lands, a tight crop from a glass door. A profile, the soft jaw, a face that expects forgiveness. My jaw tightens until it hurts. *No entourage.* Misha adds a line. *A rental.*

I stand for a moment with the wool of my coat cold from the street and her warmth still under my palm, the echo of her laugh still in the room. Then I lock the phone and slide it into my inner pocket. At the café, I told her it was nothing, a small matter that did not belong to our table, and I set the screen face down so the glow would die. It would be easy to call her back and salt the truth with the fact. But it would be wrong. She has earned a night that belongs to her and not to a ghost who once called himself her future.

I take the service stairs. Men in my seat don't advertise when they mean to hunt. Marble keeps the day's footmarks, brass keeps its polish, the house holds steady like a creature that has chosen to live until spring. Order holds, yet small signs gather—a car that lingers one meter too long, a parish door watched from the far curb. That is how a squall begins. Last time, it cost her months.

In my study the lamps are low, the clock counts a clean measure, the wall map shows docks and alleys and the old grid that taught me to read this city like a ledger written in salt. I press the silent call button built into the desk. A latch clicks down the corridor. Three rooms along, Misha steps in coatless, sleeves rolled, jaw set.

"Say it," I tell him.

"Aleksandr," he answers, using the tone he keeps for men who like mirrors. "Polite flight, no record on the ground, cash for a rental beneath his taste, and a walking loop that spells her name if you lay it over the streets. He wants to be seen by her and by us. He is definitely fishing."

"Short-term lease in Back Bay?"

"Yes."

I move a thumb across the edge of the desk until the grain speaks back. "Is he alone?"

"For now," Misha says, dropping the flourish. "New York burnt his bridges. Pride does the rest."

"Who holds his leash?" My fingers tap the table.

"I smell Sergei Vetrov." Misha's voice is flat. "He met a Vetrov runner twice. Same rental."

"His aim."

"Valentina," Misha says.

"He wants the girl," Misha says, clipped.

My jaw locks. The room narrows to the map and her name. Heat climbs my neck and goes still behind my eyes. I set both palms flat on the desk so the wood keeps me from reaching for a trigger that is not here.

Misha watches. He doesn't ask why she matters more than she should. He shifts his stance a half step closer, as if already placing his body between her and the door. If I gave one word, he would take the muzzle meant for her and call it work.

"Should we pick him up?" Misha asks.

I let the question hang, meet his eyes, and give him the small shake that means no.

"Two on him. Not close. Three corners back with glass. One on the building across from the parish. One on Tremont. We log plates. We don't spook him."

This is how we kept the city from turning into coins in mouths that never paid a debt. We move in shadow and stay behind glass. Our work is not a parade. We keep the record and leave the noise to men who need an audience.

"The house." I lift a brow.

"Perimeter holds," he says. "Inner ring at dignity distance. The cameras are tuned. No one steps into her corridor unless the roster names him."

I don't sit. I think of the way she held her cup with both hands at the café, how she waited for me to lift the fork before she tasted honey cake, how she watched my face when the phone lit, trust clear, a question under it. She is not a girl and not a rumor. She is a woman who learned to tell the truth to a roof that has stood longer than most men.

I remember the winter she came back from New York with her heart bruised and her pride unbroken. Her mother was like an expensive porcelain vase too far from any hand. Her father, Boston's longest-standing Pakhan, steadied tables when talk grew rough. Valentina grew in gilded halls and under painted domes, learned four alphabets before most girls learned one, and held beeswax tapers close to her heart. That schooling did not make a soldier. It made her stand tall.

Anatoly did not roar when he saw his daughter's face. He set a glass down too hard and watched the street with the prayer rope tight in his fist. He called two men and then sent them away without a word. By morning, a folder for Vienna sat under her teacup, a childhood wish dressed as a cure. She closed it and stayed, refusing to run away from her hurt. Instead, she learned the routes from pantry to parish and from ledger to her small trips. She stood under glass and did not bow.

"No eyes close on Valentina for now," I tell Misha. "Keep rooms and routes clean. If danger speaks first, we listen. But Aleksandr carries the tail."

"So the threat roams and we hold the doors," he says, weighing it. "Understood."

I take a card from the drawer, the one that fits under a door without whispering against wood, the one cut from heavy stock that smells faintly of ink and discipline. I write six words with the fountain pen I use for ledgers that matter. I don't stop to think about the curve of the letters. I don't soften a syllable. I fold the card once, then twice, because some messages belong small, then I leave the study and take the long corridor to her rooms.

The hall glows with lamplight that turns oak into something older than patience. At her door, I listen and hear a radio low, a woman saying something about snow in a county. I slide the note under the door and imagine it sitting at her feet like a dog that has never once asked for praise. Then I turn and walk back the way I came, and nothing about my step betrays that my life has shifted a degree.

The card says, *I don't ask for love. Only your truth.*

When I return to the study, Misha has laid out three photographs. Aleksandr by the florist where men like to pretend they remember anniversaries. Aleksandr in profile near a parish bulletin board with a flyer for a winter coat drive. Aleksandr in the reflection of a café window, jaw soft, eyes bright, the kind of handsome that passes in strong light.

"He wants the city to say his name," Misha says.

"He wants her to say his name," I answer, and at that my mouth tightens because anger is a tool and must be kept sharp. I think of hands on her shoulders that never learned restraint, and I plan from there.

I set pieces in motion the way a man sets a table. No banging, no shouting, only placement that makes sense when the uninvited arrives. The sedan we sent away tonight stays away until I call it, but a driver walks the block fence to fence in a coat that looks like a man going home. Two of ours sit in the little shop by the parish and talk about hockey until anyone who listens decides they are harmless. The streetlight opposite her gate gets a new bulb at one in the morning, the kitchen staff at the estate receive a revised delivery schedule so no crate arrives without a known hand touching its lid, and anyone who tries to slide into a service door meets Sasha's eyes and remembers he has a family to feed and God to answer to.

We make our moves. We don't post about them. That is how men who think crime is glamor lose their grip and begin to pose. This is not a theater. This is our house.

I send one more line to Misha. If Aleksandr speaks to her, I want the time and the light, not the words. We will not catch her voice in a machine. She will not forgive me for that, and I will not forgive myself.

"Understood." He keeps it short and leaves me with the sense that a door has been opened by someone who believes charm is a universal key.

I walk to the chapel because now I can. The icon looks down from a face worn smooth by mouths, the lamp burns clean, the red cloth on the rail holds no ash. I stand under the dome and speak one sentence, because I believe that what we say in here rewrites us out there. *Guard her name.* It is one line in a book I have carried longer than I have carried a gun. It belongs to Valentina and to every woman whose breath was ever turned into collateral by a man pretending he was built for power. I protect because vows are the only fence that keeps the wolves out of a chapel. Then I touch brow, chest, shoulder and shoulder, and the old motion resets something in me that city and work like to unhook.

Men like me don't practice sleep as art. I sit with the night and write lists for morning. Two trucks need new tires before the next run. The longshore steward needs an apology for a slight he earned and doesn't deserve because living with that kind of irritation breeds rebellion. The choir wants a folded table so the altos can rest mugs without spilling on the hymnals, and I will procure it. The obshchak ledger has two entries with handwriting I don't know. I will ask for the hand. The guard on the west lawn has grown lax in the third hour. He will learn to rotate if he wants to keep his post. I write and the list grows. It calms me more than tea would.

At five, the city pulls its first lights up out of the dark. I lace my boots and pull on a shirt that keeps a vow that is not complete yet. Then I walk the outer hall with a cup in my hand for show. The house stirs. The cook hums, the steward clicks keys, the boy who empties ash pails drags a metal bin along stone and tries not to scrape. The day begins with a rhythm that feels like law.

By eight, we have three more sightings. Aleksandr at the North End, where he doesn't belong unless he is shopping for sentiment. Aleksandr near a bench where I once asked a question and received a yes that tasted like a new road. Aleksandr in Back Bay at a building with a friendly doorman who has already told a cousin that Boston used to know how to dress. He leaves a florist with nothing in his hands.

Misha comes back with a look that says this will not end in conversation at a cafe. "Anatoly asked whether we will handle this with noise or with results," he says.

"Results," I tell him. "Noise is for weddings and funerals. Vows are quieter. This is a rat that wants to dine on memory."

"What do you want me to tell him regarding her?"

"Nothing," I say, and the word is hard because I prefer her to hear me first.

At noon, a driver brings a sealed bag from a downtown office I trust with small items that don't belong on a server. Inside is a single photograph printed on glossy stock. Aleksandr in profile again, now beside a phone booth that doesn't work, hand cupped to his mouth as if he were in a movie about better men. The caption Misha wrote in the margin reads, *He is calling no one. He wants watchers to believe he calls.* I smile because pride is free intelligence.

The knock at my door comes later, measured and swift. I open the door.

Valentina stands on the threshold with her hair down and her coat unfastened, the corridor's warmth still on the wool. Her face is pale from a night that did not take her, fury held tight enough to look like control. She holds the note between two fingers as if it were a match that has not decided whether to burn her.

"Why was Aleksandr followed?" she asks. Her voice is soft, but it cuts.

10

VALYA

*A*re *you really marrying him?* lands on my screen like a coin tossed into a well no one believes in anymore and still cannot help listening for the splash. I stare at Aleksandr's name until the letters stop meaning sound and go back to being shapes. The little green bubble glows against the dark, soft as deceit. I don't answer. I don't delete it. My thumb hovers, and my mind runs.

Another bubble appears. He writes in that coaxing register he saves for mirrors and soft rooms. *Your wolf trails me from parish to tram stop, kitten, from Tremont to the harbor. I'm harmless. I only want you to know the truth.* He adds a pout in syllables, a smile made of vowels. He says he feels eyes on his back and virtue in his pocket. He says Dmitri is turning the city into glass and asks if I enjoy watching men follow the wrong man. I let the words sit. I don't feed his performance with mine.

How would he know?

The answer arrives in pieces I have set aside all day like teacups I don't want to break. The man downstairs with his face neatly corrected by a wall. My father's rage turned cold enough to set the room. Dmitri's steadiness at the cafe while his phone lit and he fed patience to the flame. A word escapes a door in this house, and it grows a body and a price before the incense fades.

Aleksandr would know because someone wanted him to. He would know because someone in a service corridor mistook a sacrament for gossip and carried it to a name outside of family. Wolves don't open gates. Hands do.

Heat climbs my neck. I press the cold of the window to my forehead and take it away before my grandmother would scold me about marks. The room is too warm. The city is too quiet. The house breathes the way it does when it has made a decision.

A sound at the door. Paper whispers, the polite scrape of an envelope finding its way under the threshold like a fox under a fence. I don't need to bend. I'm already on my knees because I drop faster when I'm angry. The paper is thick and clean. The handwriting is not elegant. It is exact. One line. No signature. No plea.

I don't ask for love. Only your truth.

I don't put it down. I fold it once and carry it in my palm like a live coal, the paper warming until I can feel my pulse through the crease. He is order with a cross under his shirt. I saw the traitor bound at my father's feet, my father, the Pakhan, keeping vigil, and the room holds Dmitri's order, no spectacle, only truth. He is also the hand that corrected a Moscow import on the terrace without turning my name into a spectacle. He will call this protection. He will call my anger weather. I slide the folded line beneath the band of my sleeve, against the small bone of my wrist where my grandmother's red thread used to sit, and I tell the walls to stay out of my face.

I don't wait. I don't rehearse. I go.

The corridor light is chapel-dim. The carpet catches my steps and keeps them. I knock once because courtesy is a choice I'm still willing to make. He opens on the second heartbeat. Warm hall air lifts the ends of my hair. I have not slept, and it shows. My skin feels thin, my eyes ache, and old tea sits on my tongue. I carry his line like a coal in my sleeve, and I'm torn between truth and the fables my grandmother taught me to survive.

"Why was Aleksandr followed?" I ask. My voice is soft and exact. The kind of soft that cuts.

He doesn't deny it.

We are two quiet animals in a room full of maps. He says words like vow, honor, protection as if they are planks laid across a river. I don't step on them yet. He says he will not let my name be eaten by a man who treats promises like currency, that shadow is not the same thing as control, that dignity has a distance and he intends to keep it. He doesn't say the word love. He doesn't have to. The note under my sleeve stings like a truth I have not confessed yet.

"I'm not a vassal," I say. "I don't need a leash to be safe."

"You need a roof when it snows," he answers, and it is infuriating how calm his mouth stays when he is telling me the world will not change because I want it to. We go in circles that are not circles. They are a spiral around a center neither of us will touch. I leave before my pride learns his voice. The paper burns against my pulse the whole way back to my room.

In the morning, the city forgives us both by snowing. We wear civility like coats. The pretense is charity. We go to the North End for the auction our center is running, in a borrowed hall over a bakery where the floor tilts like an old deck. It is the kind of place where the stage needs nails every other week, where Reza catalogs donations by smell because labels lie, where strings of lights make even hard faces look kind.

I tell Dmitri he cannot wear the coat that makes him look like a verdict. He lifts an eyebrow and puts on a navy over-coat with a collar that says banker instead of soldier. I pretend not to see the way the fabric still understands the shape of a holster.

Inside the hall, tables wear checkered cloths, lot cards are hand-lettered, and a raffle drum clicks like a small engine. Reza posts bid sheets with clothespins. Toma ferries boxes from the stairwell. The parish ladies stack paper plates beside a tray of arancini that fogs the panes.

Paper snowflakes hang over folding tables labeled with marker, *Books*, *Toys*, *Winter Gear*. People nod because my name sits on pantry lists and coat drives, not on gala cards. A child in a knitted hat sells paper stars for two dollars to fund her school's heater. Dmitri buys five and folds them into my pocket without looking like a man who can be sweet. I make him hold a paper boat of arancini so hot the steam fogs his breath. The first bite burns his tongue, and he bites back a laugh like it is a secret he is not allowed to have. I catch it anyway.

"It is good to watch you pretend to be human," I say.

"I'm never pretending," he says, which would be funny if he did not mean it.

We stand under a string of lights that flickers with the obstinacy of old wiring. I hand him my glove so I can tuck a strand of hair back into the ribbon. He holds it like it belongs to a ritual he respects. Later, I will forget to take it back. That will be my excuse for walking into his room without knocking.

I stand at the front with a microphone and smile toward the direction of donors who want their names pronounced correctly. Dmitri stands at the back and pretends he is not a wall. Reza mouths *thank you* from behind a stack of tins wrapped in cellophane. Someone's grandmother bids a shocking amount for a quilt that smells like lavender and stubbornness. We sell a handmade wooden sled to a man who has never fallen in snow. I'm good at convincing people to be better than they planned to be for one night. Dmitri watches me work like a man who has never seen persuasion as a weapon.

Toma moves fast between the dais and the back room, arms full of donations and small prizes the volunteers hope to sell. It will not touch my father's gala numbers, and that is fine. When he sees Dmitri, his eyes brighten. He gives a neat nod and a quick sign of welcome.

After, we don't bolt for the door. The argument from before the auction still hums, but the night has hands. It smooths a corner each time we thank a volunteer, each time he lifts a box without being asked, each time I catch him speaking gently to a child who pretends not to listen. By the time we step outside, the edge has thinned.

We walk because the city asks for it. He buys me a hot drink from a cart with a small blue flame. He warms my fingers with the paper cup before he lets it go. We find a bench under string bulbs that hold their notes.

I speak first. The words feel risky and clean. I tell him I want a small kitchen with an open window and a table that stays busy. I want a child who thinks saints can be found in laundromats. I want work that smells like bread and printer ink and wool. He listens. He says he can fix leaky faucets. He says he cannot bake bread.

"Liar," I say, because I have seen his hands and I know what they can make behave.

There is a soft gravity to the afternoon that makes me forget we are not ordinary. I forget for exactly four blocks. It feels like a sin and a kindness.

Night folds the city back into itself. The estate receives us with old wood and locked memories. I remember the glove halfway up the stairs. It feels like an excuse. I go back down the hall, lift my hand to knock, and then don't, because I'm my father's daughter, and I have lived my life under doors that rarely answer the first sound.

The office is not locked. The lamp is low. The room smells like black tea and the bitter edge of toner. The glove sits on the desk corner, set neat and square. Beside it lies a folder with my name typed in a neutral font. The first page is a report. The ink is crisp. The clipped photograph shows my profile, head down, scarf high, a timestamp that matches a morning I thought was mine. The next is Aleksandr outside the chapel, snow in his hair, mouth arranged in that old apology. The third is a grainy shot of a driver I don't know.

Heat rises behind my eyes, unhelpful and honest. I make no sound. I set the glove where he left space for it and back out. The note under my sleeve is a small press I suddenly fear.

In my rooms the night is clean and useless. I light a candle because my grandmother told me to make a fire when anger comes. The flame sits up and behaves. I hover a finger at its edge, count to three, pull back, and call it discipline, not fear. I take the leather prayer book from the shelf and open to the ribbon my father slid in place, as if color could pace a life. The line waits with the patience of a saint who knows the end of the story.

I come to you with no secrets between us.

I speak the words into the room because the room keeps secrets whether I ask or not. I press my thumb to the crucifix at my throat. He asks for truth. The book asks for the end of silence. My pride asks for distance. All three are heavier than I look.

I sit on the edge of the bed and slide the note out from under my sleeve. The paper has warmed to the shape of my skin. I unfold it as if the ink might run if I hurry. I read the line again and again until the letters blur into a single demand. If I bring him everything, what does he do with it? Does he build a roof or a cage? Does he believe a woman's truth is a sacrament or a weapon? I don't have the luxury of waiting to be sure. Men in my family never waited. The women paid for that.

I rise and pace the length of the rug. The candle lowers itself by degrees. Snow taps the window with a patience that could be mistaken for gentleness. I breathe and smell beeswax and a winter that refuses to end.

The door opens without a knock because only one person would risk that and keep his fingers. He steps in like he owns the corridor and claims the room. His eyes go straight to my hands. He sees the book. He sees the note. He understands everything I'm thinking and acts like none of it changes the work.

"I'm watching Aleksandr for your own good," he says, nothing soft about his voice except the part that refuses to be cruel.

The candle throws our shadows across the icon like two people who have forgotten the choreography and are waiting for the choir. My jaw finds its line. My chest finds its anger. The note in my hand feels lighter than it did a moment ago... and more dangerous.

He says protect, I say include. He says roof, I say key, and the words spark until the room feels bright with argument, so I step into him and let my mouth choose for me, a long, greedy kiss that drags heat up from the floor. His hands find my waist and the small of my back and teach my body the shape of yes.

11

DMITRI

Her mouth meets mine like it's an argument she intends to win, and for a moment I let her. I let her press anger into me, teeth sharp behind soft lips, her body taut like a bowstring. Then I close my hand around her wrist and answer back.

"You come to me with fire," I murmur against her mouth, low, rough. "And you expect me not to burn?"

She tries to pull back, but my other hand is already at her waist, drawing her closer. The note slips from her fingers and falls between us like a witness. Her breath is hot, sharp with defiance.

"You don't own my truth," she says.

"I don't want to own it," I answer, tracing the edge of her jaw with my thumb, forcing her eyes to mine. "I want to hear it from your lips while you're too honest to lie."

Her pulse beats under my fingers, fast, betraying her. She tries to cover it with a laugh that sounds too thin.

"You mistake hunger for confession."

"And you mistake protection for a cage," I say, pushing her back just enough to pin her against the desk. The candle behind her throws firelight along her throat, and the sight drags something hot and old out of me.

Her hands fist in my shirt, not pulling me closer, not pushing me away. Waiting. Testing.

"You watch Aleksandr," she whispers. "You watch me."

"Yes," I admit, bending until my breath grazes her ear. "Because I want no man touching what I intend to touch."

She shivers, then bites down on the sound that wants to escape. I catch it anyway, catching her chin and drawing her back to my mouth, slower this time, deeper.

The desk edge digs into her hips as I press her harder into it, her thighs tightening against me in reflex. I taste resistance and need in equal measure. "Say it," I tell her between kisses, voice rough. "Say you want me here. Say you'll give me truth with your body, not just your words."

Her nails rake lightly across my neck. She doesn't say yes. She doesn't say no. She leans in and bites my lower lip instead, dragging heat from me in a growl. I half expect her to pull away, but instead she smiles, not softly or kindly but like a woman who knows exactly how far she can tilt the balance. "You think you lead this," she whispers. "You don't."

Before I can answer, she slips out of my hold. The sudden absence of her body against mine is a sharper cut than her teeth. She sinks slowly to her knees, deliberate, her eyes never leaving mine. My breath catches—not because I'm unprepared, but because I know exactly what this means.

"Valya," I start, my voice lower than I want it to be.

"Don't command me," she interrupts, fingers already at my belt. "Not here. Not now. You wanted truth? Watch."

The sound of leather sliding through brass fills the room, louder than the candle's hiss. Her hands are steady, purposeful, and when she frees me, the cool air of the room is nothing against the heat that surges from her touch.

I brace a hand against the desk behind me, the other curling reflexively in her hair. She tilts her head just enough to make it clear. She allows my hand there, nothing more.

Her mouth hovers, breath warm, tormenting. "Still think I need a roof?"

My throat tightens around a laugh that comes out rough. "I think I need mercy."

She doesn't give it. Her tongue drags slowly along the length of me, unhurried, deliberate cruelty. My body jerks despite every effort at restraint. She watches me over the curve of her cheek, eyes burning with triumph.

"Tell me," she says, lips grazing, voice thick with defiance. "Tell me you're in control."

I grit out her name, but the sound breaks when she takes me fully into her mouth, all the way, her hand firm at the base. Fire floods me, and control becomes a story I can't sell to myself anymore.

Her rhythm is steady, merciless, swallowing down every ounce of command I thought I carried into this room. Each drag of her mouth is an argument she is winning, each flick of her tongue another truth forced out of me.

"Valya—" My hand tightens in her hair, not to stop her, but because if I don't hold something, I'll shatter.

She pulls back just long enough to wipe her mouth with the back of her hand, eyes gleaming, lips wet. "That's truth," she says, then takes me again, fiercer, as if she intends to break every vow I've ever made by the sound of my own breath. Her mouth seals around me again, and the sound it makes —wet, raw, a low choke when I push too far—scrapes fire straight up my spine. I grit my teeth, my hand flexing in her hair. She thinks she's setting the pace. She's wrong.

"Open wider," I growl, pushing her down until her throat protests with a gag. The vibration nearly undoes me. She claws at my thigh, not to escape, but to hold steady as I drag her back and forth on me.

The room fills with the slap of my hips against her mouth, the wet pull of her lips, the muffled, desperate noises she makes every time I bury myself deeper. Each sound drives me harder, until I'm fucking into her with a rhythm that feels like punishment and prayer at once.

Her eyes water, mascara smudging at the corners, and I swear she's never looked more dangerous. She tries to smile around me, a garbled hum that sends a violent shiver through me.

"Do you hear yourself?" I rasp, pumping her mouth slowly, then hard again, savoring the way her throat takes me. "That's not defiance. That's surrender."

She gags when I hold her there, my grip iron in her hair. Her nails dig crescents into my thigh and the sound that rips out of her throat is obscene, perfect. I ease her back just enough to let her breathe, strings of saliva catching the candlelight between us. Her chest heaves, lips swollen, spit smeared across her chin. "Not surrender," she gasps, voice wrecked. "Choice."

That word makes something snap in me. I fist her hair tighter, drag her back down onto me, thrusting deep, faster now, the desk rattling under my grip as her gags turn to wet, helpless sounds. The noise fills the room like confession. Every shove into her throat is a demand, every pull back a denial, and still she takes it, still she lets me.

"Choice?" I snarl, hips jerking, her throat wrapping tightly. "Then choose to choke for me."

Her throat works around me, gag after gag, spit slicking her chin, dripping down onto her blouse. The wet choke of it, the obscene suction, the slap of my hips—it's a symphony of ruin, and I'm the one playing her.

Her eyes roll up for a moment when I hold her down too long, and the gag that tears out of her is so sharp it almost breaks me. My jaw locks and my thighs tremble with the effort of not finishing right there.

"Fuck," I snarl, yanking her off me, my cock leaving her mouth with a wet pop and a strand of spit snapping between us. She gasps, coughing, mascara streaked, lips red and swollen.

Before she can smirk her victory, I've got her hauled up by the wrist, spinning her into me. Her body collides with my chest, and I slam my mouth down on hers, tasting myself on her tongue, tasting the wreck I made of her.

"You think you're the only one who can take control?" I growl against her lips.

She tries to answer, but I'm already lifting her, setting her on the desk, shoving her skirt up and dragging her panties aside in one brutal sweep. The smell of her—hot, wet, waiting—wrecks every ounce of discipline I thought I had left.

I drop to my knees.

Her breath catches, a sharp intake, her thighs tensing around my shoulders. "Dmitri—"

"Shut up," I mutter into the heat of her, tongue flattening and dragging slowly from the very bottom of her to the slick ache of her clit. Her hips jerk, a strangled sound ripping out of her throat.

I lick her again, harder this time, then suck, pulling her into my mouth until she cries out, the sound half broken, half furious. I want her ruined on my tongue. I want every noise she tries to swallow.

Her fingers knot in my hair, not to stop me—never that—but to anchor herself as I work her open, lips and tongue relentless. Her taste floods me, sharp and sweet, and I growl against her, the vibration making her buck. She gasps my name like a curse, head falling back, thighs trembling against my grip. I drag my tongue in hard circles, sucking until her breath fractures into jagged pieces. Every sound she makes, every whimper, every muffled cry, I take it in, swallow it down like proof. "Truth," I mutter into her, tongue flicking mercilessly. "This is your truth."

Her body arches under my mouth, thighs tightening hard enough to bruise against my shoulders. She's panting, broken sounds tumbling out of her throat, one hand fisting my hair, the other clawing the edge of the desk. I know the moment she's at the edge. Her breath catches, her hips grinding desperately against my face, her voice breaking into a sharp, pleading cry she can't hold back.

I pin her thighs wider and bury my mouth deeper, tongue lashing her clit until she shudders. "Come for me," I growl into her, and the command tips her over.

Her whole body jerks, back bowing, a strangled scream tearing free as she comes hard on my tongue. I drink it in, the taste, the sound, the way she shakes as if she's fighting it and losing anyway.

And when she's still caught in that quake, when her orgasm is tearing her open and leaving her raw, I don't give her time to breathe. I rise in one motion, cock already taut, and slam into her with a single brutal thrust. Her cry breaks again, shock, pleasure, the last ripples of climax colliding with the sudden stretch of my filling her. Her nails rake down my back through the fabric of my shirt, her head snapping forward to press into my shoulder as I drive into her, deep, hard, unrelenting. "Dmitri." It comes out a gasp, half protest, half prayer.

"Say it," I snarl against her ear, hips pounding, desk rattling beneath us. "Say this is where your truth belongs."

Her reply is a scream caught between my name and a sob of pleasure, her body tightening around me, milking me as I thrust harder into the wet heat that's still spasming from her climax. I grip her jaw, forcing her to look at me, her lips parted, her pupils blown wide. "Look at me when you come again," I growl, slamming into her until her words dissolve into sound.

The desk shudders under us, papers scattering, the candle guttering in its glass. My hands lock her hips in place as I drive into her, deep and brutal, every thrust dragging another broken sound from her throat. She's still trembling from the first orgasm, but I don't let her down, don't let her catch her breath. Her pussy grips me tighter with every stroke, pulling me deeper, making it harder to hold the line. I grit out her name against her ear, sweat sliding down my temple, jaw clenched as I slam harder.

"Again," I order, voice rough, teeth catching her skin. "You're going to come for me again."

She shakes her head, gasping, "I can't," but her body betrays her, clutching me tighter, clenching around me in helpless pulses that say she's already close.

"You can," I snarl, grinding into her, pressing deep, my thumb finding her clit and circling hard, merciless. "You *will.*"

Her cry splits the air, high and sharp, nails carving fire down my back. Her legs lock around my waist, heels digging in, and she breaks, her second orgasm tearing through her, body convulsing, every squeeze around my cock dragging me closer to the edge.

"Fuck!" The word rips out of me as the heat coils tightly, snapping, and I spill inside her in heavy, violent pulses. I hold her hips down, buried to the hilt, feeling every spasm of her cunt milking me, pulling every last drop.

Her head falls back, throat arched, the sound she makes somewhere between a sob and a moan. I can feel her heartbeat through her body, frantic against mine. I stay inside her, chest heaving, hand still gripping her jaw so she can't look away. Her lips are parted, her face wrecked, but her eyes burn, furious, triumphant, alive.

I kiss her once, savage and slow, tasting everything we just burned through. "You wanted truth," I murmur against her mouth, still buried deep inside her. "That was mine."

Her body softens under me, the tremors fading into slow breaths, her nails leaving shallow crescents in my skin as she loosens her grip. I keep my weight braced on one arm so she isn't crushed, my other hand sliding down to smooth her thigh where I've left the muscle trembling. She leans into me, sweat-damp hair clinging to her cheek, and for the first time since she walked in, her voice isn't sharpened for a fight.

"If this is going to work," she murmurs, her lips brushing the side of my neck, "you have to trust me."

I lift my head, searching her face. She holds my eyes steady, no flicker, no hesitation. "You have to take me at my word when I say I hate Aleksandr, that I see no future there." Her tone is steady, but there's an edge under it, the kind that comes from exhaustion as much as defiance.

I breathe out slowly, thumb stroking along her jaw, memorizing the steadiness she's giving me. The words are what I want to hear, but wanting and believing are not the same thing.

Jealousy is an ugly thing, and it has grown inside me like a root that won't cut clean. Aleksandr's name is in my blood now, sour, bitter. Every time I hear it, I see him too close, his mouth forming apologies he never earns, his shadow stretching over her like it belongs.

"I believe you hate him," I finally say, my voice low, careful, "but what I can't believe is that he's finished with you. Men like him don't let go. They circle. They wait for weakness."

She closes her eyes briefly, as if she can already hear the argument forming. "Then you'll just have to believe me when I say his weakness isn't me anymore."

I want to take that and hold it, but suspicion gnaws at the edges of my mind. Aleksandr has always been clever with silence, with patience. I can feel it like the weather turning —some ulterior motive curling behind his smile, some play I haven't seen yet. The thought of it makes my jaw tighten.

Her hand presses to my chest, steady, grounding. "Trust me, Dmitri. Or you'll break this before Aleksandr ever can."

The words land harder than her nails or her defiance. I kiss her forehead once, lingering, my mouth against the heat of her skin. I want to give her what she asks, but the truth is already written in the back of my skull. Jealousy has teeth, and suspicion keeps them sharp. I stay there, holding her, but the thought of Aleksandr does not leave the room.

12

VALYA

I see him before he sees me because winter wastes nothing. Footprints hold their edges and even sound carries farther than it should. Ghosts do not.

For three days, he is everywhere I'm not supposed to look—a reflection in a bakery door, a shape at the end of a block I cross without hesitation, the suggestion of a coat at the turn of a corner. It is not romantic. It is annoying in the way a song you used to love becomes a pill. I tell myself I'm imagining him because memory is thrifty and has good aim. It uses a reflection, a coat shape, and a corner and calls it a man. The small parish off Myrtle, where my grandmother used to pray and where Father Gavril keeps hours and icons hang low, sits just outside our perimeter. Aleksandr waiting there is a dare, not romance. It is the exact place a story would put a test.

Snow falls, slow and fat, the kind that keeps what it catches. It settles on his shoulders and on a hat he never wore when he was a boy with ambition. Now, he dresses like a man of forms and signatures. Same cologne, cedar with a sweetness that burns a little at the end, a bottle chosen to be expensive and remembered. Same mouth, soft at the corners to make promises slide. He knows how to stand under a streetlamp.

"Valya," he says, and the old name wants to be an endearment, but it sounds like a hand checking a lock.

"Aleksandr," I answer, and I'm pleased that my voice is steady. I set my back to the chapel door because I like the feel of oak behind me. The icon inside lives at my shoulder height, and I'm not above borrowing courage.

"I heard," he says, stepping closer as if the snow were a curtain meant to reveal him. "About the engagement. A farce. Your father is desperate. This is a performance in a church you don't even believe in anymore."

He speaks softly, like he is still the boy who stole afternoons with me under the shadow of scaffolding and made me feel like fire, except fire in those days had no work to do. There is something new in his gaze now, a slickness he thinks looks like confidence. My grandmother would have sniffed and said, *Oil on ice.*

"It is not your business," I say. I could say more. The sentences crowd behind my teeth, then discipline walks them back into the room and shuts the door.

"Everything about you is my business," he says, and it has the ring of a line he has rehearsed in another mirror in another city. "Your father has made a mistake. Dmitri is dangerous. He will turn you into..." He pauses as if searching for a word that might get him back what he dropped. "Into a symbol." He lets the last syllable land softly, like a blanket over a question he doesn't want me to ask.

I'm loyal by habit and by will. I hate the Bratva when it is cruel, and I will defend the parts that remember a vow is sacred and a bargain is for sale. I hear my father's voice arguing with God in the chapel and Dmitri's low order on the terrace when his hand closed over a problem and taught it manners. Aleksandr calls Dmitri dangerous as if it is news. He has never understood how roofs work.

"And how would you know about the engagement?" I ask. A test. "You and my father don't share confidences, last I checked."

"Boston is small," he says, smiling like a man who has mistaken a rumor for power. He breathes out and lets the cologne do half the work. He is still the golden boy in an expensive coat, his smile crooking just enough to taunt without giving me anything to hold. "People talk. A poor, sad house clinging to old ways. Candles and Latin and a puppet in a black suit."

"Church Slavonic," I say, because if he wants to mock a thing, he should at least name it correctly. "Latin is for the other neighbors."

He doesn't smile at that because the joke doesn't love him. He steps close enough that the snow in his hair melts along the line of his jaw and leaves a shine. "You don't belong to this," he says with the voice that once taught me how to ignore the forecast and take the umbrella anyway. "Come with me for a coffee. Ten minutes. I have so much to tell you."

"Ten minutes to tell me what?" I ask because I don't refuse cleanly when part of me wants the argument. I learned that from the men in my family.

"That I can help," he says. "That you don't have to pretend to be a statue on a staircase. That there is work in New York that suits you. I know you still run that baby program at the center." His eyebrow tilts like he is offering me back a piece of myself I forgot. "You always loved the babies."

I don't move. My throat goes cold. It is not the weather. He left before there was any program at all. The work came after, when I came back from New York with a silence I could not spend, when winter was a room and I needed a door. It grew out of mismatched cribs and donated formula. Reza and a handful of trusted people know it breathes. I did not tell him. I don't give men in glass offices what belongs to a basement.

"How do you know that?" I ask, and the sentence drops between us like a brick into clear water.

He lifts one shoulder, easy. "I hear things," he says. "A man who cares keeps track of what his girl loves."

His girl. The two words rub the wrong way along my ribcage. I step back until the chapel door says stop. I fold my arms because I have nothing else to do with my hands that wouldn't escalate this into a scene I will have to admit to later.

The snow collects on our shoulders like patience.

"I'm not your girl," I say. "Not now. Not then, if we are honest about it."

He flinches, so small most people would miss it, and then the softness pours back over his face like a trained trick.

"Valya," he says again, shaping the syllables as if I'm still the girl who wanted to be a saint and a match at the same time.

"Come on. This" —he gestures vaguely in the direction of Beacon Hill— "this makes you smaller than you are."

"You mistook quiet for small." I meet his eyes until the charm blinks first.

There is a line between protection and control, and I have spent my entire life walking it in expensive shoes I did not ask for. My core wound is practical. Being loved means being owned.

Aleksandr carries ownership in the tilt of his chin. He was always good at it, even before the alliance ring that bought him streets. Dmitri guards like a vow he keeps close. He shows it when it matters. Neither house, ownership, nor oath is easy to live in.

"Congratulations," he finally says, finding a new angle. "On the farce." He lets his gaze drag along the chapel stone and the iron fence and then back to my face like he is measuring.

"When you are ready to stop playing altar piece, I will be where the real city is."

"Keep it," I say, and the words arrive without ornament. "I already have a city."

I step around him and let the snow take some of the heat out of my skin. He doesn't touch me. There is a car idling at the curb with windows too dark for a January afternoon. The plate is a rental and the driver's hat is cheap.

The sight makes me think of the narrow room below our floors where metal sleeps and men learn to speak in short sentences. I don't look back. I don't give the car a second glance. But I count the seconds it takes for the engine sound to fade because habit is a religion.

The armory basement is square. Oiled steel rests in its racks with the hush of things built to obey. A ledger lies open to a page that welcomes a fountain pen. In the corner hangs a small brass icon. Men who count bullets don't forget to cross themselves before they carry them.

Dmitri is speaking Russian to two men. I know Misha by the weight of his consonants and Sasha by the careful echo he gives to orders. The words cut and settle.

This is not the language from the ballroom. This is for rooms where decisions have muscle.

I hear *shape. Perimeter. Tail. Window. No heroics. Morozov.* Misha answers with a sentence that sounds like a lock sliding. Sasha repeats a time and then shuts his mouth like a man learning.

Dmitri stands across the room, coat off, sleeves rolled just enough to show the edge of ink that lives in his skin. Even the tables sit square to the walls. A map is pinned flat with steel clips that don't slip.

He sees me and finishes the sentence he is in without urgency or haste. His hand goes flat. The men read it as dismissal without insult. They file past me and pretend not to breathe. I don't pretend. I breathe carefully because something is coming.

"I went to the chapel," I say. I don't sit. "He was waiting."

Something flickers along the angle of his mouth and is gone. He doesn't ask which he. There is only one whose presence turns the street into a camera. He meets my eyes, lines true up, and I keep my footing. That is his trick, and it is why I'm still standing.

"What did he want?" Dmitri asks. His voice is level, all record and no claim, like a ledger line waiting for ink. He stands a step away and leaves it there.

"To be seen," I say. "To tell me my engagement is a farce. To tell me my father is desperate and you are dangerous. To ask about the baby programs." I watch his face for that, because I want to see what control looks like when it is surprised.

He lets nothing break the surface. A beat. A count. The smallest tightening at the corner of his eye as if something in the machine acknowledges a new gear. "He asked about the program," he says, repeating, which is either a confirmation or a prayer. His hands lower to his sides. One finger taps his thigh once and then is still.

"He knows things he shouldn't. That is a leak. Someone is feeding him." I kept my voice even.

"Good," he says. One syllable, flat and edged, not praise and not quite relief. He steps close enough that the distance thins, then stops because I'm the one who will decide how far this goes.

"Dmitri," I say, because I'm tired of rooms that require me to talk around the center. "He will keep coming. He thinks what he lost is a trinket he left under a chair."

He looks at the icon and then at me as if the two of us belong on the same wall. He holds my gaze until the seconds lose their place. The moment squares and waits.

"You shouldn't see him again," he says.

The sentence lands like a hand on a hot pan.

13

DMITRI

I say it in the armory basement, steel and maps swallowing softness. *You shouldn't see him again.* The words sound like a field order in a room that smells of oil and cordite. I watch her jaw set. I feel the damage land. I have put a command where a vow should be. I clear the room, send the last report upstairs, and wash my hands at the slop sink until the water runs cold as repentance.

The service stair threads the bones of the house and trades iron and cordite for wax and myrrh. I take it to the undercroft that keeps its own hush. Tall tapers mark the icons. Red glass lamps hold their small planets of fire on dark wood. I send a message to Father Gavril. When he comes, I ask him to begin the rehearsal so I can turn what I broke with authority into something that lives under God. He studies me in silence, the way a craftsman tests a blade. Then he speaks. Rehearsals are not punishments. They begin only with the bride's willing presence. Invite her. Don't compel.

Lamp oil breathes honey into the stone. Father Gavril's hands move with the economy of a man who has folded grief into service. On the little table, beeswax tapers wait, their wicks trimmed and patient. A red thread lies in a neat coil, the silver crowns rest in their velvet box, and a small blade sleeps under linen. The Gospel carries a faint breath of myrrh and salt.

Here, the room is older than our passports and steadier than our politics. The saints look down with eyes that remember hunger and don't despise order. I touch my brow, chest, shoulder, and shoulder and ask for the discipline to make my mouth worthy of the work.

She steps in, her braid low, ribbon red as a mark that says, "I belong to my dead and to myself." The chapel lamp catches amber in her eyes. She bows to the icons, crosses herself with the small exhale of a woman who was taught to keep breath for prayer. Only then does she look at me, and what I see is not defiance for its own sake but the hard edge of a woman who will not be owned and who suspects I might try.

"I spoke as a guard, not as a husband," I say before the priest speaks. "It was the wrong shape of care. I will guard without closing your door."

Her chin lifts a fraction. The ribbon trembles once, then stills. She gives me no mercy in reply, only her quiet that says *earn it*.

Father Gavril clears his throat, says the Pakhan will not crown his blood, that the honor belongs to two elders of the *obshchak* who stand as witnesses, hands on the Gospel, hands on the iron key, while brigadiers hold the aisle. He reminds Valentina that the red thread binds, the silver crowns bless, the salt cup seals, the black ribbon marks widows, the wax seal closes secrets, and the bell calls truth. Then he opens the service book to the marked page. "We rehearse words," he says. He reads the first line in Old Church Slavonic, consonants like river rock, vowels like open candles. He nods to me. "You know the cadence. You will carry her through it until it holds."

I answer the line with the weight it needs, not louder, not softer. The room receives it. He gives her the same line. She stumbles at the old shapes, tongue catching on a cluster that doesn't belong to modern speech. Her eyes flash irritation at herself. I stand half a step behind her and to the side. "Listen for the breath," I say softly. "Two beats here. The vowel opens, then you close it like a door against a draft." I show her with my mouth, not with touch. She takes the breath, opens the word, and the old syllable lands cleanly.

We move line by line, vow by vow, with the small and patient corrections that belong to work done honestly. Her voice grows sure within the antique grammar. Mine moves as if bone learned before muscle. I keep my hand at my side because she is not a soldier and I'm not a drill master. When she forgets to breathe, I breathe a measure where she can hear it. When she tenses at a word that cuts too close to an old wound, I say it first so the echo is mine, not Aleksandr's.

The red thread waits between us, the silver crowns asleep in their velvet box. Father Gavril gives the vow that lives nearest to my marrow, first in the church tongue, then in ours. *To guard her life with my own.* The syllables gather like storm light on the icons, deepening every color until even gold seems solemn. She looks to the icon of the Mother, then to me, a woman at a ledge searching for the next stone.

"I will speak it as truth," I say. My mother's hand is on my shoulder again, thin and warm with fever, three fingers pressing a cross into a boy's chest while a prayer turns his anger into a blade and not a stone. The vow is not new. Tonight, it has a name.

Valentina repeats the line. It breaks once on her tongue, then holds. She closes her eyes, and I see the past move through her like water. When she opens them, the silence is the kind that belongs in a temple and in a battlefield just before the first order. Father Gavril lets it sit. He doesn't hurry holiness.

We circle the rites. He touches the crowns but doesn't lift them, shadows crisscrossing his hands. He names the sequence for clarity—red thread at right wrists, shared cup, threefold circling, crowning by witnesses who will stand when we cannot. The small blood vow, a pinprick on each thumb, is because the Bratva insists that oaths tie families and not only lips. He says that any man who bends these words into leverage will be refused communion and protection both. Here, those are the same punishments.

I listen with my soldier's ear and with the part of me that kneels. I hear the policy in the prayer. The house will reduce access to the sacristy to two keys. Separate hands will fold the flower order and the choir list. The date will sit on no phone. Elders will sign the registry by initials, not by titles. Any mouth that repeats the altar's words for gossip will eat alone for a very long time. There is tact in this. There is steel in it. It honors the line between God's business and ours.

"To honor her heart above ambition." My throat tightens as if I have tried to swallow a dagger hilt-first. Ambition has always been the cleanest tool in my kit. To place her above it is a correction. I can see Anatoly in his office, silver hair bright against the window, deep lines cut by winters he refuses to name. He sees me as a threat. Still, he set his daughter above the seat, choosing a roof over a throne. I respect that choice. It mirrors my own.

Her voice quavers and then hardens. "To trust him with my secrets." She doesn't look at me. I don't ask for her eyes. Trust is a word I earn by refusing to pry where it would feel like trespass and by taking blows I could have avoided if I had chosen cowardice. I don't tell her any of that. She wants my discipline, not arguments.

When the last line closes, Father Gavril gives us the old Russian blessing that begins as a command and ends as an invitation. He ties the red thread around our right wrists without tightening, a rehearsal of binding with room to breathe. "You will carry this to the door," he says. "don't untie it until you touch the hall. Train your hands now not to pull away."

We walk the aisle with the red between us. It is such a simple thing. A thin strand that knows more history than I do, lying lightly over skin and pulse. She glances at me once, an angle of brow that asks whether I notice what she just learned. I do. She releases the thread first, at the line where the chapel ends and the house begins. I let it fall so the lesson belongs to her hand as well as to mine.

We cross the music room. Darkness clings to the walls, and the standing lamp beside the old piano keeps a small vigil. I go to it, drawn by the same unseen hand that lit a lamp in my soul today. The brass casts a gentle halo across ivory and ebony. I sit, place both feet where they belong, and let a simple hymn loosen into a lullaby. The melody moves in slow, clean phrases, each note laying a path for the next.

She rests her palm on the back edge of the instrument and watches the rise and fall of my knuckles as they travel the keys, the motion steady as a river under ice. When a man watches a mouth, he seeks persuasion. When a woman watches hands, she seeks evidence.

She lowers onto the bench beside me, her heat settling through me without touch. I shift a little so the piano doesn't creak. She looks at my mouth then, perhaps to see whether the shape of the truth suits me.

I let my left hand hold a drone and draw a line with my right that moves like a slow path through new snow. Her breathing lengthens, and the circle of lamplight flickers in her irises, kindling the golden flecks of her eyes. Her eyes almost drop their guard. I keep the tempo patient, letting each phrase settle before the next arrives, until even the old piano seems to grow quiet. Outside the door, the house recedes, as if lenses had gone to sleep.

"Again," she whispers like the first hush of snowfall in a chapel yard, and I repeat the vow in Slavonic and then in English so that both parts of her faith can carry it. She mutters the second half under her breath. The sound wraps around the room like silk that remembers being a flag.

She turns her face toward mine. There is no snap or storm, only the small tilt of a woman deciding to find out whether a mouth can be a home. I stop playing with my right hand and let my left hand hold the last chord open until it fades. Then I take her chin gently. Violence has taught me two kinds of strength, and the second is the one she wants. I kiss her slowly, with the certainty of a man who knows the floor will hold.

She makes a sound that lives somewhere between a prayer and a call to war. I answer it with my mouth, not with my hands. She tastes of clove and clean winter air and leans closer and doesn't flinch. I wait, and waiting turns into permission. My cross is a cool weight under my shirt, a reminder that reverence is a better teacher than desire ever was.

I rise, bring her with me, and don't break the kiss. The room beyond the music room is ours because I hold it so. The door stays open because secrecy is for strategy, not for love. I let her set the pace, and I keep it. When she steps back, I stop. When she comes forward, I meet her without taking the distance for free. Her fingers find the edge of my collar.

We cross a short stretch of shadow and lamplight toward the room that has a bed in it and no need for it to be an altar to anything except consent. I place my hand at the small of her back, light and steady, asking only. *Yes*, she answers with her body leaning into mine. Cloth yields. Skin finds air. I peel her blouse open, buttons scattering against the floorboards, and her breasts rise into my hands as if they were meant to be claimed there. Her breath stutters when my thumbs brush over her nipples, hard already, a sound catching in her throat that makes my cock ache.

She drags my shirt up and over, lips breaking from mine only long enough to tear it off me. Her nails trace the scars across my chest, sharp little reminders that I'm still flesh and not just steel. When her mouth follows her fingers, teeth grazing my skin, I growl low, the sound vibrating against her cheek.

I hook my hands under her thighs and lift her, pressing her back to the wall. Her skirt rides high, and I grind against the damp heat of her through lace, the friction making her moan into my mouth.

"Off," I mutter, yanking the panties aside until they tear, the sound loud in the quiet room. She gasps, half laugh, half outrage.

"You'll answer for that," she whispers, but she's already rolling her hips into me, already wet and open.

I sink to my knees again, this time not for patience but for hunger. My mouth seals over her, tongue driving deep, then dragging hard up to her clit. She cries out, hands flying to my hair, her thighs trembling around my ears. I lap at her, suck her, make her sob my name until her hips jerk and her slick runs down my chin. Before she can fall apart completely, I stand, grip her ass, and line myself up. Her eyes fly wide as I thrust into her in one stroke, burying myself to the hilt. Her cry tears through me, nails digging into my shoulders as her body clutches me tightly, hot, wet, greedy.

"Dmitri—oh, God," she gasps, back arching.

"Not God," I growl, pounding into her hard enough that the wall rattles. "Me."

Each thrust drives her higher, her cries turning ragged, wet sounds marking the rhythm of our bodies. I slam her down onto my cock, again and again, her cunt gripping me like a fist, dragging me deeper. "You feel that?" I rasp, teeth biting her throat, marking her. "That's mine. Say it."

She gasps my name, over and over, brokenly, her voice sharp with need. Her pussy clenches tightly, milking me, and I know she's close. I angle my hips, grind against her clit, and she shatters, screaming into my mouth, convulsing around me, every squeeze dragging me closer to the edge.

I push away from the wall and carry her toward the bed. She clings to me, legs locked around my waist, our bodies still joined, every step a drag of friction that makes her moan into my throat.

I lay her down, but I don't let go. I keep driving into her, slow and deep, savoring the way her body flutters around me after that first violent climax. She whimpers, biting her lip, and I catch her wrists, pinning them above her head against the mattress.

"You're not done," I murmur, rocking into her, drawing out another soft gasp. "I'll take you until you can't say his name even in your dreams."

She arches under me, eyes blazing even through her shivers. "Then don't stop."

I don't. I pound her into the bed. Her cries rise higher, each thrust dragging her closer, until she's trembling again, clenching around me. I release her wrists, and she grabs my shoulders, pulling me down for a kiss that's more teeth than lips. Then she flips me. I don't resist. She straddles me, hair falling like a curtain, breasts bouncing as she rides me hard, her hands braced on my chest. The sight makes me snarl, my hands gripping her hips tight as she slams herself down, taking me to the root with each stroke.

"You look at me," I rasp, staring up at her, sweat slicking her skin. "Don't close your eyes."

She doesn't. She rides me harder, faster, until she's crying out again, grinding her clit against me, chasing her own release. I thrust up into her in rhythm, and when she breaks, screaming my name, I grab her and roll us, keeping inside her as I take control back. This time, I put her on her hands and knees, fist in her hair, yanking her back onto me. Her scream muffles into the pillow as I slam into her from behind, the angle brutal, my balls slapping against her with each stroke. Her slick gushes around me, dripping down her thighs, her ass slamming back into me in rhythm with my thrusts.

"Tell me," I growl, tugging her hair so her back arches. "Tell me who you belong to."

"You," she gasps, breath hitching with every thrust. "Only you."

Her cunt clenches, spasming again, and I feel her gush around me, soaking the sheets as another orgasm rips through her. The sight nearly undoes me, but I'm not finished.

I drag her down flat onto her stomach, still buried deep, my weight crushing her into the bed as I fuck her slowly and grindingly, forcing her to feel every inch. She sobs into the sheets, overstimulated, shaking, but she doesn't tell me to stop. Her nails claw weakly at the mattress, her body quivering under mine as I keep her pinned and full.

Then I pull out, flip her onto her side, hook her leg over my hip, and slide back in. She gasps, eyes wide, the new angle hitting deeper, sharper, dragging another strangled cry from her. I pound into her like that, my hand around her throat, thumb brushing her pulse, and I feel her tighten again, unbelievably, ready to break one more time. "Come with me," I snarl, thrusts growing ragged. "Now."

Her orgasm milks me mercilessly, and when her teeth sink into my shoulder, I lose it. With a roar, I slam into her one final time and spill inside her, hot, violent pulses filling her until it runs down her thighs. Her head drops against my chest, both of us shaking, breaths ragged, sweat slick between us. I stay inside her, holding her pinned to the wall, her heartbeat hammering against mine. "Valentina," I murmur against her hair, voice hoarse, "I meant it. To guard your life with my own."

She looks up at me, eyes glassy, lips swollen, and for the first time tonight, she doesn't argue. She just holds my face in both hands and kisses me like trust.

14

VALYA

Morning arrives like a hymn I know by heart. Light pours through the high panes and lays clean bands across the floor. It tastes like honey that is not there, and before I remember myself, I hum the song my grandmother shaped over bread dough and small sorrows. Yelena carried it after her, low and steady, the nights she tucked me into bed while men downstairs turned oaths and debts into iron talk. My body feels both new and known, as if a door long stuck has remembered its hinges and begun to swing true.

I lie very still and let the room come into focus—linen and lace, a whisper of lavender from the wardrobe where fur kisses wool from a bygone winter. I touch the little cross at my throat. The hush inside me is not empty. It is the kind a church keeps after the last footfall has faded and the lamps go on burning.

I dress without ceremony because I don't want to break the spell by thinking too hard about it. A simple sweater, a skirt that lets me move, wool tights, and flats I can run in if I must but hope not to. I part my hair cleanly and let it fall in loose waves. From each temple I braid a narrow strand and join them at the crown with a thin red ribbon, tradition stitched softly in a modern line. The mirror holds a woman I recognize and a girl I don't want to lose. Both of us are smiling.

There is a knock at the sitting-room door, polite and quick. Not family. A houseman stands there with a crystal vase in both hands, careful as a man carrying a crown. White blooms spill over the rim, thick as cream, petal upon petal. He nods and sets them on the console when I step back.

"From a courier, Miss," he says. "No name given." He leaves me with the flowers and the choice of what to do with them.

Gardenia. The scent hits like a hand on my collarbone. My grandmother dabbed the oil behind her ears on feast days, a secret she pretended was nothing. The smell filled the pew while she prayed, little moons of scent that rose and fell when she bowed. Something cold drops into the pool of my morning and makes rings. There is a card tucked among the leaves, plain cream, and the morning holds its breath.

I don't set the card on the table. I slip it into my pocket and feel it like a splinter.

The flowers are beautiful. They are also a message I did not invite into a morning I meant to keep honest. I lift the heavy vase, carry it to the small hearth, and kneel. The matches wait in the drawer Yelena keeps for simple dignities. I strike one and tip it to kindling. Dry wood takes fire with an obedient hush. I feed the flame until it is truthful and high. The gardenias don't belong to this room. They belong to a memory I refuse to loan to a man who traded me for a family with better stationery.

I pull the blooms one by one from their stems. I lay them on the fire and watch the white turn brown. The edges curl, the perfume thickens into something sweet and choking. I open the flue wider and let the smoke find the cold. I burn them all. When the last petal blackens, I set the empty vase on the hearthstone and wash my hands until the scent is only a thought.

Yelena taps and peeks in. She takes in the vase, the ash, my face. Her mouth tightens and then softens.

"Breakfast," she says, as if that word can balance the rest of it. Perhaps it can.

I take tea with honey and toast with marmalade at the little window where the light makes the city look gentler than it is. The card feels heavier than paper in my pocket. I fold it once without looking and slip it under the back cover of my grandmother's prayer book, where old paper has learned to keep other people's certainties quiet. It doesn't belong to the room any more than the flowers did. If I keep it, I keep it on my terms.

By afternoon I'm in the South End, the morning and the flowers shut behind me. The driver lets me out a block from the center because I prefer to arrive on my own feet. The cold is clean and doesn't promise what it cannot give. The brick building looks more forgiven than funded, and the door sticks the way it always does until I lean my shoulder into it and remember that nothing worth keeping opens the first time you knock.

The inside smells of coffee and the stubborn comfort of old linoleum. Reza lifts his head and smiles. The children run at me. Little hands tug at my coat. A girl in a purple hat shows me mittens that are two sizes too big. She is proud of them anyway. I kneel to praise their courage and fold them so her hands don't drown. A boy with a gap-toothed grin demands to know whether Santa can drive in snow. I inform him that Santa operates a fleet. Two mothers push warm bread wrapped in clean dish towels into my hands. They insist that I take an extra loaf "for your old man," which makes me laugh because I cannot decide whether they mean my father or the god who keeps being asked to do too much work in this city.

I take inventory in my head while I hand out oranges from the sack I brought this morning—sizes in coats, the count of dolls with both eyes, how far our gift cards will stretch if I can coax one more vendor with a smile and silence. Reza reads the Wednesday pickup list. I hand Toma lunch and wool gloves. He taps his throat, shakes his head, and smiles softly. That smile, not words, brightens the afternoon. For two hours, I'm exactly who I like to be—useful, invisible, and believed.

When I step out for air, the light is already lowering toward that blue that belongs to Boston in winter and no other city. I tuck my hair into my collar and watch the fog of my breath drift. The street is ordinary, a man scraping a windshield with a credit card, a woman arguing with a Labrador about a puddle, someone singing two streets over where a window is open against cooking smoke. Ordinary until my skin tells me the first true thing it has said all day.

There is a man across the way who is not from here. He wears a black coat of good wool. His haircut looks like he got it from a barber who charges for silence. His stance is military, without the slouch of bad pride. With his hands bare in the cold, he chooses grip over comfort. He is not looking at me, which is how I know I'm being watched by someone who knows his work. In the bakery window, our gazes meet only as reflections, and his mouth tilts as if the glass has told him enough. He flexes his bare fingers once and strolls up the block, a spectator walking away from a winter show before the last act.

I stand for another half minute to see whether my mind is making a poem out of nothing. When he shifts his weight and the poem becomes a report, I turn back into the center and take the back exit through the hallway that smells of bleach and crayons. In the street behind the building, my driver is exactly where I told him to be. He watches my face and doesn't ask.

"Loop," I say. "Slowly." We take the long rectangle around the block. The man is gone by the time we pass the front again, which only means he remembered to leave before I gave him a number plate. I put my hand on the bread in my lap and feel its warmth bleeding away.

At the estate, evening arranges itself in candles and the silver that appears only when important men require proof that time obeys. I don't change. I take the narrow stair behind the kitchens, the one that threads the house's bones, and descend until the air cools and the lights stop pretending to flatter. I know where he will be at this hour, and urgency carries me there. Stillness lives among steel and maps, in the space between one order and the next.

Dmitri is there, sleeves rolled, speaking with three of his men, the consonants clean and low. He looks up when I step into the doorway. He takes in what I'm wearing and the set of my mouth and dismisses his men with a look. They vanish into the hall without the usual shuffle.

"Valya," he says. He keeps his hands visible. His voice is level.

"Am I being followed?"

"Yes," he says. No preface. No apology. "It is for your safety."

I stand very straight so that I don't sway with the anger that promises more relief than it can deliver. "How many times have you said that?" I ask, then, "Do you trust me?" I'm surprised by how much I want the answer to be the right one and how much it will hurt if it is not.

"More than I trust myself," he says. I believe him because he doesn't blink when he says it, and because his mouth doesn't move the way a mouth moves when it is trying to be pretty.

His eyes are ice gray, ringed darker, winter still until they land on me. Then the surface loosens, thin ice to quick water. Heat slips into my veins as if a match has been struck under the skin. I slow my breathing and bank the flare like coals under ash.

"Don't make me a ghost in my own life," I say. It is the only concession I will make tonight.

"I will not," he says. "I'm trying to make you visible only to the eyes that matter."

I leave before I say something I will regret, because my tongue is quick and my dignity deserves better than a speech given to the wrong audience. I climb the long stair-case to my room, where the brass knob keeps a trace of heat and the walls hold the ghosts of winter mornings. The house hushes around me. I take off my coat and hang it with more precision than necessary. I unpin my hair and shake my head. This small pocket of stillness should settle me. It doesn't.

I open the dressing-table drawer for the comb I usually forget to put back, and my fingers meet paper where there should be none. Not the little square of cream I hid under the prayer book. Not a receipt. Not the note from Dmitri, which I still have not decided how to answer. A letter, old cream turned almost ivory, folded in thirds the way he used to fold things to make them feel like secrets.

Aleksandr's hand is so sure of itself that it borders on parody. The same generous loops. The same straight, decisive lines. The same habit of pressing too hard on the down-strokes so the ink darkens like a bruise. I don't have to open it to know it is the one he left in my coat pocket the winter we thought we were better than the houses that built us. I kept it for a while after he left because people who lose faith keep relics even when they know better. Then one day, I hid it so it could not keep staging the past. Bottom of a jewelry box. Back of a closet. Another map. Not here. I did not put it in this drawer.

My heart does a small, ugly thing, the kind of lurch that happens when the floor remembers it is stairs and not a plane. I sit down hard on the rug because my knees have decided they would prefer not to participate.

"He was in my room?" I say it to no one, and the room hears it like a bell that cannot be unrung.

Footsteps in the hall, quick and controlled. A knock that is not a question. The door opens. Dmitri steps in, eyes finding mine on the first breath and then dropping to what I'm holding because he reads rooms to survive. His coat is unbuttoned. He has frost in his hair. The holster sits against his ribs, unashamed of itself.

I'm on the floor with an old letter in my hands and ash still under my nails from the way I chose to start my morning. I hold the paper up so he can see what I shouldn't be holding. My voice is steady because I have learned how to make it so, even when my bones are not. I give him the only sentence that matters.

"He was in my room."

15

DMITRI

The door gives under my hand because vows have a way of teaching wood our names. She is on the floor, back against the bed, legs folded under, hair loose like a pennant after a storm. Charcoal shadows the crescents of her nails, proof of a fire no sink has yet washed away. My gaze narrows. The room sharpens around the letter she holds between two fingers. Her face is set too carefully. The eyes are the only disobedience, bright, wet at the rim, furious in a way she hides from the mirror and doesn't bother to hide from me.

She lifts the paper so I can see what I should never see here. Her voice is level because she has trained it that way. The steadiness hurts more than any cry.

"He was in my room."

The words strike like incense on live coal in a censer. I see the red thread, the crowns sleeping in velvet, the priest's old cadence. My heart lurches as I fully realize that the promise

I spoke is not a contract but a sacrament—to guard her breath, her bed, her secrets, the altar of her life. Anything that enters unbidden profanes us both. My heartbeat drums behind my ear, a slow, relentless hammer. I press my thumb to the iron of my cross and make it kneel. Rage is noise, and vows are order. The prayer grips me before the rage does.

"Give me the letter," I say.

She releases it into my palm as if she is handing me a license to strike a match and a plea for mercy at once. I don't read it here. I slide it into a clean envelope from my pocket, seal it with my thumb, and take out a fresh glove for the ash on her skin. I kneel and hold my open hand under hers. She hesitates, then rests her fingers in my palm. I brush the ash into a sheet of white paper and fold it. Evidence lives better without our breath on it.

"Look at me," I say softly.

She does. Fury lives there, but not at random. She wants answers, and she wants boundaries changed. She wants both without giving an inch of herself away. I take her terms as binding.

"He will not cross this threshold again," I tell her. "Not with keys, not with any shadows, not with the arrogance that thinks a woman's room is a corridor." Amber eyes with gold flecks hold their guard, then soften by a notch.

Work begins before I stand. I signal the hall with two fingers. Two men appear and don't stare. "Seal the landing," I say. "Soft steps. Access is mine and the steward's only. Hold a respectful span from her door, three paces, no closer. Eyes forward, lenses clean. If you crowd that line, you forfeit the post."

I step into the corridor, and the house shifts around the order. "Double the guards on this wing," I tell the captain. "Rotate on short watches. Fresh eyes every two hours. Anyone who yawns on post goes home and doesn't return."

To the systems man, "Door contacts on her suite change now. Add vibration to the sill and mercury tilt to the balcony latch. Motion sensors in the dressing room and the prayer corner, and route every sensor to a silent alert that goes only to my device and to one deputy I will name. Keep the security panel dark. No lights, no tones, no status change visible to staff or intruders."

To the key master, "Audit every master within the hour. New pins for this floor before dusk. Anyone late to the exchange is already fired."

To the quartermaster, "All gifts and deliveries are quarantined in the service room by the north door. No scent crosses the threshold. Anything botanical is inspected and logged, then burned outside after photographs."

To the matron who raised half this house, "I need two trusted women to sweep her wardrobes and bed for lenses, threads, or insult. I require gloves, patience, and respect, and if you find a thing, you put it in my hand, not your story."

To Misha on comms, "Build a circle around Morozov. *Tishina, bez shuma.* Silence, without noise. He breathes near this block, I want the air report at once. No contact. No theater."

He answers once. "*Ponyal.*"

I go back in. She has not moved. Her thumb rubs her little cross in a small rhythm that says she is building a wall brick by brick and choosing not to hide behind it. I sit on the carpet across from her, lower than the bed, level with her knees. No shadow thrown, not from me.

"Say what you need to say," I offer.

"I need my life to be my own," she says. "I need my room to be a room and not a ledger."

"It will be," I answer. "The ledger lives with me."

"I'm not a ledger entry," she says.

"No," I say. "You are the page I keep clean."

Her mouth turns as if that answer angers her and steadies her in the same breath. She says nothing more. I don't force words into a room that has had enough of men's certainty. I stand, set the envelope and the folded ash on her desk, and rest my hand on the chair back to anchor my next sentence.

"I will be outside until sundown," I tell her. "Then I will come back. This house will feel different by night."

"Different," she repeats, not a question.

"Safer," I say. "And yours."

I bow once to the icon in her corner because that is how I leave rooms that matter. The corridor receives me like a sheath.

The next hours are iron and paper. A locksmith's cart hums like a hive. Brass pins spill like small coins into new cylinders. We chalk hairline seals on window latches and lay a red thread on the inside of her knob, an old sign, not superstition, a mother's mark that tells you if a door has been turned. We replace the runner outside her suite with a split layer that listens for weight where it doesn't belong. We move a lens in the far sconce to give me the line I want on the service stair. I sign for new badge lists with a pen, not a password. I hold the master key in my palm and feel its teeth. A key is a promise, not a convenience.

The gifts that arrive are logged, opened, photographed, and set in a cold room with a bulb. White lilies to the fire out back. A box of candied fruit that smells like an apology to the bin. The card with her name goes into a file with the others I keep. Men like Morozov forget that a house is a mouth that can testify.

By twilight the perimeter has a new temper. Men stand two doors down from her corridor with shoulders relaxed and eyes aware. They are fed. Hot food clears the head. The chapel lamp burns without wavering. The house breathes beeswax and winter through the vents, old wood settling its bones around the new lines I have drawn.

I send one last message to Misha.

Shadow holds?

Holds, he replies. *He is angry. He will make the next mistake for us.*

Let him, I answer and put the phone away.

Night deepens into the kind I like—few cars, honest cold. I take the back stair with my jacket unbuttoned so the holster sits easily. The guards on the landing look at my shoulder, not my face. The thread on her doorknob lies exactly where I left it, unbroken, a thin line of red against wood. I touch brow, chest, shoulder, shoulder, and feel the cool cross under my shirt. The quiet fury wraps itself back into discipline.

I open her door and step inside.

16

VALYA

Snow freckles the window like breath on glass and his hand rests warm and heavy across my stomach as if my ribs are the only shore he trusts. He smells of soap, cold wool, and the clean bite of gun oil that refuses to become perfume. I let myself drift off again. In the dream, the house key hangs on a ribbon. Keys decide who may cross a threshold. When I wake, he is dressed for war—black knit under the jacket, holster settled, boots that speak in stone. He bends to me. The chain lowers with him, the cross grazing my hip through the sheet. It is cold as iron, stubborn as faith.

He moves his palm on my lips once, slowly, a benediction without theater. Last night settles into something I don't have language for yet. Reverence has a temperature. That is my discovery. He lifts his hand away, and the absence he leaves feels colder than the window.

"Where?" I ask because I'm my father's daughter and because I refuse to be a girl who pretends her house is not a city with a pulse. His gaze searches my face like a man checking a door he already locked.

"Out," he says. The word is deliberately small. He leans and presses his mouth to my temple, then he is gone, boots softened by the runner as he vanishes into a corridor that eats sound for breakfast.

I lie still and watch the snow settle into a steady fall. It is the kind of day that would forgive almost anything if asked correctly. I reach for the little leather book on the table, my grandmother's prayer book with the cracked spine and the red ribbon flattened by decades of thumbs. Last week, the page with the vows felt like a threat written in beautiful penmanship. Today, I open it without bracing. The ink has not changed. I have.

"To bind my fate to his," I whisper, waiting for the old recoil, the reflex that says binding is ownership and ownership a velvet word for prison. It doesn't arrive. Perhaps because last night, he kissed like a believer, not a thief. Perhaps because he did not try to bind me with hands. He spoke his promises like instructions for holy work, each one meant to be carried, not worn. Perhaps, I'm tired of treating love as a classroom where I pass or fail by how well I disappear.

"To trust him with my secrets." As a girl, I learned to set my mouth in the shape of a smile while I hid the ledger behind *Vogue* and taped the charity boxes shut with my handwriting turned into armor. Trust is expensive in this house. I press my thumb to the page and wait for the flinch. It doesn't come.

I dress without the costume. Black sweater, wool skirt, hair braided low, twining with a red silk like an anchor. The crucifix warms in my palm before I fasten it. When the chain settles, my heart finds the old rhythm it taught itself.

The morning chooses silence for company. I take the back stairs past the linen closets that smell of starch and clean hands, past the service door where deliveries arrive on schedule, and sometimes what should never have crossed our threshold. The chapel waits the way bread waits under a cloth. The carved door gives with its polite groan. The air inside is beeswax and lamp oil, incense clinging to wood the way perfume lives forever in a shawl.

The icons watch with patient calm, a gaze that once frightened me and now feels like being seen by those who have already forgiven me for forgetting names. I bow, touch brow, chest, shoulder, shoulder, and light a taper for women who survived men and for men who remembered how. The wick catches with a small sound, and the flame stands up and behaves.

I set the *Book of Vows* on the rail and practice. The Old Church words are river stones in my mouth, rounded, resistant. Father Gavril told me to follow breath more than consonants. They stand firm and soften only when placed where they wish to rest. He is right. I keep the pauses he taught and put muscle behind the syllables until they bear my weight.

"To bind my fate to his," I say in English as well, because a woman should hear herself clearly at least once in a language she uses to order bread and tell a child to go to sleep. The sentence lands without banging into the walls. I say it again, louder. The saints keep their silence, and the Mother's mouth almost softens.

"What I bind," I tell her under my breath, "I will bind on purpose. Not because a man thinks protection is a cousin to possession. Not because my father wants to remake the city in my bones. On purpose."

I stay long enough to know the words will come when I call for them. Then I take the long, warm corridor back to daylight. The house this morning holds the expectant hush of winter households—silver faintly clinking in a far room, a broom soft against stone, the distant punctuation of laughter that has not yet remembered why it should be quiet.

Back in my room, breakfast waits on a low table—buckwheat kasha with a softening square of butter, two *syrniki* sugared lightly, sour cherry jam that stains the spoon, black bread cut thickly, salted butter, and pickles at breakfast because this is a Russian house. I pour tea and taste the jam. When it doesn't satisfy, I open the small box I hid and eat the honey cake I kept back, the last of it. Food is sweeter when it belongs only to my hands. In a house where trays are counted and slices are offered with names, a secret piece is a small crown. The sugar melts like a lullaby, and the only rule I break is that I keep something for myself.

By afternoon, the snow thickens. I stand at the window with a book held open and unread. The line between stillness and waiting holds like a note under glass. I hear his hand on the knob, the soft turn that tells me he will not ask. The door swings. He steps in. He only takes that right when it is his. Today it is. His coat carries a skin of snow, and beneath it, a darker bloom spreads along his left side. The wool drinks it, and still the color shows, too black where black should be flat. The stain sits three inches above the belt, low and mean. He shuts the door with a careful hand that steadies the room before it can think to sway.

"Sit," I say. The word belongs to me right now. He sits on the edge of the chaise and undoes the coat. His mouth is a straight bar, pared of softness. He shrugs the jacket off, pulls the knit up enough to bare the damage. It is a clean tear along the ribs. Not a puncture. A slice, a warning, a lesson. Whoever taught it will not be proud of their work for long.

"Sergei?" I ask. My fingers are already moving, scouring drawer, tin, thread, the kit I keep for other people's children with bike accidents and for house guards who bleed in the wrong places because this house eats its own when it is hungry. I wash my hands in the bathroom sink until the heat stings, then come back with gauze and a bottle of spirits with that honest sting.

He doesn't answer because he doesn't lie to me. This should annoy me more than a lie would. I feel that odd sureness again, like the sensation of stepping onto ice that holds, until it doesn't. My brain, naturally contrarian, reminds me that ice is still ice. I ignore it.

"Don't be heroic," I still say. "Be still."

He leans back just enough to give me the angle I need and braces his forearm against the curve of the chaise. The muscles along his stomach tense and release, a controlled tide. He keeps his eyes on my face and not on the needle. I have to admire a man who knows where to put his attention when something hurts.

Alcohol, gauze, pressure. Blood is not romantic. It is iron and salt and stubbornness. I clean the edges, which are clean because the blade was clean. I thread the needle like my grandmother taught me to thread a prayer—enough slack to move, enough tension not to fail. The first stitch pulls his skin together. The second stitch coaxes the edges to meet. He never makes a sound.

"This is not a complaint," I say because talking helps the hands, "but do you know you are impossible to explain to women at my center? They ask me about the man with the shoulders. I tell them you are a complicated metaphor for public infrastructure."

"I'm flattered," he says dryly. The low humor in it eases my shoulders. He doesn't move while I tie the knot. He releases the breath I did not realize he was holding only when I pat the skin clean again.

"Stitches out in ten days," I say. "Unless you behave and make it seven."

"I don't usually behave," he answers. The corner of his mouth admits warmth and kills it neatly before it can run wild. I tape the gauze and set my palm over it for an extra heartbeat. His skin is very warm.

"It will scar," I say, and the stupid softness I sometimes hate leaks into my voice.

"I know," he says. "They all do."

I want to ask where else. My thumb slides once along the edge of the tape. My crucifix slips forward. He catches it with two fingers and holds it away from blood. The gesture is so absurdly reverent that my ribs ache.

"Was it Sergei?" I ask again, softer now, because I cannot pretend I don't know the names of our enemies.

He shakes his head once. It is not a no. It is a *not here*. I hear what he doesn't say—the politics, the cost of naming, the way a word dropped in a house like this can become a blade before it hits the floor. He has learned my values well enough to refuse to make a spectacle where I have to walk. I'm relieved and insulted in the same breath. I'm an efficient contradiction.

I clean the tin, cap the bottle, throw the spoiled gauze into the metal bin. He pulls the knit down, sets the line of his clothes back into order. When he stands, the window light casts him as a saint a parish would trust to carry candles. He buttons his jacket and is suddenly again the man who makes rooms stop lying.

"You are pulling away," I say, not because it is true, but because I need to make the sentence solid so I can test it. His gaze lifts. A thousand decisions sit in his eyes and don't ask for applause.

"I'm placing you where stray fire cannot reach," he says. "It is a wall."

"A wall cuts both ways," I answer. "It keeps wolves out. It also keeps women in." The temper in me lifts its head like a dog who recognizes an old enemy. I stroke it once and tell it to lie down. "I will not be kept. Not even kindly."

He doesn't argue. He never argues when I say something that is more oath than opinion. It is infuriating and one day might be the reason I forgive him for everything he has not done yet. He steps close enough for my pulse to notice and not close enough to crowd. His hand lifts as if it has a right, then waits. When I don't move, he sets his palm on my cheek, thumb at the hinge of my jaw, pressure so light it could be a question. The look in his eyes is not ownership. It is inventory, the way a man measures his gear before a fight so he doesn't lie about what he can carry.

"I keep vows," he says. "I will not lie to you. I will not barter with God on your behalf to make my work easier. If I'm silent, it is because speaking would put your name on my blade. I will not do that."

"Do you trust me?" I ask. I hate the need in my voice. I hate how fast my grandmother's voice arrives to say that wanting truth is not weakness.

"More than I trust myself." He plants it like a stake. It lands and doesn't ask for discussion. He lets go of my face and steps back into the armor of his posture. The distance is both courtesy and strategy. I forgive it more than I want to.

When he leaves, the room loosens by a shade, as if the walls release a held posture. I make tea and forget to drink it. *The Book of Vows* lies open on my lap, the red ribbon cutting the page like a small wound that refuses theater. I trace one line with my finger. *To keep no secrets that could undo us.* My mouth flattens. I'm thinking of something I don't want to speak into this room. I'm thinking of Aleksandr.

I don't want to summon him into my day, but I have learned hard lessons about ghosts that smile too softly. They use silence like a weapon and politeness like a bridge. He waited outside my parish last night as if the street were a parlor and the snow an invitation. He smelled the same. He wore the same apology I once mistook for courage. I gave him nothing then. I'm giving him my attention now. I will not give him the canvas to draw lines in my life with his presence. I'm done building altars to what-ifs.

I open my phone. The screen lifts my face in winter light. I type slowly because speed has cost me before.

Don't wait outside St. Nicholas. Don't stand near the community center. Don't send flowers. Stay away from me.

I don't explain the difference between a vow and a leash. I don't ask whether he knows it. I press send and set the phone down on the window ledge, where the cold can bleed the heat from my hand. The text leaves with a charge that feels like relief and like a risk.

The afternoon sulks toward evening, blue leaking into the corners like spilled dye. The house changes timbre the way water changes temperature between one tile and the next. Somewhere, dinner becomes steam and garlic. In the corridor, boots walk past in a pattern I now recognize as his men at a distance that respects my steps. It should feel like a cage. Today, it feels like a roof.

I pick up the book again. The lamplight turns the gold leaf on a saint's halo into a soft coin. I hear my grandmother hum her washing-day song as if she were standing behind me pinning towels with hands that never stopped working. I practice my half of the vows once more, quietly, because saying them out loud in my room feels like inviting God to sit on the chair by the window and watch me try to be brave. "*To bind my fate to his,*" I say. I keep my voice steady and my back straight and refuse to apologize to my younger self, who swore she would never give any man that much leverage. This is not leverage. This is will.

The phone buzzes. The tone is brief and indifferent. My stomach drops before my hand moves. Intuition is a witch who lives in my bones and never misses her cues. I pick it up and see the name I thought I had escorted out of my day. Aleksandr writes like he speaks—measured, polite, calculated to make words vulnerable in good lighting.

He cannot protect you from what is coming.

17

VALYA

The phone buzzes, a plain vibration on wood, impersonal as a stamped envelope. I turn it over and read Aleksandr's line again, the one he favors when he wants to pass cruelty off as wisdom. He cannot protect me from what is coming. The words look like clean snow. Then a truck rolls through. I set the screen face down, press my palm to it until the haptic beat quiets, and listen to the house breathe.

Morning arrives colorless and exact. Snow lifts from the iron fence in thin veils, the way flour hangs above a baker's table before it settles. The pane is cold against my forehead. I take care not to leave a mark because my grandmother swats my hand from the glass even now. My feet carry me into the hallway, my veins seeking the warmth of a strong cup of *zavarka,* the black tea concentrate she swore by. Beeswax and faint myrrh thread the hall, a chapel smell that clings to winter like a blessing that refuses to fade. Halfway down, I taste metal, then nausea, then air. I press a hand to my stomach, then to my chest.

For a week, I have woken with a queasiness nested under my sternum, a small, steady bird. Some mornings, it is only wings. Today, it has claws. I'm not fragile, and I'm not dramatic. I am, however, a body. I go to the bathroom, with its green stone tiles that look wet no matter how long the heat runs. The cedar soap lifts a resinous clean that steadies me. Even washing my hands feels like putting one thing right.

The mirror is Empire-era gilt, foxed glass ringed with acanthus leaves, heavy with inherited judgment. It offers me my face without sympathy. I smile at it like a woman who belongs to herself, because I always have. The queasiness answers with a quiet *No* and persists. I count backward in weeks and don't like the number.

In this house, privacy is a rumor. Housekeepers empty every bin, sort recyclables, and report anomalies. I don't leave evidence that fits in a palm. I leave my phone facedown on the charger with the radio low so the room keeps breathing in my name, then slip an old flip in my pocket for emergencies. I dress in thrifted wool that disappears among the furs and wrap the red scarf low, not as a flourish but as a mask. A narrow thread of red ties my wrist, luck by inheritance, a promise the size of a seed. I choose boots and no perfume.

In the service ward, I lift a staff parka from the linen cage, pin my braid under a knit cap, and clip on a catering badge from last winter's gala. The badge is a prayer in plastic. No one reads it. I take the freight elevator to the laundry level, pass through steam, and let a cart hide my outline when a houseman turns his head.

The cloister stays dark in winter. I keep to the balcony's shadow and count two cameras and the dead spot to the garden, then cut to the coal door. The metal is cold through the glove. A delivery truck noses into the alley and coughs once. The sensor chirps into the engine and dies. I step out with my head down and the parka hood up. I don't look toward the corner where the sedan idles, the car Dmitri uses. I turn downhill, away from our frontage and the driver's sightline.

Beacon Hill lifts its chin and pretends the wind was invented elsewhere. A woman in a fur hat passes, older than the day. She nods. I nod back. For a moment, we are queens of parallel kingdoms moving in opposite directions.

City rules take over from here. I slip through the florist's back room, say hello to the owner who knows me only as a woman who buys ribbon, and out to River Street. I buy a newspaper and a pack of gum with cash so my hands look occupied. A dull, persistent ache settles under my ribs, and another answers behind my eyes as I cross the line of shadow where the chapel wing ends. My grandmother would call that a sign. I call it data. I walk to the T stop by the river, tap a stored card that is not tied to my name, ride two stops, and come up on a block my father doesn't own with glass.

The clinic is three floors above. The stairwell is the color of old pistachios. A paper star hangs from a string and insists it is festive even though the tape is losing the war. I knock twice. The woman who opens knows my other names, the ones that never make it onto party place cards. We have worked together in community centers where coffee is currency and lists are sacred texts. She is a doctor by train-ing, a neighbor by temperament, and a friend by stubbornness. She says nothing more than hello because discretion is a better vitamin than C.

She opens the door with that particular calm a good doctor wears like a uniform. She gives me a hello that lands like a hand on a shoulder and asks nothing that would bruise.

Her office smells of lemon and printer ink, no shrine to degrees, only one crooked frame and a wall clock with a red second hand. A clean counter. She gestures to the chair, checks the clock, and sets a paper cup by the sink. "This first," she says, voice low and practical. The test is simple, a strip in a small window. The second hand that has forgotten how to hurry ticks the seconds. She draws two vials of blood because she believes in numbers that don't flinch. Needle in, needle out, cotton and tape, no fuss.

She probably knows why I'm here and not in my home, checking this myself. Her gaze touches the clipboard by the door, then the street through the narrow window, where news outruns buses. A house like mine keeps ledgers on souls. This place keeps only charts.

Through the glass panel, I watch the paper star in the stairwell sway each time the elevator opens and closes. I try to count tiles. It doesn't help. When she returns, she carries the strip in two fingers the way a midwife carries a candle in a power outage during a storm. Her mouth is kind and undecorated by sympathy. She sets the result down between us as if it were both a gift and a summons.

"Positive," she says as she would to a keeper of story and shield.

The word fills the room without raising its voice. Outside, the street keeps its errands. A bus exhales, a child calls, a woman laughs too loudly, and none of it pauses for my news. Life insists on itself with or without poetry.

Pregnant.

My friend puts a clean hand on my elbow and says congratulations as if the syllables could cushion a fall. I nod because she has given me kindness wrapped in accuracy. I say yes when she offers tea. She talks about vitamins and rest and how bodies tell truths our heads bully them out of. I hear every third word and all of the tone. She doesn't ask who. The next appointment lands too close to a gala on a calendar the estate staff will never see.

I'm not naive. I'm not ready. In one instant, I'm changed. The slow burn under my ribs settles into a pulse. On the walk back, I stop at the parish that is not ours, the one where old women hold the door against wind and strangers the same way. The icon of the Mother with three stars meets my eyes without blinking. I light a candle from the flame that refuses to die and set it down. I say what I can say without lying to any heaven that might be listening—keep the work of my hands clean. Keep my mouth worthy. Don't let fear make me cruel.

I come to you with no secrets between us. The vow moves through me like winter light, clean and unforgiving. It is a line I have been rehearsing in a book that smells like salt and beeswax. The words were supposed to be hard in theory and simple in practice. A child turns them into a labyrinth. If I tell him now, will he marry me out of duty? If I wait, will he have to forgive both the secret and the fact of me? If I say nothing and the world says everything, will that break the altar under our feet?

I leave a coin because it is practical and a piece of thread because I'm my grandmother's girl. The world outside the parish is whiter than it was when I went in. The street is muffled, soft. I walk through it as if it will hold me. I'm not hiding from Dmitri. I'm also not ready to arrange his face around this news and see the shapes it learns. He is built of vow and winter and iron. He believes what he says to God is more than sound. If I tell him today, the marriage becomes a shelter he must build around us immediately. A roof is good. I want walls with windows. I want to step into that chapel knowing there is no corner shadowed by obligation. I want our names to be said with oil, not with ink.

The estate's gate recognizes me the way dogs know the hands that feed them. Inside, the afternoon lies pale on the marble like the open palm of a statue. I pass two men who carry flowers for the front hall and a girl from the kitchen with a tray of something that smells like dill and butter and the end of any argument. I nod. I keep walking.

I go upstairs with my hand sliding along the banister worn smooth by ghosts. In my room, the green stone looks less wet than usual. I sit on the floor where the light hits and open *The Book of Vows* to the page that waits. *I come to you with no secrets between us.* The line used to feel like a cathedral door I could not push. Today, it is a key in my fist, heavy enough to matter, mine to decide when to use.

I imagine his face when I say the words. First, surprise. It always registers in the set of his mouth, not in his eyes. Then a quiet that is not distance. It is calculation, the kind that protects before it acts. Then anger, not at the child or me, but at the thought that I would let him speak holy things into the air that held something unsaid. He wouldn't forgive that easily. I wouldn't ask him to. The solution is honest and terrible. *Tell him now.* The fear that lives in my chest is wicked and simple. He will step into vows like a soldier into formation and refuse to examine the hope that has been growing between us because duty is cleaner than tenderness. Clean is not always kind.

A knock at the far end of the hall breaks the thought. Somewhere, a door opens. Somewhere, silverware touches cloth. The house flips its hours. I stand at the window and pretend the glass is a river I'm about to enter. I whisper a line from a lullaby because the silence needs a spine.

The text lands at dusk, not from the number that carries chaos but from Reza, who never uses exclamation points. *Need more mittens,* he writes, and ruins the deadpan with a photo of three children in dinosaur hats. The picture steadies me the way a palm steadies a heel on ice.

Yes, I answer. Mittens, wool socks, storybooks, and a box of cocoa packets.

He sends back a mug emoji and, after a beat, a line that reads, *You get quiet when storms circle. Want to tell me which cloud?*

I type, *Inventory,* then delete it. Then I erase the word and send, *Delivering tomorrow at noon.*

He lets that pass. *Good. I will leave the back door unlatched. If you knock, I don't need to know why.*

Evening drops early in this city. It always has. The lamps along the back hall are already lit, pale circles along the runner like saints with low batteries. I step out because four walls will start to talk if I let them. The corridor that leads to the small library and the armory office turns left and then left again. I'm thinking of a line from a fairy tale about a girl who held a skull for a lantern and learned how to look directly at the things that wanted to scare her. I'm that girl when I want to be. My body makes the turn while my mind argues its case.

A sound tears the quiet in half. A body meets marble with an ugly finality. Someone curses in Russian in the tone that puts knives back into sheaths and then takes them out again anyway. I walk faster because fear shouldn't be allowed to decide how quickly a woman arrives at her own life.

The next sound is something heavy striking hard. A frame, a chair, or a table edge loses the argument. The third is a breath pulled in and swallowed. I turn into the main corridor, marble squared by men who worshiped order even when their ghosts chose silence. Tonight, the house refuses it.

Two men knot and break apart on the floor, their shapes known to me the way a childhood name is, learned once and never lost. The scuffle is tight, leather skidding on marble. A shoulder hits stone, a short, ugly sound. The guards hold the edges like statues that know their job, faces still, hands ready, letting the correction find its shape.

Aleksandr's mouth shines red, a sharp slash that makes his face look almost honest. A narrow thread of red ties my wrist, luck by inheritance, a promise the size of a seed. The smile slips when Dmitri's weight settles a fraction deeper, a law enforced. Time slows the way it does when a room turns holy or toxic. The crucifix at my throat feels heavier. *The Book of Vows* upstairs is open to a line that is not a metaphor. There is a child inside me. I don't yet know where this scene belongs in the story we are writing. I do know a house built on vows will not stand if lies are allowed to rearrange the furniture.

I step forward until the heel of my boot touches a drop of blood that is already setting dark. Dmitri's head tilts by a degree, enough to register where I am without surrendering control of the situation. The dark in his eyes makes room for me.

I stand square, spine tall, chin lifted, mouth closed. The snow outside presses its face to the glass like a curious child. The moment holds, tight as wire, and then it decides. *Dmitri has Aleksandr pinned to the marble, blood on his fists, eyes black with rage.*

18

DMITRI

The marble is cold through my knee, Aleksandr's coat bunched in my fist, his pulse jumping under my knuckles. A drop of blood darkens by my boot heel. Snow crowds the glass, pawing at the seam like an intruder I mean to bar. Valentina steps into the blue light and sets herself square, chin lifted, mouth closed. I take her in before I take myself in, and the circle of my vision, hard and iron, eases for her and widens. I don't take my hands off him yet. Rage is a storm. She doesn't need to see it loose. She needs to see it bridled.

"Get out," I order.

"No," Aleksandr manages, foolish even now. He tries to turn his head toward her and make a scene. I hold him with my forearm and leverage to put his gaze back on the stone. This began five minutes earlier. The hallway sensor logged an entry that shouldn't exist. Melt marks freckled the runner on the north landing. The lower post radioed the code that means come now. I put Misha on the stair and Sasha at the arch. We closed the angles and let the room tell us who had slipped its seam.

I step into the foyer and find him exactly where I knew he would be, staged for an audience. He came in on a weak seam. We will close it. I don't rush. Anger is noisy. I read the room as if it were a map under glass—the angle of the stair, the shine on marble where a heel slipped, the guard's shoulder turned just enough to screen a line of sight, the shadow under the arch that should be empty and is not. I place my feet where sound will not travel. I let the seconds work for me. When judgment arrives, the room already understands it. Valentina is here, so I keep the floor clean of theater.

"Dmitri." Valentina doesn't plead. She doesn't command. She names me, and in this house, that is enough. I look up, give her the tilt that means I hear and I'm not conceding the room. Then I look back at the trespasser who thought the door to her world was a lever he could pull.

"You trespass my house and her peace," I tell him, low so the marble hears it first. "*You* bring her a letter that drags a grave into my hall. You wait for a witness. You will learn to do none of those things again."

He tries to twist out and finds plain mechanics where charm should be. I could break something small in him and teach him to love stairs differently. I don't. Restraint is not mercy. It is order.

"You will not speak to her," I say. "Not here. Not anywhere." He drags his eyes toward her again. I deny him the audience.

"Up," I say. I take his wrist, turn, and lift it enough to make breath a lesson. I keep him moving so he cannot choose a word. The door to the courtyard opens onto clean cold. Snow dusts his hair, trying to make him look like a penitent. He is not. I set him on the top step, not dragged, not paraded, simply removed.

"You will carry this message," I say into his ear. "You will tell the man who sends you that a soft angle will not open this house. You will tell him that if he touches her name with rumor again, the answer will not be words."

His mouth tries bravado and finds blood. I close the door on it. Misha shoots the bolt. The marble goes still. Order returns to where it belongs.

I turn back into the corridor. The envelope is still there. I take it with two fingers, slide the card half out, see seven practiced letters that pretend intimacy, no flower, only ink and nerve. I slide it back into the sleeve. I will hand it to the only person whose plumb line this ink has already bent.

"North landing seam," I say, back in the corridor, with Valentina standing at the console out of the traffic line. "Eight seconds of blind on the motion. Replace the chain on the service stair. Rekey that door. I want the gap dead by nightfall."

"Already moving," Misha answers. He has a way of making obedience sound like cooperation. He glances once at Valentina, a respectful glance that measures her stance without weighing it. Then he takes the team down the service hall.

I meet her eyes. The fire inside them is not shock. It is calculation and fury braided with control. She sees all of it—my hands and his blood and the envelope. The way the house listens to me. She doesn't speak here. I give her the decision.

The corridor belongs to protection. Conversation belongs in rooms. She turns without a word and takes the long way. I let her.

I send Sasha to wipe the lens halo and reset the cameras. The captain changes the watch without noise. The old key set goes into a canvas bag. New pins come up from the bench. Housekeeping is told nothing and sees less. Incoming gifts are diverted to the cold room. The chapel register closes for the unrequested.

Then I walk. Down the long spine of the house, gilt frames holding faces that never blink. Sconces pour honey along plaster and pick out the seams in old paint. A high room to the right remembers orchestras, crystal fields hanging over polished parquet. Another keeps velvet and talk, low chairs turned toward a mantel where carved fruit shines. The next holds a long table set for campaigns disguised as dinners, silver in ranks, linen crisp as frost. A run of tall windows holds the night, and no one stops to look. The carpet takes the sound out of my steps as I stop at the door she will choose.

The library is paneled in old oak that keeps the polish of other winters. Gilt titles climb the shelves in foxed reds and browns, their letters thinned by careful hands. A brass lamp with a green shade makes a steady circle on the long table scarred by pens. Valentina takes her grandmother's chair as if called to it. The rug under her feet is Persian and worn where generations stood to choose words. Firelight plays along her braid. I don't envy it. I stand just inside the door and allow the room to measure the man I am now.

A clock on the mantel counts like discipline. Above it, a winter portrait watches, silk gone soft with varnish. I'm no longer the boy who would have thrown a body down the steps and called it justice.

"You cleared a path because you could," she says, voice level and slow, each thought tied to the next. "You took a man to the door and taught him the correct exit, and for that I'm not ungrateful. But you did not leave me a place to stand." Her gaze doesn't flicker. "In this house, I have rooms that taught me how to speak for myself. You cannot turn them into corridors that belong to your orders." I look at the ladder, resting on its brass rail. Then at her hands, still on the table.

"Next time, ask me. Ask even when speed bullies you. Ask even if it costs you minutes. I want my voice in the room before the door closes." Her eyes hold steady, warm amber with small gold flecks. "Keep the threats out. Don't keep my answer out with them. I will decide how I stand in my own house. I will decide when I say no and when I say yes in the matters that touch me."

"You are safe," I say. It is a fact, not a request for gratitude.

Her gaze moves to me. The line of her mouth changes shape. She places the blade of her words on the table between us with perfect politeness.

"You did not ask what I wanted."

I let it cut. I earned it. "No," I say. "I asked what was required."

"What if what I wanted was to tell him to go to hell myself?"

"I would have stood behind you and kept the room honest." I meet her eyes. "I will remove threats. I will not erase your voice."

She looks into the fire. The logs shift and throw sparks. She stands at the edge of a choice.

"You throw him out like trash. You build a world where nothing touches me unless you allow it. Then you say it is not about want."

"This is not about what I want. I'm keeping your choice free of fear and pressure. When the pressure is gone, I will ask. Your yes or your no will be yours."

She doesn't give me the kindness of believing me on the spot. She gives me the decency of not lying. The chair creaks under the history it has held and under the weight of a woman who refuses to be turned into a story. The fire throws light on her lashes. Her jaw moves once.

"There may be another hand in this," I say. "I have no proof yet. The angle is chosen to divide a house. I will close that hand without noise."

She turns her head then. Her eyes sharpen, the darker possibility landing. Seconds tick on the wall clock. Her silence rests on the wall, heavy as a Pavlovsky Posad shawl. Snow taps the panes. At last, she rises, smoothing a skirt that doesn't need smoothing. She takes the slow route to the door.

She stops in the doorway. "It is not only my door. It is my life. Next time, ask me." She doesn't look back. The latch settles with a small, clean click.

I keep my answer behind my teeth. The place where her hand rested on her grandmother's chair still holds a trace of warmth. I don't reach for it. I have mastered fear. Trust is the thing I have lost.

19

VALYA

I lie on my bed for a long time, staring into the dark where the ceiling should be. When I sleep at last, I dream in black and white and garnet, the dark red of my mother's brooch. My father sits over a board of streets. His fingers move bishops and rooks. He pushes a pawn along a winter avenue, threads a knight through alleys, appoints a councilman as a queen who knows she is replaceable. He doesn't look at faces, only angles. When he tips a piece, the board bleeds. The blood runs in a clean ribbon down the altar steps of my childhood, redder than any rose, and finds the cradle in the side chapel and climbs its legs like ivy. The cradle rocks though no hand has touched it. I try to reach it, and my boots stick to wax that looks like ice.

My mother sits in the front pew, motionless, placed like a figure in a niche. Light falls on her face and leaves her without a voice. She turns a fraction toward me and hardens to porcelain, a museum vase with flowers that have faded to memory. I shout her name. The sound goes up and dies against the gold leaf. I call her name and run, tears hot on my face, and I strike a small, solid body at the end of the aisle. My knees slide on the waxed stone. Work-rough, gentle hands lift me.

"Why, Valya," she croons and wipes my cheeks with the corner of her apron.

She is thin and strong, a little woman made of wire and will. Gardenia clings to her skin. Flour lives in the fold of her sleeve. A thread of incense rides the wool at her collar. I press my face there and know the pilled knit, the clean soap, the faint salt of dough on her cuff. Her thumb, nicked from knives and winter, finds my temple and rests. My eyelids are heavy from smoke and crying.

"Grandma," I whimper. Her hand cups the back of my head and finds the old spot like a key finding its lock.

She smells of raised bread and beeswax and the cold that follows a door from the nave. She hums the washing-day tune, low and sure. The note settles in my chest and steadies it.

"Can you draw it, *Babushka*?" I whisper, my eyes closed. She draws a small cross on my brow with a flour-dusted thumb. The rosary at her pocket clicks once against the pew.

"Good girl," she whispers, the words warm as a loaf. "Stand." My feet stagger, then learn her rhythm.

She smiles, and the room thaws. It is the first light at the edge of winter, a small sun breaking and then another. Light runs along the pews like water under new ice, a promise folded inside it. Honey and clean starch, a living warmth I could cup in my hands. I don't see blood on the steps, only Grandma's hands on the altar rail and a red thread in my palm as if it were a secret and a blessing at once.

"Ribbon for remembering," she says. "Prayer for crossing. Sweet for strength, *zolotko*." She breaks a honey cake with her thumbs. The steam carries clove and orange across the nave and pushes the iron smell back. She ties the thread around my wrist, not tight, never tight, and looks straight at me, eyes bright as winter stars that fireflies borrow in their little lanterns.

"Fairy tales teach you the rule. You keep faith, and the forest keeps you," she recites, her voice like the rustle of birch leaves in a thaw. "Forget the rule, and the forest eats you. Now wake, my little wolf. There is work."

The blood floods the steps. The cradle is empty. I wake with my hand curled around nothing, iron on my tongue. The ceiling is pale and ordinary. The room is not. It is where the child in me grew up into the woman I am. Winter presses its face to my windows like a child who wants to be let in. I'm hot under the duvet and cold under the skin. Sweat has dried along my spine in a thin salt map. The small clock on the mantel throws its careful tick into the stillness. I sit up too fast, and the floor tilts. The small curve in my stomach complains. I slow my breath until the room settles around me.

The doctor's voice returns as if I had called her on a rotary phone that connects to reason. *You are healthy. But stress is not your friend.* She speaks in the gentle firmness of women who see too much to lecture.

I pad barefoot across green tile that always looks wet and is blessedly cool. I pour water into the basin. My mouth is ash and metal. I drink slowly, steadying each swallow with the edge of the sink. In the mirror, I'm not a woman in a novel. I'm a woman whose face forgot to sleep. The braid I slept in has loosened into a low twist. The ribbon slipped, its red a thin line across my shoulder like a promise that wandered out of a knot onto my skin.

I light a small beeswax taper on the sill, the frost on the pane giving it a halo. I have learned to build my morning like a chapel—flame first, then breathing, then food. I whisper a prayer, the kind my grandmother taught me when I was six and convinced that God listened most closely to small girls with sincere intentions. So confession comes next on the list I never write. Not for absolution. I'm not that foolish. It is to put into the room what I cannot carry in silence, because silence sharpens what it holds.

I manage bread and jam in the smallest of bites, more ritual than breakfast, then button a thrifted wool dress that refuses to flatter and is therefore honest. The scarf my aunt sent is checkered black and ash, the kind that vanishes in hedges and stone. I don't choose perfume. Today, I want to smell like soap, not forethought.

I take the service stairs that smell of old lye and boiled tea. The guard on the landing shifts his gaze to my shoulder, as the code teaches. Respect worn like a uniform is still a kind of cage. He is not my enemy. I give him a small smile, the kind that honors his post without inviting speech. Grandma would say house discipline can serve as a handrail or as a chain. Today, I take the handrail and move on.

The parish sits a walk away, brick shouldering brick, a modest nave that keeps winter out with more faith than insulation. Inside, the lamps usually make small faithful circles of light. Today, they are dark. The confessional door is open on an empty box. A small paper is pinned neatly near the sacristy. *Father visiting the hospital. Vespers as usual. Confession by appointment.*

I sit in the fourth pew, where my grandmother liked to slide a child beside her and keep a hand on my knee when she thought I would wriggle. The icon of the Mother with three stars looks as if she knows everything and is too kind to say it before I'm ready. I try to pray. The words will not land. I leave coins and walk out with two kinds of silence—the easy stillness of an empty church and the hard stillness of what I have not yet said.

The courtyard at home is a winter chessboard, boxwood frosted, gravel crushed to sugar. I mean to cross it fast. I cannot. My father stands by the chapel door, a black silhouette cut out of winter. His coat hangs like it has seen storms and won. Opposite him stands a man in a fur collar, hollow cheeks, dark sunglasses in a gray afternoon, smoke leaking from his mouth. His vowels carry Chicago.

Two long coats hold position ten paces off. Hands in pockets. The hard shape of metal is unmistakable against wool. No one raises a voice, but cold strips the words and scatters them like ice dust. I don't intend to eavesdrop, and I will not announce myself. The yew hedge offers shadow, and I take it.

"Optics," the visitor says, the word dragged through his nose as if it were money. "Chicago cannot carry your optics any longer, Anatoly. Old rites look quaint on Christmas cards. In boardrooms they look like weakness."

"Weakness looks like needing paper to stand," my father says, voice low and dry as winter dust. He coughs, a brief fit. When he straightens, he adds, quiet and clear enough to reach me, "The rites kept us when paper burned."

"The world likes to see a chair with a young back in it," Chicago says. "Boston is changing. Investors prefer clean hands. Your insistence on blood vows makes donors nervous."

"Investors like Grekov?" My father scoffs.

Gravel snaps under a shoe and then goes still. I slide deeper along the yew and the iron rose trellis. The canes are bare, but thorn and lattice break a silhouette better than leaves ever could. The men fall hushed. They never needed volume. One coat angles a look across the beds with the slow sweep of a man who counts sightlines. He doesn't see me. I know this garden's seams the way a seamstress knows bias. I keep to shadow and stone.

"People like him buy headlines," my father says. "Vows buy peace."

"Peace is expensive and doesn't scale," the visitor replies, as if discussing software licenses. "The families will not vote for a museum. They will vote for a modern house."

"The city speaks a new language," Chicago continues. "The bloc wants optics and predictability, Anatoly—clean head-lines, clean sheets. Not crowns and candles."

He lets that settle, then adds, "And after you? Who takes the chair? Who holds the knife when the chair begins to wobble? Investors ask for succession, not incense."

My stomach locks so hard, I brace a palm against the coping. *Knife. Daughter. Theater.* The words taste bright and metallic. He is speaking of blood, of heirs, of a pageant they want filmed. My father doesn't look toward the hedge. He looks toward the chapel. He always does when he needs help he will not ask for.

"The chair will go to a spine that understands what keeps a roof on," he says, voice iron, neither mercy nor cruelty.

"And whose spine is that?" the man asks, too smooth. "Your health is not what it was. The city sees it."

"I tie my daughter to a man who understands vows," he says, his voice iron, neither mercy nor cruelty. "Old ways are not a costume here. They are a roof. I will not replace a roof with a brand."

"Then your roof will be pulled down around you," Chicago says, and there is nothing dramatic in it, only an accountant's grim satisfaction. "You are losing favor. Tradition is admirable from a distance. Up close, it looks like rust."

My father's breathing shortens for half a second. I know that sound as I know my own name. When he speaks, his voice is softer and more dangerous.

"Rust is a word men use when they want to sell a house they did not build," he says. "Tell your council this. If they want a younger spine to hold the chair, they will need to take it without God's blessing. We will see whether optics hold in hard weather."

Chicago's eyes flick toward the door, toward the cold, toward the hedge for one calculating heartbeat. He touches his collar, a man who likes his fur to be stroked, and offers a showroom smile with no pulse.

"Modernization or a quiet retirement," he says. "Consider which you prefer on your plaque."

He leaves with the efficiency of someone who likes to end conversations before they become scenes. The coats melt after him. My father stands very still, the chapel door to his right like a witness. He puts a hand flat on the stone. He looks older and more himself than he has in weeks. I want to go to him and say I heard everything, that I'm sorry, that I'm furious on his behalf. I want to tell him that I will be the roof as long as the roof doesn't turn me into a ceiling.

The sense lands like cold water. He is not trading me. He is roofing the house with my life. Dmitri is a roof he trusts to hold in a hard storm and a hand that will not sell the altar for paper. Where does that leave me? Pawn or daughter? He thinks protection is sacrifice. I carry the women in our line in my bones, and I carry a child now, small as a coin, already bending the path under my feet. If I choose these vows, I choose them as a crown I lift and not as a chain I accept.

I don't step out. He doesn't need my body as a shield. He needs me as a vow he did not coerce. I leave the hedge to the shadows it belongs to and slip into the chapel instead, a daughter returning to where the women in our line leave their honest fear.

The warm air reminds me of beeswax and old wood. I light the lamps to hold their steady little flame. The icons listen the way they always do, without judgment and without indulgence. I bow, cross myself as I was taught, brow so I remember to think, chest so I remember to love, shoulder and shoulder so I remember I'm held. Then I light a taper. One for my father's breath. One for Dmitri's hands. One for the small life I'm hiding from both of them because my courage is not as obedient as my mouth.

My voice is rough when I try the line. I clear it, and it behaves. *To bind my fate to his.* The Slavonic follows, slower, older, the consonants like river rock, the vowels like open windows. When I first read it, the words looked like a knife disguised as lace. Today, they are a lifeline in hard water.

I lay my palm flat on the Gospel and don't ask for permission to be strong. I ask for the patience to be honest in rooms where honesty is not a currency anyone respects. I look at the Mother and say without words that I'm trying to be both a good daughter and my own person, two desires that have always shared a bed uncomfortably.

Outside, footsteps cross the stone. A guard coughs into his sleeve. Somewhere in the house, a door closes with a hush that is too careful to be an accident. The city holds its winter like a balance on a sharp knife. I take the quiet with me when I rise, and I take the heat of the little lamp in my hands until my skin remembers it is not made only of alarm.

I choose the long corridor to my rooms because I want to pass the windows where the light falls in hard bars. On the landing, a housemaid is polishing a banister with attention that counts as prayer. We exchange the smallest of nods. The world is lurching, and yet it lists. The brass still wants to shine. I find that comforting in a way that makes me laugh at myself under my breath.

My door is unlocked, which in this house is ordinary. Dmitri's men hold a dignified distance in the hall. The locks have been changed twice this week, the cylinders rekeyed and tested, and the motion alarms tuned so drafts don't masquerade as danger. I'm meant to feel safe, and most days, I do. Today, a different awareness rides the room, the sense of being watched the way a cat watches from the top of a bookcase, a presence with claws, not hostile, only patient.

The room is tidy, the kind mothers teach when God notices a made bed. The chair by the window holds the throw my grandmother embroidered in red and black—wheat and birds. *The Book of Vows* lies where I left it. I sit and open it, and the handwriting looks different to me now, less like instructions, more like a map with the dangerous shoals circled in pencil by a hand you trust.

I will come to you with no secrets between us.

The sentence is blunt and luminous and not a suggestion. My stomach tightens again, not with nausea this time, but with clarity. I'm carrying a small truth that wants to be born into light. I'm also carrying a fear that if I speak it now, Dmitri will stand with me because he is honorable, not because he has chosen me. I don't know whether the difference matters when it is snowing and enemies have learned our doors.

The worst thought is the gentlest. What if he does choose me and still feels bound by obligation, not by desire, and I cannot tell the difference because duty and love wear the same coat in this house? My grandmother would say love is not a coat. It is a stove. It warms, or it burns. If you tend it well, it gives both steady warmth and sometimes, a clean, honest burn.

I read, "To bind my fate to his." The words fall like a bell, binding me to a man who keeps vows like bone, to a house that doubts my father, and to a future that asks more than a face. I turn the page. "I come to you without secrets between us."

"I will," I tell the room and my life. "I will. Soon."

The question that has been gnawing at the root of my sleep tightens like a hand. If my father's roof is being pulled down, if the council whispers rust, and if the men who trade favors for headlines decide our vows are theater, who protects my child if not the old lion who made Boston hold its tongue when he entered a room? *Dmitri will*, my bones answer. *The Bratva will*, my fear argues, until the ledger says there is more profit in forgetting us.

Snow brightens. The day goes blue. I set the book down because my eyes burn. I walk into the dressing room to find a shawl. There is a sweetness that is almost soap, almost sorrow, the ghost of a flower that used to live in my grandmother's hair on feast days. My chest stutters. I don't want to look where my nose says to look. I do anyway.

My fingers go cold from the inside out. *The Book of Vows* on the chair in the next room is open to the line about secrets. The house is so quiet that I can hear the small click of the radiator. My body remembers the corridor, the blood, Dmitri's hands, and the way he shielded my name and skipped my say.

It sits centered on the dressing table as if the room itself arranged it—a single gardenia, heavy-headed and impossibly white, opening in a silver bud vase that belonged to my mother, the little dent still on one side where a mover's cuff met it a decade ago. No card. No note. The thing itself is the signature.

20

DMITRI

Chicago's cologne clings to the courtyard long after the men are gone, sharp musk threaded with ash, the kind that tries to overwrite candle smoke and cold stone and misses by a hair. I step from the cloister into the thin winter and read the stone the way other men read paper. I had watched from the cloister arch until the coats cleared the gate, counting cadence and vowels through stone while Misha held the perimeter, because a Pakhan speaks alone and a vor keeps the knives sheathed until the talk ends.

Boot marks pause where the chapel door throws its little shadow, a heel turns, a toe points toward the gate. The yew hedge has one clean break where a body leaned and listened, small and careful. I file it. Wind presses its face to the glass. The lamps in the nave burn like patient teeth. I lower my gaze. The house keeps its prayers.

A guard on the lower landing lifts his eyes to my shoulder the way I taught him. He coughs into his sleeve and says nothing because nothing is safer than almost anything. I already know what was said. Councilmen carry two weapons into old houses. The first is numbers, and the second is the word "modern" spoken like a cure. They will call vows theater, call fear prudence, parade optics, and pretend the market has a conscience. They came to tell Anatoly to put the altar in storage.

Misha slips out of the service corridor with a folder that looks like a grocery list and is not, jerks his chin toward the back office, and keeps his voice in that low register he reserves for rooms with icons. He lifts the folder a fraction, eyes steady. "The Bratva councilman pushed optics and modern. The Pakhan answered with roof and vows. No names near the chapel, nothing on tape. The Pakhan wants you in the back office. Two council members. Closed sit-down. No phones." He taps the folder with one finger and steadies his feet.

"Now?" I ask.

"Now," he answers.

The small office behind the long room is older than the estate, a pocket of stone and wood that still remembers when a boy could not buy his way out of winter. Anatoly is already there, standing with his hands behind his back, the cross at his throat a dark line against the white of his shirt. Two council members occupy the chairs like men who are used to better furniture. One has the careful tan of a banker who skis in February. The other wears his coat even with the radiator on. His collar is fur and his smile is all teeth.

"Volkov," the fur says, as if he is greeting a new model of something he intends to purchase. "We were speaking in the abstract. Optics. Continuity. You understand."

"I understand continuity," I say. "I keep it for a living."

The tan spreads his hands a fraction, a gesture that pretends generosity. "Anatoly has built a brand that is almost a relic," he says, mild and deadly. "Museum quality. Donors love museums. Investors don't. There is concern that Christmas crowns and blood vows read as pageantry in a city with cameras."

"Vows read as reliability in a city with knives," I answer. "You are here because this house still holds the vigil on nights when the docks want to shout."

The fur considers me as if testing glass for a flaw. "The families are watching," he says. "Vetrov is adaptive. He hires boys who speak developer. He sponsors youth leagues. He is happy to attend a vigil with a camera if there is an endowment attached."

"Vetrov launders cowardice through novelty," Anatoly says, voice low. His jaw tightens once. "He will not kneel in a church unless the floor has mirrors."

The tan tilts his head in a way that asks for mercy without conceding anything. "Update the picture, not the creed," he says. "It requires optics that reassure a board. It requires a chair that will travel well. You have a daughter who is... luminous. You have a right hand who is efficient. Perhaps you consider a transition that reads as continuity. New back for the chair. Same crest on the door."

Anatoly looks at me as if he is remembering a boy who once stood in this room with scabbed knuckles and a hunger that argued with prayer. He doesn't speak. The choice hangs like a bell and waits to be struck.

"I serve the Pakhan," I say. "The chair is not empty. The roof stands. The Vigil will proceed." I let my gaze rest on fur and then on tan. "If the Council wants to drag a chapel into a boardroom, they can use their own table. This one belongs to a house that still knows how to kneel."

The fur exhales through his nose, a small sound that means irritation held on a leash by calculation. "There is also the matter of Aleksandr," he says, savoring the name the way men savor a wound they don't have to wear. "His presence unsettles donors and soldiers both. He is a complication Vetrov did not have to pay for. Perhaps you should manage that picture as well?"

"I'm managing him," I say.

"With your hands," the tan murmurs, not a question.

"With my hands last night," I say. "With shadow after that. He is not the root. He is a branch that wants to think it is a trunk."

The fur smiles in that way men do when they think they are being charming in a house that respects decisiveness. "Speaking of trunks, they fall when roots rot," he sneers. "Think about new roots, Volkov. The city has fewer trees than it did."

Anatoly raises two fingers, and the room obeys. "Enough," he says. "I will speak with my council when I'm done speaking with my house. The Vigil stands. If the families want a younger spine, they can ask for it without insulting this altar. We are finished."

They take the dismissal because men who like to win don't often recognize when they have lost a point that matters.

The door closes behind them, soft and absolute. I stand with Anatoly in a silence that is older than any of us. He looks at me, broad through the shoulders, silver hair cut close, the deep lines around his mouth and eyes carved by winters that never forgave. His next inhale is shallow and careful, one hand resting on the desk a heartbeat longer than pride allows, and I can feel the duty of a line he doesn't want to give away and doesn't want to keep alone.

"They think I'm rust," he says.

"They think rust is what happens to iron when men stop oiling it," I answer. "They don't know what iron is for."

He nods once. The little motion is more private than a blessing. "If the chair wants you, it will come with knives under the cushion," he says. "If you take it, you will bleed through your suit every day. Make sure you are not bleeding on my daughter."

"I bind to her first," I say. "I will pay that price without asking for change."

He studies my face as if it were a ledger and he has found a line he did not expect. "The council will test you and call it due diligence," he says. "Vetrov will test you and call it progress. Aleksandr will test you and call it love. Be certain of your language."

I leave him with the window and the prayer rope and the decision that is already written in his bones. The corridor puts lemon oil on my fingers and old wool under my palm, the paneled walls giving back a soft gleam from gilt and glass, the stair's carved volute meeting my grip like a known sigil, velvet pile pushing against my step so that tradition and touch move together as if the house itself were built to be held. I don't go to the chapel. I go to the rooms where maps hang and metal sleeps.

The armory office is warm because heat likes steel, and steel likes to be reminded it is alive. Misha has the wall already open, pins like small red prayers along a grid of piers and alleys and corners where men get brave after two drinks. He hands me three pages without throat-clearing.

"Two nodes on Aleksandr since last night," he says. "Short lease in a name that shows up on a tattoo shop in Hell's Kitchen. The card on file bought suit service and a florist order that we will not say out loud. The driver's plate belongs to a dental hygienist in Everett who doesn't own a car."

"Who has the lease and the car?" I ask, my eyes narrowing over the pages.

"The lease and the car sit inside a shell company that receives wires from a fund we already mapped in a Vetrov structure on the New Jersey side, with two cutouts between, enough to mark his hand."

"Two steps is camouflage, not distance," I say. "Show me the money trail."

He turns the second page. "Wire from a consultancy whose only clients are three charities with overlapping boards. One board member drank with a man we like in 2014 and said the word 'modernization' five times in one cigarette. The signature on the wire is nothing." His finger taps the line. "The routing is not nothing. It brushes the same corridor we closed when we took the pier back in September."

"Soft angle," I say. "Not muscle. Narrative."

"Sergei is putting on a suit," Misha says. "He is paying boys to speak developer."

"And gardenias." I let the word hang. "He is paying boys to speak 'Grandmother'."

Misha's mouth turns at the corner the way it does when he hears a song he doesn't like. "Her room," he says. "I have the list of hands that touched the wing today. It is short. The housemaid with the banister. The steward with the keys. The linen boy. The electrician for eight minutes. The guard is at a dignity distance. None of them is wrong. Someone else touched it last night when your hands were busy on marble."

"Then someone else had a key," I say, and the old orphanage tightens in my chest the way it did when cold walked up my sleeves and sleep felt like a rumor. "Or someone outside learned our keyway and impressioned a key."

"Katya will have the cylinder apart by noon," he says, like a quartermaster reading stock. "The pin scars will tell us if it was an old master or a fresh street copy."

"Good," I say. "Give me the third page."

He slides it across. It is a stack of cell-site pings that look like static until the pattern resolves. Aleksandr's phone sleeps for hours, then wakes long enough to make a loop that touches the parish where women keep their prayer, the alley that feeds the florist who sells remembrances in vases, and the curb where the courier loitered, burner heating his glove, the night a consecrated secret left our house and tipped him. The loop repeats every other day. No calls, just presence. It is the softest kind of threat and the most effective, the kind that expects belief without proof.

"Sergei is spreading the net," I say. "He wants the council to say 'rust', for donors to say 'optics', and for Aleksandr to say 'love'. He will pull when the room is most crowded and the altar is lit. He wants the crowns to fall and for the cameras to say Boston is old and in need of an upgrade."

"Proof," Misha says, voice flat.

"Almost." I grin. "We have a bank window, a consultancy wire, a shell, and a schedule. It is not yet a spine. It is enough to move men into places where they will see the rest when it arrives."

He nods. The move from talk to muscle is easy because we have rehearsed it for fifteen years. I put my hands on the table, and the city answers my touch like a live panel, circuits waking where I press. I'm not elated, and I'm not surprised. I'm what I am when work begins.

"Perimeter stays at dignity distance," I say. "Double the inner ring at night. Rotate the men so no one writes a habit with his feet. Lenses get cleaned and brought two degrees down so shadows look like rooms, not excuses. Any delivery that smells like flowers is water-tested in the service sink, then burned. No cards make it to a reader without my eyes or Misha's." I look up once. There is recognition in every pair of eyes.

"Good," I say. "The chapel corridor goes dark on a timer. We own the light, not the cameras, and the lamps return only when a hand I name brings them up. Motion alarms on the landing are calibrated to ignore winter drafts and to trip on human stride and heat."

"On Aleksandr?" Misha says.

"Shadow only," I say. "Staggered tails, three corners behind, with reflection and bus glass. No eye contact. If he reaches toward the parish door with a hand that knows how to pick locks, we let him show us where he learned. If he waits outside where women cross themselves, we learn who sent him the address. If he whispers the word 'Eve' into a phone again, I want the tower and the time and the man who paid for the minutes."

"On Sergei?" Misha cracks his knuckles, and the lamplight catches the letters inked across them.

"We don't hunt him in a suit," I answer, my eyes on his hands. "We hunt the men who buy his suits. Pull donation lists for the three charities with the consultancy."

To Sasha, I say, "I want names of those who sit on two boards and visit this city more than once a quarter. The florist on Tremont knows the difference between a man who buys roses for a fight and a man who buys gardenias for a knife." Sasha nods once.

"She gets a number that bypasses every layer between her and my hand. The code word for gardenia orders is 'frost'. Any frost on her books comes to me before water."

Misha writes *frost* and underlines it. He has learned that some words do more work than a paragraph.

"The docks," I say. Misha lets the corner of his mouth lift.

"East Boston gets widened by a block. No new trucks go under canvas without a photograph of the tires and the man who signed for them."

I reach for a glass of cold water. Then I add slowly, "The longshore union man who owes me for his nephew's mess will get a message that reads like friendship and feels like obligation. We don't stop a shipment for show. We only stop lies that want to wear our logo."

He grunts assent. He enjoys his work when it is clean. He enjoys it more when it involves making a liar apologize. "My sister," I add, and he lifts a brow because I don't often name family in a room with maps.

"She pulls the core, strips the cylinder clean, reads the bitting, and maps the keyway and warding, then puts the metal back together so the door forgets she was there. She lays those cuts over the issuance book line by line, flags any twin that never should exist, and tags the clerk or steward who signed it out without a witness."

Artem, the key master, tips his chin, understanding bright in his face. "We will know if a key is gone," he says.

"We keep that dark, no notices, no memos, because silence makes the rat move, and movement makes a trail." I keep my tone even.

"We salt the street with three dummy codes, one through the steward ledger, one through a shop whisper, one through a driver text, and the first code that wakes chatter or a locksmith ping or a burner light tells us the route and the hand. Do you understand?"

"Council." Misha says, hands flat on the table like a man measuring grain. "You don't want to court them, and you don't want to provoke them. Which is it today?"

"We don't court men who use God's name like a season," I say. "We don't provoke men who vote on whether a roof stands. We answer questions with results. They want modernization. We give them a week with an empty slab, quiet dispatch, and corners that go to ground."

Misha smiles without moving his mouth. "You speak developer now," he says.

"I speak *krysha*," I answer. "Everything else is signage."

He leaves to walk the orders through the bones of the house. I take the chair for one minute and let the map rest under my hands. The seat has lived in a corner of my mind for twenty years, a clean shape cut from iron and patience, something I could carry because I learned not to be afraid of burden. It looks different today. Not because I doubt the strength of my back. Because I understand the cost to the room where a woman lays a prayer book open and believes a man will not put a committee between her and God. The chair would ask me to be everywhere. Vows ask me to be here.

There is no conflict in the equation once I name it correctly. I bind to her first. If the chair comes, it comes under a roof that belongs to the two of us. If the council wants something else, they can eat at another table.

I stand and pick up the phone that looks like a museum piece and is safer than any encrypted toy the young guns like to bring me. The first number is a dock foreman who is older than my boots and still stronger than the men who mock him. The second is a sacristan who keeps a key under a stone at the parish and knows the faces who don't belong. The third is the courier dispatcher the florist uses, a neutral hub that fingerprints every bouquet before it ever hits a doorstep. I give them one sentence each and a codeword that sounds like a shipping note if anyone else is listening.

I send two more lines by hand, folded and sealed, one to an elder who still keeps a ledger with a fountain pen and will be flattered to be asked to witness a clean correction, and one to a beat cop who owes me a debt and likes to repay it with silence, not praise. No names on paper. Sergei thinks he is fishing with silk. He has never watched winter pull the rope.

At the window, the long hall holds its even squares of light. Radiators tick. The chapel lamp keeps steady below. In the glass, I catch my face and the small cross under my shirt, iron and memory under wool. No thrill. No surprise. I'm the man I am when the work is clean and the vows are speaking. I alert every loyal contact I have.

21

VALYA

The next day

Dmitri is taking me out on a date today. The word alone feels strange in my mouth, like something borrowed from someone else's life, but I don't fight it. We are both aching for a little normalcy in the middle of everything, one evening where I can pretend there is no Aleksandr, no suspicion, no dossiers with my name typed neatly on the cover. Just us, the city, and the taste of something beautiful.

He meets me outside the estate in a navy coat, nothing about him shouting soldier or sentinel. The sight of him this way, unarmed in appearance and softened by choice, unhooks something in my chest. He offers his arm as if we are any ordinary couple heading out for the night, and I take it.

The restaurant is small, tucked away on a corner that smells of bread and strong coffee. A chalkboard menu leans against the window, promising gnocchi with sage butter and pears poached in red wine. We sit near the back, where the candlelight catches in his eyes and the world feels far away.

We start with fresh burrata, its center spilling like cream when the knife cuts it open. Dmitri pushes a piece toward me, bread still warm in his fingers. I take it from him, bite, and close my eyes at the salt of olive oil and the sweetness of tomato. He watches me with a look that makes the whole room disappear.

By the time the gnocchi arrives, pillowy, rich with browned butter and crisp sage, I'm laughing at something he said about the stubbornness of Reza's parish committee. He takes his wine in slow sips, his hands steady on the stem, his voice quieter than usual, as if this place has granted him permission to be something softer.

We share the poached pears last, their skin stained deep red from wine, the flesh tender. He lifts a spoonful to my mouth, and when I take it, the sweetness lingers on my tongue. It feels like communion.

Walking out into the cold night, the air sharp with woodsmoke, I feel lightheaded—not from the wine, but from the luxury of ease. His hand settles at my back as we approach the car, not possessive, just steady. When he opens the door for me, I see the reflection of us in the window— two people who, for once, could be mistaken for ordinary.

We don't speak much on the drive. The city blurs by in streaks of light, and I rest my hand on his thigh, just above the shift of muscle. His knuckles whiten on the wheel, not because he resists but because he feels it as sharply as I do.

At a quiet stretch of road, he pulls over, the hum of the engine filling the silence. My heart beats too fast, and the stillness between us breaks all at once when I climb across the console into his lap. The leather seats creak, my skirt riding high, my thighs straddling him.

"Valya," he says, low, warning and want tangled together.

"Shut up," I whisper against his mouth, kissing him hard, tasting wine and winter air. His hands grip my hips, pulling me down against the hardness straining his trousers. I grind against him, heat sparking sharply where our bodies meet.

The windows fog quickly, our breaths misting the glass. I tug at his shirt, needing skin, needing him. He groans when I roll my hips, the sound raw, the kind of sound that feels like it belongs only to me.

His hand slides up my thigh, pushing fabric aside, fingers brushing where I'm already slick and aching. I moan into his mouth, biting his lip, the car rocking slightly under us. His other hand fists in my hair, holding me to him as if the world might try to pry us apart. The gearshift digs into my hip, the space too tight, but I don't care. I want him here, like this, where nothing exists but heat and hunger. His fingers slip against me, teasing, and I cry out, the sound muffled against his shoulder. "Don't tease," I breathe, nails dragging across his chest. "I'll lose my mind."

He smirks against my neck, but his breathing is ragged, and his fingers press deeper. The car fills with the wet sounds of me opening under him, the windows trembling with each gasp and grind. The cramped space forces us into angles that feel desperate and obscene. His fingers leave me wet and throbbing, and when he draws them away I whimper at the loss. He pulls at my hips, guiding me forward until the head of his cock nudges against me. I gasp at the heat, the thickness, and then he thrusts up, sliding deep inside with a force that makes the breath tear out of me.

The car rocks with the impact, the leather seat squeaking beneath us. My skirt is bunched around my waist, my blouse gaping open, my bra pushed up so my breasts spill into his hands. He squeezes them hard, rough palms circling my nipples until I cry out, his mouth swallowing the sound in a bruising kiss.

I brace one hand on the fogged window, the other clawing at his shoulder, while he drives into me from beneath, the angle sharp, filling me so deep I can't think. Every thrust grinds my clit against the hard muscle of his pelvis, every stroke pulling a louder moan out of my throat.

I shift, arching my back, and he seizes the chance by pulling my body closer, pushing me down until my knees press into the console on either side of him. The position opens me to him completely, no hiding, no defense. His cock slams into me with a loud thrust, and I ride it, riding him, breasts bouncing against his chest, my lips crushed to his in frantic kisses. "Look at you," he groans against my mouth, one hand pinching my nipple, the other dragging down my spine. "So hungry for me that you'll take me in a car like a sinner at confession."

I bite his lip hard enough to taste blood, grinding down on him until he snarls. He pulls me into his mouth, kissing me so deep I forget my own name, and then he thrusts up harder, pounding into me until the seatbelt buckle digs into my thigh. I wrap my arms around his neck, my breasts pressed to his face, his tongue circling my nipple even as he fucks up into me. The sensation makes my whole body quake, moans spilling from me without thought, every nerve caught between his mouth and the relentless drive of his cock.

The windows are opaque now, fogged completely, the outside world erased. There is only him, only this, only the rough slide of his cock inside me and his mouth at my breast, sucking until my back arches in helpless pleasure. He breaks from my nipple to kiss me again, hot and messy, tongues clashing, our teeth knocking. His breath is ragged, his words swallowed between thrusts. "You feel... so fucking good... Valya."

The gearshift jabs my side, but I don't care. I roll my hips against him, angling until the head of his cock drags right against the spot inside that makes me scream. He feels it, knows it, and slams into that place over and over until my nails rake down his back and I'm shaking in his lap, but then his grip shifts. With a growl he seizes my waist and flips us, dragging me forward so my chest hits the fogged window. My palms slap against the glass, warm with my breath, the cold night just beyond.

"Stay there," he rasps behind me, and before I can catch my breath, he's inside me again, driving deep from behind. The new angle makes me cry out, cheek pressed to the glass as the car rocks under the rhythm of his thrusts.

The window rattles with every slam of his hips. My nipples flatten against the cold surface, sensitive and aching, and he reaches around to squeeze one breast hard, pinching until I sob. His mouth is at my ear, his teeth grazing, his breath hot against my skin.

"You love this," he growls, pounding harder. "Pressed up like a slut where anyone could see if they looked close enough."

I moan, the sound breaking into a scream as his cock hits that spot deep inside, relentless, sharp and perfect. My hand smears the condensation on the window as I claw for purchase, my body arching helplessly.

He thrusts faster, one arm wrapped around me, palming my breast, the other hand between my thighs, rubbing me as he fucks me into the glass. The pressure is unbearable, sweet and violent all at once.

"Dmitri—" I gasp, voice strangled. "I'm–I'm going to—"

"Come for me," he snarls, thrusting so hard the car jolts. "Now."

I shatter, my body convulsing, the orgasm ripping through me like fire in my veins. My cunt clamps down on him, pulsing, gushing down his cock, and I scream his name against the window as my vision goes white.

He groans, a sound torn from his chest, and drives into me with punishing force, holding me flush to the glass as he spills inside me. Hot, deep, filling me in heavy pulses until my legs buckle. He keeps me pinned there, his weight anchoring me as his cock throbs, grinding into me until every last drop is buried inside.

For a long moment, there is only the sound of our breathing, ragged and harsh, the fogged window trembling under our bodies. His forehead rests against the back of my neck, his chest heaving. I can feel the smear of sweat where his mouth presses to my skin and the slow, lazy aftershocks still pulsing through my core.

"Valya," he mutters finally, voice hoarse, almost reverent. His arms tighten around me, one hand still cupping my breast, the other splayed across my stomach as if he could keep me there forever. And though no vow is spoken, it feels like prayer.

He stays inside me for a long moment, his chest pressed to my back, our breaths rough and tangled. Then he eases out, his hands steadying me when my knees wobble. He pulls my skirt down gently, smoothing it over my thighs, then cups my face and kisses me softer than he has all night. His lips taste of salt and sweat, of something that feels almost like apology. He strokes damp hair back from my cheek and tucks it behind my ear, careful, patient, as if we have all the time in the world. "Come," he says quietly, and helps me settle into the passenger seat. He straightens his coat over me like a blanket before starting the car again. The engine hums low, carrying us through the quiet streets, headlights spilling across snowbanks.

Neither of us speaks. His hand stays on the wheel, but sometimes, his knuckles brush against mine where they rest on the console. Each touch feels like a word he doesn't know how to say out loud. At the estate, he walks me upstairs, not letting go until we reach my room. I should let him go, I should remind him that I can sleep alone, but I don't. He undresses me slowly, not with hunger this time but with something close to reverence, and then pulls me against him under the covers.

His arm curls tight around my waist, his breath warm against the back of my neck. In the darkness he asks, "Are you afraid?"

I keep my eyes open, staring at the ceiling. The answer rises like smoke. I whisper, "No."

It is a lie. I fall asleep anyway, his arm heavy across me.

Morning light pushes through the curtains, pale and cold. My phone vibrates on the bedside table. I blink at the screen, bleary, until the words sharpen into clarity. An encrypted text from a blocked number, stark against the quiet of the room. *If you want the truth about your fiancé, meet me at the old bell tower. Come alone.*

22

VALYA

The message lands and hangs there like a threat spoken softly. I read it once and then again. *If you want the truth about your fiancé, meet me at the old bell tower. Come alone.* At the top, the phone shows an unknown sender, a small closed padlock sits in the corner, and the reply field stays gray. I open the details pane and find nothing, no name, no number, no card to add, only a blank tile where a face should live.

I touch the padlock, and a help screen tells me the message is protected end-to-end. I go to *Settings* like a woman checking the stove twice, scroll through *Filters* and *Blocked*, hunt for the seam that might explain how this slipped past our net, and meet only clean menus and closed doors. I return to the thread. The words wait. My thumb hovers, and my mouth dries. I ask myself if I should go. I must go, and still my mouth is dry.

My hands move before the fear can name itself, reaching for plainness the way a thief reaches for shadow. I know how to be forgettable. A black windcheater that eats light, a gray cap pulled low, hair twisted to a hard knot under the hood, flat boots that keep quiet on stone, no scent. The red scarf becomes lining, not banner. I coil it under the collar where it warms and doesn't speak. The crucifix rests warm at my collarbone.

I leave the room breathing in my scent, the lamp low, the radio murmuring at a whisper, a shawl over the chair, *The Book of Vows* open to the line I have been practicing, the bath porcelain wet as if I have just washed my face. My coat stays on the peg.

I take the service stair. On the second landing, the lower post lifts his chin, and the dome camera begins its slow pan. I wait until both gazes slide away and slip into the chapel's shadow, where the lamp behind glass keeps its small moons. Yelena's careful hands have already steadied the wicks. Incense threads the half-lit corridor and climbs into my head in a way this new body refuses. I set two fingers to the doorframe for blessing and apology, then cross to the court-yard where hedges wear sugared edges and the iron gate waits like an old rule. The right hand doesn't tell the left.

No sedan idles at the curb. No shadow peels off the fence. The street offers only a plow's distant scrape and the hush that falls over brick when morning holds its tongue. I cut down alleys the house cameras don't see, past a shuttered bakery that smells of fennel and heat, past a parish with a paper star taped crooked in the window. I carry my small charity laptop in a canvas tote with paint on the straps. It is ugly enough to be invisible and clean enough to trust.

The bell tower waits where the North End forgot to finish what it started, a stack of brick with seams fretted by ice and mortar turned to powder. The old crossbeam is split and feathered, a place where pigeons once turned hours into rolling coos and the quick slap of wings, then left it to weather. The bronze is long gone. The mouth is a black ellipse, and the wind threads through and draws a note that sounds like longing.

I step inside the arch and stand beneath the broken timber. The masonry presses its chill through the wool of my coat, the wind running with it until my skin learns the patience of stone. Every childhood rule rises—never meet men who prefer corners, never go to a second location, never confuse courage with recklessness, and still I stand. I'm a Kirov daughter and a woman who knows when information will not come any other way.

I hear the scrape of a sole long before he shows. My stomach rolls once and settles. My mouth tastes like pennies and tea. He steps out from the negative space behind a pillar. Not Aleksandr. Wrong posture. This one carries his shoulders as if he learned to march on gravel. Hair close to the scalp, a line of scar down the cheek that did not heal well, a coat that looks like income spent on durability, not show. No ring. No visible gun. A bulge that could be anything. He doesn't come closer than two arm lengths. I let the crucifix warm under my palm.

"For you," he says. A Baltic Russian, consonants neat, vowels narrowed, English almost school-perfect until a *ch* hardens where it should soften. He holds out a small black drive between thumb and forefinger. Latex glove. The etiquette of people who don't plan to be remembered.

"From whom?" I ask.

"From a man who prefers you not to marry wrong." He smiles without his eyes. "And a man who loves timing."

Sergei Vetrov lives in that sentence like a wolf at the edge of a field. I don't flinch. I take the drive like a communion wafer. Steady, deliberate, no shaking. The plastic is colder than the air. I slide it into my tote.

"If you think this scares me into your church," I say, "you don't know what I have survived in mine."

He nods as if pleased I used the word church for both worlds. "Look soon," he says. "Metadata is a kind of hourglass." Then he folds back into nothing, steps placed so carefully, the grit barely moves.

I don't linger. The tower has the temper of a trap. I cut across to the little cafe that saves me when the center's heater sulks. The bell on the door rings like a coin dropped into a brass plate. The barista clocks my face and my need for a table near the outlet and pretends not to. I take the corner seat. I pull the laptop from the tote, flip the lid, kill Wi-Fi and Bluetooth, and feed in the drive.

Filenames bloom, efficiency as orders: *SUBJECT_V_- Tail_Week1, SUBJECT_V_Tail_Week2, Comms_Transcripts_Extract, Clinic_Prenatal_Valentina.pdf, Access_Log.*

My hand goes slick. I click the first folder. Telephoto shots pour out like a film of my life seen through a rifle scope. The community center loading bay, me carrying a box marked *Books.* The North End charity auction, me with a paper boat of arancini, laughing at something I don't remember now. The park bench with lights netted over the branches. My coat collar up, Dmitri's profile bent toward me, the angle of his shoulder protective, not possessive. Every picture framed from just far enough to be plausible and just close enough to steal.

The barista drifts over with a pencil behind her ear and tilts her head toward the machine. "You need anything?" she asks, kind and brief.

"Just water, with ice," I say, giving her my best smile.

I open *Comms_Transcripts_Extract.* Time stamps line the left margin. The language is clinical. *SUBJECT V departed service door 08:32. Contact at Tremont 08:51. No unusual movement.* A different hand has annotated certain lines. *Note: Annex code appears again. Who is the driver?* It reads like logistics, as if I'm a payload and the city is a string of waypoints.

The girl arrives. She sets a glass on a napkin and leaves me to the screen. The ice clicks against the glass, and only then do I see my hand shaking, cold climbing my wrist as heat gathers under my collar. My thumb hovers over the trackpad for a heartbeat. I click *Clinic_Prenatal_Valentina.pdf.*

The logo at the top belongs to a clinic that sends fire and ice down my spine. The font loads half a second late, like a blink before guilt. My name. My birthdate. *Result: Positive.* Blood slips from my head and pools in my chest. The report marches, cold and aloof. Bloodwork ranges. A recommendation for folate. A reminder to avoid alcohol. The file carries the shape of my body in grayscale numbers.

A second window opens on its own. A tidy list of logins scrolls past. One line glows like a confession. *In-house network, West Wing access point, user tag steward, 07:14.* Five minutes later. *In-house network, Library access point, user tag guest.* In the margin a note reads, *pulled off our network.* A faint white wolf sits in the corner like a maker's stamp. It wants me to blame my own house.

The room tilts. Not the floor. Me. I swallow, and it catches. There is a taste in my mouth like old copper and mint tea gone cold. Heat flashes across my skin, then recedes as if the building inhaled me and changed its mind. I feel the thin drumbeat under my palm. I hear my grandmother's voice. I hear *The Book of Vows* as if it were thundering in my ear. *I come to you with no secrets between us.* It is ink in our book. It is a line I was raised to honor. Now, it is a cliff.

If he knew. If he has known. If his men read my body off a server while I was still deciding whether joy was safe to touch. If he said nothing and watched me practice vows with clean diction and an unsteady soul. If he decided protection includes reading me like a ledger and assumed I would thank him later.

Or this is a play. Sergei loves thread pulled through a family seam. He feeds ten truths and one poison and tells you to choose fast. The Baltic courier's vowels, the latex glove, the neat handoff, and the white wolf in the corner like a maker's mark all smell of Sergei's new church—only leverage and no vows. No saints, only shareholders, a *krysha* built from glass towers and foreign wires that never bend a knee. He wants the council to call our altar rust.

What if he wants Dmitri's devotion to vows to read as a weakness he can price and buy? Did Dmitri set a tail to keep me breathing or to keep me owned? Did the house steward open a door for God or for a fund with a foreign spine? Did Aleksandr carry Sergei's message because he is a fool or because he is a partner? If the wolf is real, why show me the trail now? If the trail is false, what part of me does Sergei want to move first, my fear or my faith?

The access log could be dressed to look like home. Or it could be home. I know enough to doubt everything and not enough to calm anything.

I close the lid. The bell rings. Someone leaves with a sugared pastry. The smell lifts and turns my stomach. I stand too fast, and the room goes gray at the edges. The glass spills water on the table. A hand moves near me. The barista. She slides the water closer so the ice touches my knuckles and eases a second chair in with her knee as if inviting the room to sit down for me. "Breathe," she says softly, fishing a clean napkin from her apron, laying it beside my hand, the way to lay a small mercy. I nod, swallow, and let the cold find my mouth.

"Thank you." I hold the tote close like a child with a bad secret and cut back into the street.

My legs know the city when my mind doesn't. I pass a store that sells wedding crowns in the window as Christmas ornaments. I laugh once, sharp and wrong. I pass a pawn shop where a ring sits under glass with a tag that says *Estate*. I pass a parish where a woman kneels with her forehead on wood, and for a second I envy her the clarity of a posture that knows what it means. The crucifix at my throat is hot against my skin.

The estate rises with its familiar brick and its gargoyles dusted with powder, as if the city put flour on old mouths to keep them from speaking. I push through the gate. I don't smooth my face at the door. I want him to see the truth. The marble catches my steps and sends them back up the stairs like an announcement.

He is there. The foyer frames him like a portrait, suit black as the space between stars, coat open, holster hidden but present, cross under his shirt a cold geometry I know by touch. Men place themselves at the edges the way his presence teaches them to.

His eyes find me. They go to my hands, to my throat, to my face, cataloging harm, logging air. My eyes touch the black knit at his throat, a narrow lick of ink climbs toward his collarbone, the first stroke of the bleeding cross I have traced with my mouth.

His eyes travel to the tote. His gaze holds no elation and no shock, only winter kept still by discipline, a reading that measures distance and decides who belongs inside it. Bell dust flecks my sleeve, cold rides my hair, and he reads trouble without the map. When he shifts, a cuff lifts, and a thin bar of ink flashes at the wrist, a fragment of words not yet earned, then disappears.

"Where were you?" he says. Not raised. Not gentle.

Something in me snaps like thread cut too close to the knot. Nausea hovers like a threat and a promise. I don't choose diplomacy. I choose the only truth he left me room for.

"Don't do that," I say, and the marble drinks my voice and sends it back stronger. "Don't stand there like a judge in your own church and ask me for alibis."

His mouth tightens. "Where?" he repeats.

I lift the tote and slam it against my hip because I will not slap him with it like a child. I unzip, pull the drive, hold it up between two fingers as if it were a small bomb I'm tired of carrying. The guards slip into shadows with a flick of his finger.

"How long?" I ask. Each word lands clean. "How long have your men been following me? How long have you known I'm pregnant?"

23

DMITRI

She holds the drive up like a relic and asks how long I have watched her and how long I have known about the child. The foyer takes the words and lays them between us like the ocean.

I don't let my face move. "Give it to me," I say.

She doesn't blink. "Answer me."

"Give it to me," I repeat and open my palm.

A beat, then the plastic touches my skin. Cold. Light. Filthy with intent. I nod to the two men by the arch. "The study," I say. I take her to the study off the library, the sound-sealed sit-down with a thick door and carpet that swallows footsteps. The radiator's white-noise tap runs steady. To the guards I say, "No one enters this room until I call."

They vanish. Marble and lamp glass hold a long stillness. I could offer an explanation first. I don't. I set the drive to the console table and let the grain keep the mark.

"Where did you get it?" I ask.

"Do you care?" she says. The red scarf at her throat is a wound and a banner at once. "Weeks of photos. A transcript of men reporting my steps as if I'm a street to be plowed. My clinic results. Pulled from a system with our house on the access log. Your house."

I keep my tone level. "Our house."

"And your surveillance," she says.

"No." I let the word stand alone, hard as a stop sign. "Not mine."

"Then whose is it?" The anger in her eyes is like daylight.

"A good question," I say, because we are past comfort and into truth. "One I will answer after I see the device clean." I take out my phone, press a single button, and hold the receiver to my ear. "Study," I say when Misha answers. "Bring a field kit now. No talks."

I end the call and set the phone on the table. My hand wants to reach for her. "If I had known you were with child, I would have said it to you the moment I was sure. I would have said congratulations, and I would have said forgive me for the world I'm about to make safer. I did not know." My voice catches, and I make it plain.

Her mouth twists. "Your men have a transcript of the day I bought oranges. One of them comments on my scarf. Don't insult me by pretending you did not have the lab report."

"I'm not pretending," I say. "We have tails on threats. We don't tail you. Not like this." I let the consonants carry what my temper wants to carry for me. "There are a dozen ways to forge a log and make a house look guilty. You know that. You are too intelligent to take proof from the hand of a stranger and call it gospel."

Her laugh is one breath that snags. "And I'm too intelligent to think a man who calls my steps sacred will not map them to keep his crown intact."

The flare in my chest climbs my throat and tastes like acid. "You think this is about a chair?" My voice doesn't rise. I let each word find its place. "You think I would take your face and lay it on that altar as a prop for a world that prizes power over vows and mistakes ambition for virtue?"

"I think you don't see me unless I'm in the line of your protection," she says. Then softer, more lethal, "I think you never looked at me as anything but duty."

That lands. I don't sway. I feel the cut, and I let it stay open because closing it would be cowardice. "Duty is what kept you alive before I had your mouth," I say. "Duty is what kept the staircase empty when you slipped past the cameras to carry boxes for people who wouldn't remember your name after the cookies were gone. Duty is the spine under every vow we rehearsed." I take a step toward her. "And now hear me. You are not only duty. You are the choice I make when there is no one watching."

"Then why did I learn about my child from a file hand-delivered by your enemy?" She lifts her chin. "Why did I have to taste fear alone in a tower older than both of us while you sat here polishing order?"

I look at the drive and hate it as I have rarely hated a thing. "Because someone wants you to think I'm that man," I say. "Because Sergei Vetrov is not a fighter of men. He is a sower of rot. Because Aleksandr doesn't cross thresholds without being told which hinge is rusted."

She flinches at the name. I see it and keep going. "They want us to doubt before we bind, for the Vigil to fail before the lamps are lit."

"You are changing the subject," she says.

"I'm naming the field. On that field, I'm not the one who put your clinic file on a stick."

"Fine," she says, and the syllable lands like a ring on stone. "So I will ask the simpler thing. Why did you not ask me where I was this morning because you were worried, not because you were keeping inventory? Why did you not notice three days ago when I could not stand near lamp oil for more than a minute?"

I open my mouth and close it. She watches the failure. I force myself to say the thing that costs. "Because I'm trained to count doors before I count faces," I say. "Because I have lived a long time in rooms where care looks like a threat if you show it wrongly. Because there is a part of me that believes I will lose you if I take my hand off the perimeter to touch your cheek." I drop my gaze to the floor to give her the target she merits. "And because you held it back to own it."

She takes a step as if to pass me, then stops. "I did not tell you because I did not know how to fight your discipline," she bites out. "I did not tell you because if you married me with the child unknown, at least I would know the vow was not cornered by duty." She pauses at the edge of the rug. "I did not tell you because I'm my grandmother's blood, and the line in the book says no secrets, and the truth felt like it would turn me to salt if I spoke it too soon," she says, her voice level and wide as a winter harbor at slack tide.

"You should have told me," I say, not lacing it with a plea. "You should have come to me with your truth."

"And you should have given me a reason to believe I wouldn't turn into another ledger entry." Her hand goes to her belly and stays there. "You ask for the truth. I bring you the whole of me. I will not trade my spine to buy your mercy."

The latch turns. Misha steps to the edge of the room with a small case and a face set to business. He reads the weather in one look and speaks to me, not to her. "Field kit."

"Here," I say. "Gloves. Dead sleeve. No power. No wire. This is a black file under the icon, a closed circle. Katya runs it cold, and she runs it deep with the Monk in the grey room. Output is on paper, by runner to my hand. No copies. No chatter. Time-stamp it on your card."

I turn to Valentina. "Whatever is on this, you will see when I see."

Misha nods once. He pulls on gloves, slips the stick into a sealed sleeve that drinks signal and rumor both, writes the hour and his mark on a card, and puts the bundle into his inner pocket. "I will mark it in our highest lock, as you said. Katya will use our quiet forensics priest in the lab with no windows to the net," he repeats under his breath. He is gone in three heartbeats, the door closing without a sound.

I return my eyes to her. "I'm telling you the line no man in my seat likes to say. *I did not know.* No one on my crew was ordered to touch your clinic file. No one on my crew was ordered to tail you like a mark. If any man broke that line on his own, I will break him. If this was dressed to look like us, I will turn that dressing into the rope that hangs the hand that tied it."

"And in the meantime?" She lifts the tote and lets it fall against her hip. "So tell me how to stand with you when the proof of a leak and the proof of a theft arrived from the wrong mouth and not from yours."

I look at her and let her see what I don't give to rooms. "You hurt me," I say. The admission lands in my own mouth and tastes like copper and ash. "Not because of the child. Because you almost made me speak vows with rot under them, because you did not trust me with the one truth that would have changed how I walk through this next hour."

Her mouth falters. Her eyes slide off the lamp as if the room has shifted a degree. Her hand rises to her lips and stills.

"I did not mean to do that," she says, the hinge in her voice unfamiliar. "I meant to protect us."

"I understand," I say. "And I'm still cut."

I open the door, step into the quiet, and leave her with the lamps and the rug and the line in the book that will not bend.

I leave the study and walk the long hall alone, past the lamps that keep their small circles, past the door that remembers every hand that has turned it. The chapel takes me in with the oil and old wood. I bow, touch brow, chest, shoulder and shoulder, and kiss the icon frame where the varnish has gone soft from winters of mouths like mine. The rope waits on the ledge. The knots pass under my thumb, grain against skin, one after another until my pulse begins to hear the count.

"Lord have mercy," I say, not for an audience and not for witnesses. Breath in, name, breath out, mercy, until the iron behind my ribs stops trying to break the bars I built there. I kneel where the stone is worn to a shallow cup by men who needed more than power and less than forgiveness. I place my palms on the step and hold still until stillness answers.

The wall carries the line we trained our mouths to say, cut into the plaster where the light finds it without help. *To honor her heart above ambition.* The letters are simple, and they don't blink. I speak them once as a pledge, then again as a sentence.

I taste what the words demand. I see the chair as it first lived in me, clean, necessary, a shape I could carry because strength was the only language that kept the boy who ate fire in me alive. I see the road that brought me to her, paved with coal and heat and forged by will, and I admit what I did not wish to admit in any room that holds my name. Ambition brought me to this door.

I close my eyes and see her hand on her belly and hear the edge in her voice when she guarded herself from me. I feel the cut as if a thin blade has found the soft part under the armor. It is the trust withheld. It is the thought that she stood in winter and could not choose me with all her fear.

I lay my forehead to stone, hold the rope, and look at the carved vow until my breath steadies. I know the truth with the kind of knowing that doesn't negotiate. I began down this path for the seat. I'm here now because I love her. The hurt is clean, and it is very deep.

24

VALYA

I enter on my father's arm as if nothing inside me has come loose. The red silk folds close like a seal, the same kind of red my grandmother called a blessing against evil eyes. The dining hall is staged for ceremony, silver aligned like ranks, crystal raised like small cathedrals, the long table set with caviar, black bread, trout under lemon, and a roast that glistens as if newly anointed. Icons look down from the far wall, their gold leaf warmed by lamp oil. Outside, snow presses its white script against the tall panes and writes that this is a holy season. In here, language is older than calendars—cut, serve, watch, remember.

Anatoly sits at the head beneath Saint Nicholas, patron of sailors and thieves, his suit the color of ash, his hair clipped close to look untroubled by time. He offers his hand. I kiss the knuckles that have signed treaties, exiles, and endowments. His jaw has the set of a judge and a grandfather at once. When he rises with me to take our place, his sleeve pulls back. There is a tremor in the lines at his wrist. He covers it with the napkin as if he is tired of being found brave.

Dmitri sits to my left at a deliberate diagonal, the angle a watcher chooses so a room can be read without a turn of the head. His suit holds a strict line, the white shirt a clean oath against it. Since the argument in the foyer, he has not looked at me. He studies the crystal as if it were a map, jaw set, mouth untouched by drink. His hands rest empty on the linen. In this house, that is a signal. No reaching, no claim, a small mercy. It is also a verdict, because here, the hands speak before the mouths do.

It is the Bratva council dinner. Men arrive in pairs, in measured coats, with rings that carry histories, and a few women whose eyes move without wasting their expressions. Chicago's elder wears a navy suit that sits like armor and a smile that belongs to a banker who has survived three bank runs. An emissary from Brighton Beach has cologne that travels ahead of his voice. Two cousins from Montreal murmur in Quebec French, hands nicked by rope tar, rings dulled to the color of wet anchors, a stripe of salt on each sleeve. There are brigadiers from Worcester and Providence, the steward of the common fund, the keeper of the ledgers, and a lawyer whose tie has more theology in it than his face. No priest is present.

The last to arrive are two council members, the elder in a black sable over a midnight suit, lacquered shoes, a widow's ring turned inward on his finger. He sets his phone face down on the linen and forgets to smile. He lets his gaze rest not on faces but on the *zakuski* laid out like a thesis. He lifts two fingers, and the sommelier steps in with a dark bottle held over a candle so the sediment shows.

The second man carries a winter tan that doesn't belong to Boston. He skims the room once, a smile contained at one corner like a kept secret, and gives a curt nod easy to mistake for consent. I watch an onyx cufflink catch the light and send it back to the ceiling roses as heads turn toward him. Anatoly and Dmitri don't look.

House staff move like well-taught ghosts in dark uniforms. A parish girl I know from our parish balances a tray with small bowls of pickled mushrooms. Her eyes flick to me once, then away. She has heard the rumors before the candles have.

The first toast is Anatoly's. He stands, glass raised shoulder high, not above the head where pride lives, but not low either. "To peace when it can be kept," he says. "To order when it must be enforced. To Christmas that asks men to remember that hospitality is older than profit." He drinks half, not all. When he sits, the color at his mouth looks faint, as if it is painted from a distance.

The talk starts like cutlery, light touches and tests. Boston's business is described as shipments and shelter, the winter routes along the port, the new harbor master who may be persuaded by respect or by arithmetic. The *obschak* is solvent, the steward says, and the word travels like incense. A solvent common fund means officers will stay fed. The Montreal cousins offer trucks if customs snarls. Chicago's elder opens a hand, palm up, to invite a new arrangement that sounds like respect and smells like consolidation. It is a season for modern solutions, he says. Younger shoulders for chairs that have become too heavy. The fur and tan nod.

Younger shoulders. The phrase lands on the silver like a coin. My throat tightens. The caviar's brine climbs my tongue and burns as it goes. I don't drink water because my stomach is already attempting to climb a rope. I hold my spine and name the saints under my breath.

Sergei's name belongs to Boston, yet it arrives from Chicago as if the wind carried it across frozen tracks. He has been seen in Worcester. He has been seen in a North End cafe where no one has reason to be seen. He has been seen near a parish where no business is done unless a man asks God to gather his intentions before he speaks. No one says the word 'coup'. They say *prudence*. They say *succession planning*. They say the word *unity* and mean *leverage*.

When the talk turns to vows, the tone doesn't lift. A man with a new watch that costs an ocean says our house is too concerned with rituals that make for good photographs and poor profits. Candlelit crowns read as weakness to men who prefer neon and cards. Another counters that no structure outlives its rights. Tear out the altar, and the roof can leak. Chicago's elder flicks a glance to Dmitri as if to measure how faithfully he serves tradition when it is inconvenient. Dmitri keeps his gaze on the rim of his glass he has not touched. The muscle in his jaw marks a slow count.

Anatoly listens with his hands folded as if he is at a funeral and a birth at once. When he speaks, he chooses accuracy. "We are not a museum," he says. "We are a house. A house holds its people together with vows, not tricks." He is not loud. Men tilt toward him out of habit and because fear is a form of respect men understand. I angle my plate to see his profile and the hollowness under his cheekbones that winter has brought too early. His collar sits looser than usual. The vein at his temple that used to swell when he planned a war lies still. He reaches for his wine. His fingers miss the stem, then find it. He shakes like a man who has spent the day under a bell.

I put my hand under the linen and brace the edge of his chair discreetly so he can steady his arm against the table without anyone seeing the effort. He glances at me, gratitude banked deep, pride unbroken. It is the first time all evening I recognize my father unarmored. He is not only a seat. He is a man who refuses to admit that the end doesn't ask for permission when it arrives.

The servers bring steaming bowls of *solyanka*, tart with lemon and olives, strong with smoked meat. I lift the spoon because the room expects me to eat. The first sip sits wrong and nausea flares. I set the spoon down and press my tongue to the roof of my mouth until the surge passes. Beside me, Dmitri notices everything that moves and everything that doesn't. He doesn't look over. He shifts his glass a half inch to the left to place it between me and Chicago's elder, a small block, as if glass can be a guard. I hate that he can be tender without touching me. I hate it more that I love it.

The lawyer clears his throat and begins a sermon on compliance that uses the words 'franchise' and 'liability'. The Montreal cousins drift into fish. Brighton Beach's man tells a story about a customs officer and a child who needed a new winter coat. No one laughs. The stew smells like patience cooked too long. I fix my mask and study the way the elders use utensils to speak. A knife held in the right hand, the tip on the plate, signals skepticism. A fork set down, tines down, is displeasure dressed as restraint. When a man wipes the rim of his glass with a napkin, he is performing caution. Boston men used to signal with the way they broke bread. Now they signal with their phones face-down and their thumbs still.

Sergei comes back into the talk as a problem that might be solved by modern men who understand digital ledgers. Someone says his crew is nimble. Someone else says nimble men run fast when the first siren touches the air. There is a suggestion that he has friends in New York who would prefer an heir with ambition to a daughter with conscience and a lieutenant who takes vows seriously. The words are wrapped in compliments and pity. I hear the blade under the velvet.

I don't look at Dmitri because my face would betray me. His hands go flatter against the cloth, forearms long, veins like lines on a map that end at a chapel door. He doesn't speak until the elder from Chicago invites him with a remark about the tension between sacrament and strategy. "Mr. Volkov," the elder says, courteous as a surgeon. "You have been silent. Do you agree that sacred language invites profiteers to use it as cover?"

The table turns. Dmitri's eyes lift. For a moment, they catch mine, then pass. He doesn't save me. He doesn't ask me to save him. He addresses the question like a man who knows that clarity can sound like a threat to people who worship fog. "Language doesn't invite theft," he says. "Thieves invite themselves. We will light our candles and hold our Vigil as we were taught. We will also build a perimeter that doesn't care whether a man prays in Latin, Russian, or in zeros. If a man hides his greed behind church talk, the roof he tried to sell will end up covering his coffin."

He sits back. The room rearranges a fraction toward him and then back to its own center.

Chicago's elder smiles with all his teeth. His eyes don't change. "Boston," he says as if the city were a person he owes money to. "Your poetry remains persuasive."

My father lifts his glass again. This time, it almost slips. Dmitri's hand moves an inch, then stops because I'm already there with my own, straightening the stem, making the gesture look like a daughter fussing with presentation, not a daughter guarding a man's dignity. Our fingers brush. Dmitri pulls back immediately. I keep mine steady.

Servants bring second plates. The roast is carved and served with a relish that gleams. I take one bite. It tastes of rosemary and effort. Voices descend into small caucuses. Chicago's elder speaks to the steward. The Montreal cousins tilt a wrist to the light, admiring a thin, old-gold watch while their free hands hover over the sturgeon and dill. Under the talk, I hear my father's breathing roughen. He sets down his fork and slips his ring around his finger, once, twice, as if testing its balance. He never plays with that ring.

I start to panic in the place of my body that used to be a child. The room narrows around my father's pallor and around Dmitri's stillness, which feels less like anger and more like a wall a man builds because he believes walls are safer than truth. The chair is suddenly a throne and a hospital bed. I have the ridiculous urge to knock over the candelabra and yell at the elders to stop pretending we have not all seen an empire limp.

Instead, I turn my head the tiniest bit and study Dmitri's profile. The scar near his jaw that another woman might have romanticized looks like survival carved into bone. His cross rests under his shirt, the chain line faint through white cotton. He swallows once, then sets his napkin in precise square folds on his lap. I try to remember the last time he laughed. Was it in the North End with arancini in paper boats?

Dessert is served. Poppyseed roll with raisins, honey plums, a tower of meringues that look like snow shaped by careful hands. Someone begins a toast to Saint Basil for the new year. I raise my glass of water. I press my fingers to the scar on my palm from lighting vigil candles like my grandmother.

Chicago's elder lays his hand on the table, fingers spread, and speaks into the room. "Legacy must learn the languages of the living," he says. He glances at my father as if he is offering him a bench, not a chair. "Anatoly, your house is strong. If you bless a transition in January, markets will read confidence."

My father smiles. He looks older than he did at the start of this meal. "Markets don't read Russian," he says. "They read money. And Boston's money prefers its saints standing." He sets his glass down and presses his index finger to the stem to still the tremor. The silver of his cross flashes at his throat when he tips his head back. I feel something in me tip toward prayer.

Dmitri speaks once more. He says Sergei looks large because he spends money like it grows in the pockets of men he will later betray. By spring, the accounts will be empty. Men like that are always shocked when Easter comes. The line is a warning, not a joke.

The dinner thins into aftertalk and the small courtesies of coats and cars. In the corridor, the staff gather plates and scrape bones into deep pans. Someone in the vestibule has come in with snow on their shoulders. It drips as if the building has begun to cry. I stand with my hands folded and feel like a relic waiting to be placed in a reliquary or smashed. Dmitri passes me once as he escorts Chicago's elder toward the foyer. He gives me a short look that says I'm not a stranger and that he is not ready to speak. I take the look like bread. I don't ask for more.

By the time I reach my corridor, my head rings like the tower in winter. The carpet muffles the steps behind me. I count doors. I smell lamp oil and beeswax and roast, all commingling into a perfume that smells like a family pretending it is not a company and a company pretending it is not a family. I rest my hand on my doorknob and stand there for a moment. I don't want to open a room that will be only mine again.

The lamps are low. The bed is turned down. I sit on the edge and untie the ribbon from my hair. The red looks almost black in the lamplight. I hold it in my palm and think of the thread Father Gavril looped around our wrists. I whisper the vow line out of order as if I can rearrange fate by rear-ranging clauses. *To bind my fate to his.*

I wash the paint from my face and watch a woman emerge who looks like a girl in photographs from a winter long ago when her father still threw her into drifts and her mother still wore lipstick. I look at myself hard. Pride keeps my spine. Love unsettles everything I thought discipline could hold. I don't know how to reconcile a man who can make a chapel feel like a country and a room where he could not look at me because pain had taken his face hostage.

A soft knock lands on my door. Not a servant's double tap.

Not Dmitri's single firm call. A rhythm I know from a child-hood when knocks were codes and warmth was a prize.

"Come," I say and rise.

Anatoly enters. He has shed the jacket that carried him through dinner. Without it, he looks thinner, proportions slightly off, like a statue moved to a different plinth. He closes the door behind him with the care of a man who doesn't want to startle the room. He pauses as if parsing what posture will hurt least, then crosses to me and sits in the chair that has my grandmother's needlework in a pattern of vines and crosses. He doesn't look at the mirror. He looks only at me.

"*You must finish the vows, Valya,*" he says, voice low and precise, the kind of tone he uses when there is no room for argument. "*The moment I fall, they will come for you.*"

25

DMITRI

The clinic smells of boiled linen and lemon. A framed diploma tilts a fraction left, tired of holding everyone's certainties. I don't sit. Men who ask for chairs admit they came to negotiate.

The doctor is smaller without the coat, cardigan buttoned to the throat, eyes trained by years of giving good or bad news. Katya told me her name and that she is competent. Katya knows because she is a surgeon when she chooses, a systems analyst when I need one, and my sister always.

I came alone. Fear moves faster when it senses a committee. "Doctor," I say and set a card on the blotter. Our seal hardens in red wax. "Someone pulled a file from your system. You will confirm it now."

She glances at the seal, then at me. "You could have called."

"I don't call about sacraments," I answer. "I come."

Her fingers move to the keyboard. The screen throws pale light across her face. I keep my eyes on the doctor's right hand. It trembles once, then obeys. I say nothing while she types. In the hallway, a child coughs. A nurse laughs too loudly.

"Here," she says, turning the monitor two fingers toward me. She has removed names and dates, anything that would turn this into gossip. I don't need the identifiers. I need the pattern.

"Two logins," she says. The tremor has vanished. She has her mask back on. "One legitimate at the time of visit. One fourteen hours later. It came through a hidden return address, a network built to hide where the visitor sits."

"Show the second path," I say.

She brings up the trail. To most men, it would look like rain. To me, it looks like alleyways I know by smell. Incoming connection, a counterfeit staff pass accepted, file viewed, file duplicated, file exported. The log ends with a line of numbers.

"That is as far as I can go."

"It is far enough," I say. "The breach exists. It is not yours."

The admission costs her. Doctors guard their doors. She turns the monitor back. "You understand the law."

"I understand vows," I say.

Outside, snow lies thick on the curb. A plow scrapes by and throws a ridge against a hydrant. On the corner, a florist strings lights in a window, paper angels on twine. I stand in the cold until my jaw stops its anger. Then I call Misha.

"Grey room. Now."

The grey room sits two floors below the chapel, past a steel door that weighs as much as a man who has worked the docks for thirty years. Ash walls hold a table that doesn't wobble, a row of phone lockers, a lead-glass cabinet, and two quiet racks of drives. In the high corner, a small icon faces the stone where the servers cannot see it. Here, lies run out of places to sit.

Misha stands over a printout with red strokes like sutures. Katya works at the far bench under a lamp bent low over tweezers and a tray. She is all edges and nerve, slim as a whip, sharp-faced in the cold light, combat boots planted like a verdict.

On the center table rests Monk, our Mobile Offline Non-networked Kit. A black case open on foam, an air-gapped laptop, a write-blocker with tamper seals, and a compact printer that gives us paper and nothing else. No cables to the building. No radios. No door for rumor. The drive from the bell tower sits inside a static sleeve that eats noise. Misha taps it once with a gloved knuckle, steady as a dock man testing a crate.

"Talk," I say.

"No calls left the stick after you sealed it," he answers, lifting a page that smells of toner, and on it he lists what lives inside—images, transcripts, access logs dressed to look like our house, the dressing neat and sly and almost perfect until it slips.

"Show me the seams."

He circles three lines in blue. Our routers stamp connections with a habit the way a man bars his seven, and here the stamp is copied well and then forgotten for four entries, a forger who lost his rhythm.

Katya tips her chin, her red hair a small banner. "There is a little prayer in the file," she says, dry as salt. "A maker's mark. White wolf tucked in the margins. Some boys sign their sins." Her mouth curves, not kind. She respects a good tell.

"Sergei." I say. "Clinic?"

She clips the stick to the safe reader, hands steady and quick, a fox working a lock. "Image, verify, print on paper," I say, and she runs the Monk.

She mutters about my poetry for paper and keeps working. When the candle-blue screen settles, she leans back like a judge after a verdict and says, "It starts inside our house. Picture a thief with a borrowed sacristy key. The link went to the clinic, opened Valentina's file, made a copy, left one inside our system, then handed the rest off through a city relay. The time stamps line up. It is the same hand on every step."

"The flower—check it." My eyes are ice grey. "Gardenia shoved through our lock, white as a lie on Christmas Eve."

Katya brings the silver bud vase the maid found on Valentina's table. Her boots bite the concrete. She twists the base with a jeweler's wrench and splits the metal clean. Inside sits a resin pocket, a thin battery, and a tiny slot with a card. She lifts the SIM with tweezers and smiles like a scalpel. "Bugged bouquet," she says. "It is water resistant and has a week of life. One job only—listen and send."

"The SIM used data in ten short bursts," she reads. "Topped up at a kiosk for cash. No name. The strongest tower sits over a pharmacy three blocks away. Each time this SIM wakes, a second phone lights that same tower. The second phone doesn't do anything else. It pings, waits, and goes dark. A lookout." Her voice is a dry match struck in a church.

Misha lifts a photograph. Street shot of a rental at the curb. The date is a small ghost. The plate reads clean through the slush.

"We have it," he says, his voice almost satisfied. "The rental sits under a short-term corporate account for a 'consultancy'. That firm has three clients. All three are charities with the same people on their boards. The same boards sit on all three. We saw this path once before when we shut the pier. The wire leaves New Jersey, touches a shell we tied to Vetrov, then hops again. Two stops. Just to hide the hand."

I look at Katya. "The clinic log used a fake staff pass," I say. "Your guess?"

"Same pattern here." She taps a map with her pencil. "The touch that hit the clinic brushed our estate. Not one address. Many. Guest network. West Wing. Library. And a repeater that was not ours, alive in a service hall for fourteen minutes, then gone. Different rooms, same hand."

The stick is dressed like a carol book. The top folders sing simple. Under them sit nests of folders. One 'random' name is a tilt cipher. You angle the letters and it spells VETROV. Sloppy pride. A skim of the chapel calendar sits beside it. Whoever built this wanted dates, not gossip, the hour a girl would stand where candles are.

I ask for Aleksandr. Misha lays out the loop—parish, florist, curb, driver in an electrician's coat. Same days. Same windows. The sum is not poetry. Sergei planned. Aleksandr delivered. The clinic gave them the secret. The repeater gave them our halls. The stick gives us their signature.

Simple. Ugly. Traceable.

Katya shuts her eyes once, opens them, and says, "He wanted her alone."

"This is inside," I say, my teeth set like a bolt sliding home.

"Inside," Misha answers. "Here. A linen cart stuck in the lift while the steward signed for an unmarked box." He flips another page. "The box weighed nothing," he says, then grimaces at his own choice of words. "The box carried almost no mass."

Katya nods. "Inside was a palm-sized plug built to look like a nightlight. It seats in five seconds, no tools, no training. Anyone with access could place it, which is the point."

"The service cam hums," Misha adds, "and gives us one frame worth keeping."

A man in a navy work jacket passes the corridor mirror with the box tucked to his ribs, hat pulled low, scarf high, profile turned to the varnish so the lens gets nothing but a jaw and a shadow. The timecode matches the lift stall. The badge on his chest is real enough to fool a glance and wrong by one letter if you know our ledger.

"Same gait as the 'electrician' from the parish-florist-curb loop," Misha says. "We are not guessing."

"We pulled the service camera and the delivery slip, then walked the timestamp to the pantry vent. Sasha took the grate off while Katya held the light." Misha lifts a small nightlight plug to the light in a tweezer. "It listened to our rooms, swallowed what moved through the air, and passed it to a car waiting at the curb," he says. "When the car pulled away, the little plug went quiet and pretended to be furniture."

Sasha runs the outside lens and returns with a partial plate under road salt and a driver in the same navy, hands bare in the cold, someone who doesn't mind leaving fingerprints when he plans to disappear.

Misha lays the key log on the table.

"The lock to her room?" I ask.

Katya tilts the pulled cylinder under the lamp. Her hands work with the cool speed of a surgeon. "Fresh scratches here and here," she says. "Not a tired master. A cousin key cut too close to ours after someone held the real thing long enough to trace it."

Misha reads from the log without looking up. "The steward signed the master out for polishing two months ago, held it nine hours, one past the limit." He scoffs. "The polisher's other client sits behind a dentist's door that later received a parcel for a name tied to one of Aleksandr's short leases in New York."

Katya's mouth goes thin. "Your prince could not wire a lamp," she says. "He brought boys who could."

We bring in the steward. His freckles go to chalk, he speaks of delays, and I tell him he was careless. Careless men don't last under a roof held by vows.

Katya stands back, boots square, red hair bright as a warning flare, and watches me choose the next cut. She thinks vows are nonsense. She also thinks I keep the house breathing. Both can be true.

"I will take the burn," I say. "Truth is not a thing you ration when a life is at stake."

Katya's mouth softens. "There he is," she mutters. "The man who throws himself between a knife and a hymn."

There is one urgent thing I must do before I begin. I find her in the small sitting room off her corridor, a place with green tiles and a window that throws pale winter light across a table with a vase that holds nothing. She sits with her hands folded on a closed book. *The Book of Vows*. The cover is worn where a child once traced vines with a fingertip.

"Walk with me," I say.

She rises, doesn't touch my arm, follows me down the hall where icons hang between doorways like sentries that will not take sides. The chapel breathes lamp oil and old wood and the scent of tapers trimmed for the Vigil. I cross myself at the door and step into the hands of the saints. She bows. We stand before the low table where the crowns sleep in velvet and the red thread lies coiled, a single drop of color that knows how to bind a city.

I don't explain first. Explanations are for after the work begins. "We will practice the last line," I say. "Not because a priest asked, but because I ask, and because the house needs to hear us ask."

Her mouth tightens. "You want me to perform."

"I want you to anchor the roof," I say. "Men are trading our name over fish and strong talk. They are measuring whether this house is still a house. If you and I speak the final line, the message travels faster than any rumor. Altar words will hold."

She looks at the crowns, then at my throat where the cross lies under cotton. "You are asking for more than practice," she says.

"Yes," I say. "I'm asking for assent. Not to me. To the vow."

Her hands move to the book, then fall. "Read it," I say. I show her the page we marked. Old letters. A translation written in her grandmother's hand below, darker ink at one clause as if the older woman pressed hard there.

She sets the page on the stand. She draws in air once, slowly, on a count I know from training and from music. Her gaze finds the line. She traces it with a fingertip, mapping vines into meaning.

"To bind our fate to each other, before God and man," I say first, very low, so the syllables strike the wood and rise again. I say it as I mean it, and I mean it as if the floor were a witness.

She reads the line. Her lips shape the words. Her eyes don't leave the page. Sound doesn't arrive.

I let the silence hold. She is not refusing. She is testing whether her voice belongs to her. She lifts the page, sets it down again, then lowers her hand. Not today. I nod. Once.

"I hear you," I say. I step back. "We will finish when you are ready to speak and not read."

She closes the book. The lamplight finds her lashes and sets a thin gold on them. I want to ask for more. I don't. The house doesn't need me to plead with its future. It needs me to hunt the man who thinks Christmas Eve is a stage for treason.

I leave the chapel and let the corridor take me. The air tastes of myrrh and snow that has learned our steps. I turn toward the stairs, already pulling the next thread in my mind. Drivers to tail. Accounts to check. Guard schedule to shift without telling a soul. A decoy package with a canary word that will sing in the ear of any man who steals it. My phone buzzes once in my pocket. I don't like the time. I lift it to my ear.

A voice I trust because it has eaten out of my hand and bitten me when honesty demanded it speaks without preface. "Vetrov is planning something for Christmas Eve," my informant says. "You need to move now."

26

VALYA

I find the registry by accident and by blood, in the same sound-sealed study off the library where we already shut doors on arguments and let the carpet swallow footsteps.

Anatoly's study smells of old smoke sunk in oak and beeswax warmed by a steady hearth that this house keeps in the open. The thick door remembers every palm. The room is warm like the womb, with honeyed lamplight and air kept like a promise before an answer. I move as Vasilisa might, the girl with a doll and her mother's blessing, drifting at first, eyes skimming medals and mute bottles, dust pricking small constellations in the lamplight. The clock ticks, syncopating the house's pulse.

Then my hands begin to think. Fingertips read nap and grain. Cloth remembers, spines yield like ribs. The shelves keep their secrets as Koschei the Deathless hoards a stolen life, nested and evasive, egg within duck within hare within chest. I'm not prying so much as petitioning. Touch becomes a method, curiosity a key. I'm searching for something that will hold me fast, proof of who I am that is neither portrait nor rumor.

A bookcase along the inner wall leans as old men lean after liturgy. Bottles squat on the lowest shelf, glass green as old ponds, labels in Cyrillic that have outlived their printers. War medals hang from a nail on twine, little suns dulled by fingers and years. I sweep my hand across the spines for something I cannot name. The shelf sags, a hinge gives, and the back panel tips as if relieved to retire. On the revealed ledge sits my grandmother's sewing tin, enamel chipped to daisies. I don't know why it is here. I lift the lid. Threads pool like small galaxies—red for warding, white for linen, pale straw for flax, the colors she kept for charms. At the bottom waits a key.

Behind it waits a trunk the color of pews, iron corners, a lock that remembers authority. I pause for a tilt of night, a star's brief wink, an owl naming the hour. The key is brass, warm from my palm, the bow worn smooth, the teeth cut deep, a small crescent nick bright along the edge. I tie a loop of red thread to it and slide it into the gap. The lock yields. The lid lifts with a dry sigh. Inside lies the house itself.

I carry the books to the long library table, walnut polished to a tea-dark sheen that tames reflections. I set each volume down as a librarian settles a folio, angles squared, cloth turned back. The first is bound in black board, pierced three times, a red thread running the pamphlet stitch. The knot sits like a small heart at the hinge. When I open it, the paper whispers. My grandmother's hand holds the first page, lines precise, ink browned to umber. Names of men and wives, children recorded with feast days instead of birthdays. Notes in the margin that read like a catechism of debt and mercy. I find my mother's name written as if the pen were a match. The stroke catches at the end and leaves a scar of ink where my grandmother did not lift in time. Beside it sits a date and a single word. *Crown.*

I follow the letters until memory holds them, a clean brand in soul and stone, where oath binds crown and the house consents. The book holds the family tree, its branches spreading far and wide. I trace the branches. Farther in, the paper remembers a fire that came close. Whole boughs turn to ash at the corners. Next to one branch, my grandmother has drawn a small circle like a halo and marked a girl's name with a cross. The note below it is not a prayer. It is a sentence. *Taken in spring, returned in autumn, a voice that cannot be silent.*

I press my thumb to the ink and hear the clink of my mother's bracelets in rooms where men thought they understood what a vow costs. Beneath the registry lies a stack of letters bound with ribbon the color of dried cherries. Anatoly's hand rules here, tight script, disciplined margins, no flourish. Letters to men who now call themselves board chairs. Letters to elders who once believed doors and corners were both God's. He writes in a voice that doesn't beg. The subject repeats in different words. Unify under a sacred roof. Oaths before God. The *obshchak* as chalice, not purse. Brotherhood as rite, not rumor. He lists chapels that survived bombs. He names crews by their saints as well as by their streets, the seat defended not by cash alone but by men who would take a bullet with the Creed still on their tongues.

Replies stack under his letters. Some keep their gloves on. Some smile and slice. An elder with real clout writes with sugared hands that donors want headlines. *Crowns don't sell, scandals do.* It lands like a receipt, not advice. Vetrov doesn't bother to answer on paper. His side sends a courier with "terms" folded crisp as an invoice and the arrogance of payment already assumed. Minutes from meetings no one will admit happened. A line here—*Montreal wants lanes, not lectures.* Another, *Brighton Beach agrees to rites so long as rites don't interrupt margins.* In the margin, in a hand that is not my father's, Ivan Kostin writes that *a daughter at the altar is a risk* and initials it with a tidy K, a council elder who collects rules like medals and smiles when tradition costs other people blood.

Then deeper ink. A meeting in a sacristy with two elders and a priest whose name is not written. He records a plan to anoint the chair with oil so holy that men remember to approach it with clean hands. At the bottom, he has pressed the ring he never removes into wax. The ring left a small, perfect oval. The wax has a fingerprint in it. It is mine. I must have pressed it as a child. He kept the page.

I turn pages until my eyes ache. A ledger appears under the letters. It is not dollars. It is favors. A nephew sent to rehab, a daughter protected from a dealer whose name reads like an insult, a longshoreman rehired after a season of shame. My father turns bread and fish into columns and makes a city eat.

At the very bottom sits a small cloth bundle tied with red thread. Inside, a pair of crowns in miniature, silver pale as dawn, and a note in my father's squared hand. *If the men forget why they sit, put these on the table.*

I close the books and the trunk and rest my palm on the lid. For years I have thought of marriage as a beginning—the lesson women pass to women while men hold the power. In this room, the truth stands up. It is a last liturgy for a roof already losing shingles to men who call modernity a saint. He tried to turn us back toward the altar and oath when the city told him to learn accounting.

I set the shelf to rights and carry the first registry with me. The hall receives me like a nave. Lamps along the paneling float in small halos. Gilt frames hold ancestors who did not pose for painters, yet still manage to look judged and satisfied. I pass a houseman who has polished the same brass knob every winter since I could see over a windowsill. He dips his head with that narrow deference that is not servility. He knows where I stand now. I'm not a daughter on a staircase but the bone of a house that refuses to learn another language.

I walk the rooms as if I have never owned them and as if I always have. The map room where ports turn into lines and lines into power. The drawing room where a chair has built its own gravity. The narrow passage between the public rooms and the service hall, where decisions get made, with linen carts blocking the sightlines. The chapel door waits at the end of the long corridor. I don't enter yet. I carry the registry to my rooms and place it on the table beside *The Book of Vows*. Two books. Two spines. One city.

Sleep comes as a stranger who knows the way to the kitchen. I cut a square of honey cake, still tender at the crumb, and let it soften on my tongue until I get the clove and orange in the back of my mouth. I warm milk with a spoon of honey and a thin slice of ginger, the old house cure my grandmother favored when nights ran long. The cup fogs my hands as sweet heat steadies the pulse.

In the morning, I wake with the registry open to a page where my grandmother wrote, in small, stubborn script, a sentence that will not leave me. *A house stands only if its women decide that it will.* The old woman never asked for permission to set the record herself.

I'm not afraid. Not of councils that talk like bankers. Not of men who think crowns are photos. Not of a future that asks more of my spine than of my smile.

Rehearsal is set for late, no pageant, only the ones whose faces are allowed near the altar when the candles are lit. I dress to be quiet and clear. A long winter dress in soft dove grey, high collar and fitted sleeves, skims my frame and falls clean to the ankle. Black kid-leather flats keep my steps silent. My hair falls in loose chestnut curls down my back. From each temple, I braid a slim strand, draw the two braids together, and tie them with the red ribbon so they sit like a gentle circlet. A narrow ribbon threads the only color, garnet, that catches the light at the nape. My small gold cross rests at my throat. I look like myself, only steadier.

The sacristan sets the wick knives in a bright, exact row. A girl from the kitchens brings a basket of beeswax as if she is carrying fruit saved from summer. Father Gavril unlocks the cabinet and lifts the crowns with both hands, the way a man lifts a child and remembers his knees. He sets them on velvet and nods to me.

"I will light them," I say, and the sacristan moves aside. There is no reason for me to do this work. There is every reason. The old burn scar on my palm shows when I set a taper to flame. The sulfur touches the air, then warm wax. One candle. Then another. Fifty at least. The chapel changes with each one. Blue glass over Saint Nicholas throws a cold river across the floor. Garnet over Saint George paints the far wall as if someone had pressed a wound against it and asked it to hold. Under the icons, men have knelt with pistol oil on their fingers and vows in their ribs. They came here to make their rage answer to the same Lord as their hope. I have always loved this room more than any ballroom. The air holds my grandmother's hymn and my mother's perfume and the smoke from the censer that turns into lace above the vent.

I go to my father's study with the small crowns in my hands. He is seated under the portrait of his forefathers, his ring on his finger gleaming and a glass of black tea steaming at his hand. His color is not as it was when I was a child. He lifts his gaze, and the old fire arrives. It has not died. It has learned discretion.

"You lit them," he says.

"I have lit them," I say. He studies my face as if counting wicks, then, with a tired warmth, he murmurs that my grandmother would scold me for drafts and bless me for flame. The gentleness drains, and counsel returns, for he tells me that men who mistake chairs for crowns will try to rule the room. The chair is a tool, the altar a law. I must gather allies who kneel to the law and not to themselves.

I want to tell him I have read the letters and understood, as if watching those meetings march by, and he was shining like a man who stood through a squall and chose not to run.

"Go," he says, voice level, his eyes patient. "Set the chapel in order and let the light speak first." He lifts his glass without asking for my hand, then stands with careful breath. He slips his rosary into his pocket and adds that he will take the back pew at the cathedral for the ceremony, a witness among witnesses when the crowns are lifted.

I return to the chapel with my father's permission. Two elders arrive. They remove their hats. One crosses himself with precision, forehead to chest to shoulders, a habit so old his bones do it without words. The other bows low to the icon of Saint Nicholas and kisses the frame where the varnish holds the shine of a thousand mouths.

The steward sets silver basins under the candles in case the wax runs rebellious. The sacristan threads a red line through the little metal rings that will bind our right wrists and leaves a loop of grace. He has done this for fifty years. He never ties too tightly.

I walk the aisle and check every latch. The doors to the side chapel. The sacristy lock. The balcony rail shows no scrape where no scrape should be. When I lift my head, I find the choir loft empty and the trumpets on their hooks catching dust. I refuse to give snow the last word. Snow doesn't own this city. We carry it into our coats, stamp it from our boots, and make it serve the bread with cold that wakes a face. *Resurrection,* my father would say. That is the word they mocked when they preferred restructuring. The Mother of God carries three stars on her veil and watches with a mouth that doesn't judge the living. This is a house. It is not a brand.

I hold my hands open, palms tingling from wick and match. I remember the first time Dmitri sang under his breath to show me where to place a vowel in a prayer that doesn't belong to architecture. A council calls him a liability when it wishes to shave its conscience thinner. He calls himself mine without asking for thanks, and I have hurt him. I will not let hurt be the last word between us.

The chapel waits. The candles stand. The panes hold. I take my place on the step and look at the crowns. I don't rehearse a speech. Words arrive when I need them. They always have in this room, even when my mouth was dry and my hands were too cold to trust.

Footsteps in the corridor approach, firm and softened by the runner. No man under this roof makes that pattern except one. The door opens. He steps in with his coat on and his collar marked by the faint line of a harness. His shirt is black under the coat. Along his ribs, a darker gloss spreads, slicking the weave. The air tastes faintly of iron. His face carries the stillness that comes after an exchange of blows where both men thought they were right and at least one of them was wrong. His eyes go to my hands, then to the candles. He doesn't look around the room to count exits.

"Let us finish the vows," I say, and the words take their place and stand there.

His mouth finds the shape I have only seen when he touches the Gospel with two fingers. In one motion, he takes his place beside me. We stand in front of the table where the red thread waits. The sacristan ties it around our wrists. The elders rise in the back pew. They have won enough wars to know they must stand for the right things.

We face the icons. There is no priest yet. There is no music. There is the low tick of wax running. There is the faint ring of metal as a censer cools on its chain. There is the heat along our hands where the thread lies. There is the taste of myrrh that always moves into my mouth when the book opens. We speak. We don't mark the cadence like students. We let the line carry us as if it were a bridge cut from iron by men who expected to be shot at and crossed it anyway.

"To bind our fate to each other, before God and man," I say. My voice finds the stone and stands on it.

He answers with the same sentence, his mouth shaping each vowel as if it were an oath hammered on an anvil. His hand holds mine. The red thread lies across our pulse.

We speak the next line and the next, Old Church words that feel like river stones in the mouth. To honor, to guard, to keep, to forgive, to bring truth with no delay. When I speak the line that names secrets, I don't flinch. When he speaks the line that names ambition, his voice drops, and the room receives it as law.

Our hands don't shake. The candles don't gutter. The saints don't look away. We are not alone, and we are not many. We are exactly the number needed to make a vow binding. We reach the last clause. The crowns gleam as if they know their turn is coming. The colored glass over Saint George throws a red bar across the altar rail like a warning and a benediction at once. I hear my grandmother's hymn run under my words like a river under ice. I see my father's ring pressed into wax and my own fingerprint inside it.

We open our mouths together for the final word. A single mote of glass rests on the red thread on my wrist.

The stained glass over Saint Nicholas explodes. A single bullet pierces the blue and turns the window into a rain of knives. The shard that carried the saint's halo falls between us and the altar and shatters against the stone.

27

DMITRI

T he pane in our estate chapel is boarded, the saint's face mended with timber and prayer. The bullet that shattered it is logged and sealed. Katya runs the trail that hurt us there, tracing entry, angle, and hand. Sergei wanted that message to haunt our rehearsal and push us from the altar. It fails. The Vigil moves to St. Nicholas and goes forward as written.

The cathedral holds a winter of its own, ancient stone warmed by a thousand tapers. Candles rise in tiers like a regiment that learned to sing. Lamps anoint gold onto icons worn thin by kisses and winters. The families have come. Brigadiers with rings that carry wars. Elders whose eyes have read every ledger and still prefer faces. Ivan Kostin, who did not believe women had the permission to stand. The keeper of the *obshchak* sits with the book shut on his knees, thumb on the corner, present for order, not profit. Colored glass hums above the nave, saints kindled in carmine and cobalt. Outside, the snow thickens on granite and iron. Inside, backs straighten because God is watching, and so is the house.

I stand at the left of the solea, bandage under linen. My shoulder protests when I lift my arm, and I deny it. I have denied worse. Across the aisle, Valentina comes toward me with the unhurried certainty of a procession. Garnet pins hold her veil. Iron pins hold the city. Her red silk shimmers like a banner in a house that remembers saints and knives, and the room learns where to look. Her hands are steady, the kind a man could build seasons on, and when the priest sets the red thread between us, it settles over our wrists like a living line.

Father Gavril lifts the crowns and blesses them. His voice carries along stone, clear as a bell with its ornament stripped away. He sets the red cord across our wrists, not tight, never cruel, just firm enough to tell the room and heaven whose hands belong together. Coats whisper in the pews, a lamp kisses its chain, a cough loses its battle with a sleeve. Men square their shoulders the way soldiers do when the standard comes forward. This is not pageantry. In our house, a crowning makes two bodies a single rampart, turns bloodlines into a treaty that outlives signatures and lays law on the tongue stronger than ledgers or guns.

I look once at Anatoly. He sits three pews back, suit the color of gunmetal, face paler than it was last month, jaw square anyway. Both palms rest flat on the pew in front of him, shoulders set as if the verdict has already been signed. Glass broke in our chapel, and he answers by sitting taller, a commander who refuses the lesson of fear. He inclines his head to me. He has never loved anyone like he loves his roof.

Tonight, he hands it to me and to her with the smallest nod he has ever given a man. I answer it with my own.

The choir begins the Vigil hymn. The words lift the nave. Incense walks the center line like a herald. The rite opens. We say the first lines as we were taught—in the Church tongue, consonants like river stones, vowels opening like doors, then in ours, so every ear can hear. Elders rise to witness. Two councilmen who don't believe in God stand anyway, which is proof they still fear a covenant more than a contract.

Father Gavril lifts the crowns, and the gleam calls the room to order. Colored glass throws a piece of saint across Valentina's cheekbone, and it looks like war paint and a blessing at once. We circle the table three times, slow, measured, the old way. Each step says the same thing. This is not theater. This is a fence the house will hold.

Then the door on the side aisle opens.

Mourners appear in long black, faces arranged to pass any usher. They carry nothing and yet hold themselves as if they have just set a coffin down. Aleksandr, jaws shaven clean, wears a dark suit tailored for confession but meant for a mirror. Behind them, eight men in coats, collars turned up, hands hidden under cloth in a posture that has nothing to do with prayer.

Sergei Vetrov enters last, bald scalp catching candlelight, face mapped by old cuts, neck thick, shoulders built for breaking doors. A small crown sits on his finger with no saint on it. He carries the pistol like habit, a mean economy in every movement.

Gasps break along the pews like gulls rising off a winter harbor. No one stands. The choir falters, then falls hushed.

I take one step and put myself between Valentina and their line. My left arm has stitches and bleeds again under the shirt. I lift my pistol low. I keep my hand open at my side, where her fingers can find it if the red thread fails. She doesn't need to. She may.

Sergei stops at the transept rail as if he has paid for the front row of a play. His eyes walk my shirt to the dark at the shoulder. His mouth curves. He enjoys a man who bleeds and keeps standing because he mistakes endurance for sentiment.

"Volkov," he says, voice soft under the chant, as if he respects a church enough to keep his tone inside it. "Look around. The city has gathered to see a crown placed. Here is my offer. Lay the girl down and walk away from this farce, and I will put Boston in your hand with ceremony. Take the chair. Call it an upgrade."

Men who love power don't whisper because of reverence. They whisper because it travels better in a church.

"You should have come through the narthex," I scoff. "Men who enter from the side have learned bad habits."

He tilts his head. His eyes are broken glass that has forgotten how to reflect. "The door was poorly kept. I could not resist a lesson." His men shift by inches, suppressors like black tapers. One mourner kneels, sets a leather case down, and unzips it as if serving liturgy—magazines, cable ties, gauze, a coil of thin chain—they have brought a portable altar for desecration.

Aleksandr takes two steps forward, chin lifted, eyes bright with borrowed courage. He turns counterfeit tenderness toward Valentina. "Valya," he says, honeyed, stealing the old syllables.

"Speak to me, not to her," I snarl. I pull his gaze with the barrel.

Valentina is a stone on the step, eyes like river-found kopeks, bright where the silt has rubbed away. It steadies my aim better than any drug would.

"Ask him what she hides," Aleksandr calls to the audience, twirling around on his shiny boots. "Ask if he knows what she carries." He looks to the elders, to the staff gathered by the door, to the two girls from the kitchens who pressed themselves into a shadow. He turns back to Valentina, his voice falling into that old coaxing shape of the vowels. "You never loved him, not as you name love. You needed a roof and took the nearest hand."

Valentina doesn't look at him. She looks at me and speaks as if this is our kitchen and there is no one else in the world. "The only man who has ever loved me is the one who spoke a vow. He shed blood to keep it."

The church holds its shape. No one screams. Men who brought their mothers hold those women under their arms and lower them into the space between pew and floor with a grace that would make angels take notes. The kitchen maids hold hands. They have learned to do that from women waiting for men to come home from a winter sea. The priest lays the crowns on the cloth and draws the thin veil over gold and garnet, not hurried, not afraid, a small act that tells the room the rite is under guard.

I read the entry like a map, my mind stitching routes at a soldier's pace. The line that fits runs through the side sacristy that touches the crypt. A bought verger three parishes away, a cousin here with a car, a borrowed key. Shooters dressed as mourners walked in under a Vigil for an aunt whose name sits in the registry on a saint's day. It is inference, but the seams align. He pays well, and he trusts the word "memorial" to soften any usher. Men like him live on clerical error.

I return fire at his shoulder and miss him by a breath, chip a pew, ruin a mercenary's sleeve. Misha is already at the left flank, Sasha at the right, two more inside men peeling the black coats back from the aisle like rotten bark. Our choir has broken off mid-phrase. Then one alto keeps a descant fear cannot touch and holds the note. That thin, brave thread keeps the room from breaking. It seals my decision to outlive this hour for it.

Sergei's men lift their arms and show the metal they smuggled under cloth. They fire low for ankles to herd us. We answer high for wrists to stop hands. An usher I trained two years ago breaks a jaw with the brass finial of a candle pole and then kneels to cross himself for the fact of blood on stone. The chandelier near the south aisle drops one prism and shivers. Its chain holds because the man who climbed to test it yesterday loves his job.

A mourner rushes me with a blade dressed as a candle knife. I catch his wrist and twist. The blade clatters. I drive his face into wood, and he slides to the floor in a slow prayer that ends badly. Someone behind me fires. I feel the round comb my coat hem. Misha shouts once, "Left," a muzzle flashes, a man grunts and goes still behind the pillar.

Another burst, chalk-white plaster powders from the arch. Chips sting my cheek. A stained-glass saint gains a round hole in the palm and throws rubies and cobalt across the floor. Boots drum. Benches scrape. Someone screams a name in Russian. Someone else answers with a roar that makes the lamps tremble on their chains. My shoulder floods with heat where stitches tear. I clamp the arm to my ribs and keep moving.

Sergei fires twice. Stone spits off the altar rail, and he smiles, amused. The choir stall erupts in splinters as another round walks the wood. Smoke climbs into incense until the nave smells like a forge. I pivot and answer with a round to his lackey's knee. Aleksandr's mouth opens in a shocked "O", then he collapses into hot tears. He crawls behind a pew, dragging a red stripe like a ribbon. He sobs, curses, hears himself doing both, and clamps it shut, teeth bared, pride shaking in his jaw. He fumbles for a pistol and finds only a rosary dropped long ago by the old sacristan. He grips that instead and looks suddenly, painfully young.

The mercenary on the right flank kicks a basin, and water leaps across the floor. Candles spit, steam rises, the room smells of old myrrh turned sharp by fight. The air is close and bright and full of fast decisions. Misha shouts a count once, then switches to hand signs. Our men read them and answer with their bodies. "Door," Sasha says and points with his chin.

The side bar begins to close. One of Sergei's men dives and wedges it again with a folded brochure of feast days he stole from the narthex. He grins like a boy who has cheated a parent, and I put a round through his hand. He shrieks. The brochure catches fire where it touches the candle. Sergei steps onto the first rail step as if onto a stage. He doesn't glance down at the glass under his soles. He raises his pistol toward the Gospel as if finishing a thought. I move forward, and the shot finds my shoulder again with a punch that spins me half a step.

The elders begin to chant. The words wash across the pews and settle into the smoke of the room. It gives me permission to do what I came to this house to do. Sergei sees the elders and the chant and the way the candles refuse to lie down. He understands what he has walked into.

"Walk away from her," he says just to me. "Come to the docks. I will sign the *obshchak* into your hands. I will give you Boston and a corridor to New York. You can finish your vows on New Year's Day with anyone you like."

"Anyone I like is already here." I keep my voice level.

He smiles like a gambler who has found a man who refuses the table. He lifts the pistol a fraction and then lowers it, a small admission. "Then we will do it the old way," he says.

From the nave's far corner, a mercenary in black rises with a long rifle he broke down in a choir stall and built again while we bled. He plants his cheek. The barrel seeks a line that leads through the altar toward the aisle where Valentina stands. I see the path, the breath he takes before the squeeze. I move. There is no time for speech. I shoulder into him from the side. The shot sends the thurible stand into the air, where it flips and rings. She doesn't shrink. Her eyes are on mine that don't say thank you. She holds her ground as a daughter of a house that will not fold.

Sirens far off would be a mercy. We have none. The fight narrows to small pieces. Wrist against wrist. Muzzle against arm. Boot against thigh. Knife against belt. We press. They press. A rosary snaps under a heel and scatters beads like hail.

I look for Sergei in the smoke of candles and the churn of bodies. He is backing down the side aisle, resetting lines, men between us, Aleksandr dragging himself with his hand out. Our men hold the doors. The side hinge screams as metal finally remembers it is fallible. Misha puts a shoulder to it, and it sets true.

"Stay with her," I tell Sasha. "No gap."

Sasha nods once and takes his place a half step to Valentina's left, knife low, pistol high, posture like a vow.

"Sergei," I call. "You came into a church. Leave the way cowards leave."

He laughs. "I brought you a chair, and you brought me hymns." He scoffs. "We are at an impasse."

"You mistook hymns," I exhale, "for a lack of knives."

He lifts his pistol toward me in a little salute and winks. He knows he will not take me today. He is too much a merchant to die on a tiled floor when there are invoices to send.

Then the room changes.

A hand touches the pew behind me, and the old wood groans, a sound from thirty years ago, from a winter when a man built a city with favors and blows and the iron belief that vows outlast any ledger. Anatoly has been standing near the back, hands on the pew, ring bright under the lamp. He has watched with a face like law. He has not moved because moving costs him now in a currency none of us can repay.

The elders stop chanting as if a conductor lowered a hand. The men in black glance toward the sound because even men who fear nothing look when a king stands.

Anatoly takes one step into the aisle, then another. His coat hangs hard on his frame. His mouth is set to the line. His hand goes to his chest. A small, precise press over the cross he wears under cloth. His knees touch the pew. He folds into the wood like a man sitting down without a bench. His mouth moves.

I'm at his side in three strides, Sergei forgotten, gun down, Misha with me, Valentina already moving from the rail, Sasha shifting to keep her covered, the sacristan lifting the oil as reflex, the elders reaching and stopping because love needs space and order. I slide an arm behind Anatoly's shoulders and lower him to the pew. His eyes have the clarity of a winter sky. It is six in the evening and very late.

His eyes go winter-clear and kind, finding mine, then lifting to the altar and back, a father's blessing and a general's surrender in one look. His thumb presses a small cross into my sleeve as if sealing a vow.

"Make him better than me," he whispers.

28

VALYA

Smoke clings to the rafters like a hymn that refuses to leave. The saints in the colored glass stare through cracks that were not there an hour ago. Wax pools along the rail in fat tears that harden as the air cools.

Sergei is gone. He took the side passage by the sacristy, where steps drop into stone that remembers older wars. Two of his men lie facedown near a pillar, scarves tangled, boots askew. Aleksandr sits on the floor with his back to a pew, leg tied off with a strip of linen from the vestry, lips bloodless, pride stitched poorly across his face. Our guests stand, sit, lean, refuse to go, argue in low voices, count children with their eyes, touch crosses at their throats, and look at me.

I kneel beside my father.

His rings are cool against my palm. The line between his brows loosens. The small white scar on his cheek, put there by a bottle in a South Boston bar before anyone called him Pakhan, looks delicate now, almost fine. His chest rises, less strong, rises again, then shallower. Heat climbs my eyes. I fix my gaze on the knot of his tie, then on the icon above us, and blink until the salt retreats. He will not see me weep. I hold my face steady for him and keep my cadence even.

The cross under his shirt presses into bone as if metal could hold a sternum together by will. Someone has set the crowns back in their velvet, like children put to bed after a riot. Father Gavril hurries with oil and stole, hand steady, eyes fierce. He is too far. The nave is long and the task heavy for old legs. The prayer will arrive late.

I put my mouth close to my father's ear because friends and enemies are all within three yards, and some words belong to only two people.

"Papa," I say. My voice frays.

His eyes find me through the haze. They sharpen as if some clerk in his soul has opened the file marked "Daughter" and laid it on the desk. He summons a smile, weak as candle-light, and lets it go so he can spend what is left on speech.

"They respect Dmitri. He is a rule they know," he whispers. I must bend to hear him. Air rasps. He spends another phrase anyway. "*You*. It was always you they could not place, your insistence that God and the street can share a table. You wouldn't fold."

I shake my head once because tears choke my throat, and the staff will take their cues from my spine. He speaks again. I lower my head to hear him well. "You know how the chair thinks and how the kitchen forgives."

"You tried to make a new house with vows as scaffolding," I

whisper into his ear, words softened by tears. "They insisted on calling it a museum."

"They said rust," he murmurs and smiles. A cough robs a syllable. He recovers it without apology. "They wouldn't kneel together. So I chose a vow that wouldn't bend to councils. I did not build a cage for him." His gaze shifts toward Dmitri, then back to me. "I opened a door for you into a house where you stand first and the ledgers stand last." The smile reaches his eyes, then pain dulls it. I place my hand flat on his chest.

Oil glints at the edge of my sight. The stole slides over a priest's hands. My father knows it will not arrive in time. He looks past me to the Mother with three stars, the one my grandmother kissed with both hands and a sigh. His mouth shapes a child's prayer. He finishes half. The rest hangs in the air as our vow did a moment before glass sang with bullets. His eyes return to mine. The last of his strength climbs into his gaze and presses a command into me.

"Don't let them sell the altar," he says, eyes on mine, voice soft as snowfall on a winter night. "Don't let them turn love into a show. Keep the roof. Make him better than I was." The words are clean, a thin draw of air, then stillness.

I feel that stillness in my bones like a winter bell.

For a moment, the cathedral narrows to the width of his face and my hand over his. Then sound returns without shouting. The priest reaches us and lays the stole on my father's brow. His eyes shine. He speaks the prayer anyway. I lower my forehead to my father's knuckles as if warmth can be forced back into a hand that commanded storms. It cannot.

I rise. My knees refuse. My house requires. I turn to the room. Everyone is here, all his sons and daughters.

"Light the lamps," I tell a sacristan with ash on his smock. "Bring fresh oil. We will not leave the Gospel under gray. Yelena, fetch clothes, the best ones. Not a thread frayed tonight." My voice sounds like my grandmother when a man from the parish knocked snow on her clean floor. Women who were shaking a minute ago find their tasks.

"Father Gavril," I say softly. He looks at me as if I'm still the child who sounded out the *Tropar* line by line. "He did not make it in time."

"No," he answers. "But he began it, and that counts in heaven." He traces the sign over my father's brow, touches his cross to his lips, then to the hand that will never lift an order again. His eyes return to mine and see what is next. "You have decisions to make."

"I have orders to give," I answer. The tremor becomes current. The current becomes command. It is a wire that suddenly carries the whole city.

I look at the house—elders, brigadiers, cousins, keepers, my men, and my women. Then I look at the censer lying on its side, ash veiling the Gospel like morning frost. I give the words enough rise to reach the back, gentle under the icons.

"No one leaves this cathedral until every candle is upright and every splinter cleared from the rail," I say. "No saint looks on blood by morning. No ash covers scripture at dawn. If you eat at our table, you work at our altar. If not, you eat elsewhere."

A murmur travels that sounds like men remembering they have spines. A woman from the kitchens, hair tied in a scarf my grandmother might have owned, takes a broom. An elder removes his jacket, folds it over a pew, and kneels to gather glass with the gravity of a man receiving communion. A lawyer with theology on his tie rolls his sleeves and carries bodies to the yard with three dock men who know how to lift without theater.

"Misha," I say, and he appears with blood on his knuckles and iron that remembers grief. "Seal the catacombs. Two men at each staircase. Count heads. No heroics in the tunnels."

"Yes," he answers.

"Sasha," I say, and he is there with a knife he has cleaned and holstered because we stand in a church. "Aleksandr lives. Keep him bound. He will be tended, and he will keep silence. Move him to the side parlor, not the sacristy. I will not have politics near the chalice."

He nods, mouth flat, eyes hot, discipline like a furnace that accepts any fuel. "*Da.*" He signals two men to lift Aleksandr. Aleksandr curses under his breath and looks at me as if expecting a farewell. I give him a gaze that holds nothing he can spend.

I lift my eyes to the colored glass. Saint Nicholas breaks into three fractured rivers of blue that still pour light. I move through that light like a bell ringer checking ropes.

"You," I tell a cousin from Worcester, "find Anton in the workshop. He has tin and putty. He will panel the broken window until the glaziers arrive. Tell him to secure the break and protect the icon wood."

"You two, Ilya and Petya," to the boys who run errands and think no one knows their names, "take these blades for wax. Lift first, then cloth. Don't smear a year into the stone."

Dmitri watches and says nothing. Yelena crosses to him and lifts a brow. She already has a tin of clean linen, a bottle of vodka, a vial that smells of calendula. "Pressure will do," she says, calm as a nurse at dawn, placing the vodka in my hand. My fingers remember. I cut his sleeve, flush the wound, fold linen and pack the depth, and hold firm and even. He stands and doesn't flinch. Yelena knots the bandage flat and true, then slips a second wrap to fix the arm against his ribs.

"Hold," she says. He holds. The red eases to a stubborn pulse.

I nip two loose threads from the wrap with Yelena's small scissors, tuck the ends flat, and smooth the cloth once. "Enough for now," I murmur. He doesn't thank me. He doesn't need to. In a single motion, he steps half in front of me without crowding. With him at my side, the cathedral belongs to us again.

The stories return softly. My great-grandfather, in a village easy to miss on a map, kneeling in a church with no floor, only packed earth, holding a candle for a wedding where the priest wore patched sleeves and still brought heaven down. My grandmother crossing herself with dough on her fingers and calling it holy. My mother laughing in a parish hall and silencing two men with one look before a joke could turn to gossip. Anatoly built this altar instead of buying another boat and called it a debt to God that money could not settle. We are not pretty people. We remember what rooms are for.

I go to the iconostasis and lift the fallen chain of the censer. I gather ash with my hands. My lips sting with salt and old smoke. Father Gavril lifts the Gospel. Yelena brings warm water and lemon oil. I hold the cloth while he wipes ash from the cover. The gray lifts, returning the gold. Father Gavril hums a hymn under his breath, a tune that always felt like a road you can walk in the dark and still find the door.

Night claws at the clock and drags it slow. Men carry ladders. Boys carry linens. Women carry hot tea in enamel mugs. Ash leaves by the shovelful. The tile under the rail shines. Candle stubs retire. New wicks stand to attention. The censer hangs straight again and waits.

I stand in the center aisle and feel the house pull itself together like a man after a fight, counting fingers, touching bruises, finding a laugh under the blood. This is what we are when no one is filming. This is the mistake Sergei keeps making. He thinks a house is a ledger and a chair. He doesn't understand that a house is a cathedral and a kitchen and a thousand hands that throw themselves between a knife and a child because a grandmother once said this is the only way to live.

I return to the pew where my father lies. Yelena has straightened him. She has placed his hands over his chest, the father's pose of a man who once knew how to hold. Father Gavril has set a small candle near his right shoulder. The flame stands like a sentinel. I kneel and set my forehead to my father's knuckles. The ring presses my skin. It will press again when I wear it or when I bury it. I don't argue with God. I ask for two things. Courage. Clarity. Tonight, they are the same.

I stand. My cheeks are wet. I wipe them with the back of my hand the way a girl does. I don't replace the tears with a smile. Dmitri waits at the rail. His eyes don't demand anything from me.

"Before sunrise," I say to the room, "the crowns will be polished with a new cloth, the table set for the Vigil, the choir fed with tea and honey."

I find Misha. "Rotate the guard outside. Any man leaving post receives hot soup. Keep lenses turned from the icons." To Sasha, "Watch the inner door and the aisle. Two men on the rail. Keep tongues still near the incense." I turn and let the house hear the line it needs. "This family will meet at dawn standing."

I walk to Dmitri. He meets me halfway.

"Are you steady?" I ask. It is not about pain. It is about resolve.

"Yes," he says.

I hold his gaze and let the gathered see what they came for and did not expect to witness.

"If we are going to be crowned," I tell him, "let it be at dawn. Let them see us bleed and still choose love."

29

DMITRI

Incense and lamp oil hang in the nave, resin-sweet over cold stone. Iron is gone from the rail. Lemon and hot water have done their work, yet the floor keeps a thin memory the way a scar keeps a story. The tin panel that held the broken window through the night is gone. New glass nests in fresh lead, seams still bright from the glazier. Morning pushes through it in bands of color, cobalt on the flagstones, carmine across the rail, gold climbing the pillars. Shadows lattice and lift as the flames move. I touch my shirt once at the shoulder where the bandage rides under cotton, then let my hands fall. The old cross under my collar is cool against skin that still remembers *by honor and pain*.

The vow is older than last night. I read the line at the chapel steps. *To honor her heart above ambition.* That sentence waited for me when I was a boy with empty pockets and a spine built from orders. She stood with *The Book of Vows* open, and I traced the words with her, slow and true, the way a man points to the only door that leads home.

We spoke *practice* then. Now they are not practice and not ornament. The red thread will be tied again, but it has already chosen its work. We will circle the table three times, and the house will hear what my bones know. Vows make this roof hold winter.

They come.

Our people fill the nave from narthex to icons. *This is the Bratva as the city knows it when it stands without masks.* Elders who survived frost and indictments, brigadiers who kept docks moving through lean years and funerals, from Worcester and Providence who still count favors like coins. Cousins from the North Shore with hands scrubbed raw and rings that outlived two regimes. Brighton Beach men in dark coats, union stewards who hold cranes and gates, the keeper of the *obshchak*, soldiers who learned the code in yards and on piers, and quartermasters who can feed a hundred from a single order. Drivers who know which alleys keep secrets. Two bookmen from the archives with lists of saints' days and debts. Our choir fathers who sing and keep time with callused fingers, and the steward with his freckles scrubbed clean and his eyes down because he will not forgive himself for months. The house is present.

Women stand with them, wives with rosaries in their pockets, daughters with candles that don't shake, the kitchen girls in their best skirts, Yelena with a tray of tea for the choir. Chicago's elder stands two pews back, ring turned inward. His gaze is still like a banker who has finally come to a church he cannot price. The families are present. That is the Bratva. Not a rumor but a body, a brotherhood that argues in boardrooms and kneels in chapels, a roof of men and women who know that coin without covenant buys nothing that lasts.

Father Gavril crosses the floor with the stole folded over his arms. He pauses at the Gospel, bows, and sets the book where the ash lay an hour ago. Misha posts by the north aisle with men I trained to move only when movement is needed. Sasha holds the side door with his jaw set and his eyes alive. Katya stands at the pillar under the healed window, soft boots, dark sweater, hair bound back with a strip of black silk, like a surgeon who has decided to honor a rite. I spot Reza and Toma from the community center near the last pew, and with them stand our small allies from that world—grandmothers with headscarves, a parish priest with tired hands, and two veterans of the old regime who laid down their guns and kept their honor. The choir has taken positions to the right, boys and girls and two old men who have sung this service since the harbor cranes were new.

I take my place by the narthex for the betrothal. My coat is on a peg. The black suit is plain and clean, shirt fresh over the bandage, collar sharp. The rings wait on a silver tray by the analogion with the red thread. When I lift my head, I picture Anatoly in the front pew. His absence sits like a presence. I bow to him with breath and with spine, holding my place. Then my eyes fix on the doors.

She enters.

Valentina steps under the arch as if the nave is a field she planted, veil a fraction askew, not from carelessness but from haste born of purpose. Her hair is gathered and fixed with iron and garnet pins, the stones glowing the deep feast day red of vigil lamps, martyrs, and kings. They settle along her brow like small standards, as if the church sanctions this head for its banner.

Red silk moves without drama. A ribbon of the same thread marks her wrist. Honey light catches in the small gold flecks of her eyes and turns them to heated amber. She doesn't look for me. She looks for the altar first. Then she looks at me. Light catches the little cross, her grandmother's crucifix, and sets a clean glint at her throat.

Father Gavril takes our hands and sets them on rings that wait on a silver tray. The choir shapes a *Tropar* no paper program has ever learned to print correctly. He blesses the rings with the sign that knows east and west and above and below. He places her ring, then mine. Three times we exchange them in each other's hands, three times the metal comes and goes, a lesson the city forgot. I hear the soft intake from the pews when the light finds the engraving inside my band, a single word in Church Slavonic, *Roof*. Hers holds three initials only, a family habit older than the house. She knows what she carries.

We cross to the solea for the crowning. The crowns lift from velvet like history waking. They gleam as if nothing scarred them last night. Two elders step forward to bear witness, the *obshchak* keeper with his ledger hand and an old brigadier whose first winters took friends and made him stop gambling. Their palms flatten over the Gospel and the iron key on the analogion. A vow must have witnesses. A house must have a key.

"*Blessed is the Kingdom,*" the priest begins, and the choir answers. The service moves in slow power. We stand where men bled, and we refuse to call it anything else. The prayer that follows names crowns and joy and martyrs, not because the marriage asks for pain but because love in our city is never just a celebration. *It is a stand.*

Father Gavril sets the crowns upon us. The elder with the ledger lifts mine and places it with hands that weighed coin last night and weigh souls now. The old brigadier lowers hers, his fingers certain and gentle, as if fitting a helmet that must protect and not bruise. Red thread lies ready. Yelena lifts it from a silver plate and brings it like an aunt bringing salt to a table. The priest binds our right wrists together with one loop, then a second, then a third, drawn enough to remind each pulse that the other exists. The choir swells. Wax tears down tapers and hardens into memory.

The Gospel is read. The passage is the same as it was for my grandparents when they stood in a village that had no floor, and as it was for those who married in exile over crates in a port office where a priest came in the night. It speaks of Cana and water turned to wine, of a cup shared, of a blessing that arrived when guests had assumed the house had nothing left to give. Tradition doesn't need novelty. It needs fidelity.

We drink from the common cup, sweet and strong and ordinary. She lifts it first, lips to rim, then I. It tastes like bread and courage, like years, like the steady thing that holds when the city shakes underneath. The priest gives us three sips. Mercy can be measured yet abundant.

The dance begins, three circles before the analogion. Father Gavril leads us by the handkerchief, and we follow, left, right, left, the crowns catching light on the third turn and throwing it back in small fires across the faces of men who planned to judge and now find themselves moved in spite of themselves.

We halt. He lifts the crowns from our heads, traces a cross in the air over us, and sets them back on the velvet as if laying down swords. Then he places our joined hands in each other's palms and covers them with his stole. He doesn't give a sermon. The stole slides. The gesture says everything. God covers what we cannot mend or hold.

We turn to each other. It is time for the part no priest can give and no council can refuse.

"To bind our fate to each other, before God and man," I say first. I spoke it last night under tin and grief. I speak it now in a full church with faces that have paid for their seats.

"To bind my fate to his forever," she answers without pause. Her mouth shapes every word like a craftsman fitting a joint that must hold a thousand storms. The house takes them into its bones.

"To honor her heart above ambition," I add, and I feel the heat of my scar under the shirt as if iron remembers heat.

She gives me her own line in reply, voice clear as bells in frost. "To trust him and keep no secrets that could undo us." She looks at me when she says it. Last night held pain and misreading, fear and pride. This morning holds a correction and a promise.

"Let her light guide me through darkness," I say.

"Stand beside him in battle," Valentina closes.

We exchange rings in front of everyone. Her hand is warm and steady. The band slides home with no hesitation. Mine follows. Our joined hands lift for a breath. The red thread touches gold and lies still.

Our house kneels. We always have. We place both knees on the stone. The floor is cold. The chill goes through fabric into bone. Strength is never a posture but a habit. She sets her left hand on the altar rail with fingers open. I set my right hand over hers and feel the pulse in her wrist count out a hope—for her house and the city.

Father Gavril places his palm over our heads. He prays the last prayer that belongs to this rite and also to battlefields and sickrooms. The choir answers with a line that sounds like men who learned to sing in barracks and women who learned to sing in kitchens. The crowns rest. The candle flames rise straight.

We rise.

The word *husband* settles somewhere deeper than my ribs. The word *wife* sits there with it, as armor and balm.

The elders come forward, two only, the right ones. The *obshchak* keeper touches my sleeve with two fingers. "Roof," he says, a single word.

The old brigadier looks at Valentina with a face a granddaughter might trust and says, "Daughter." He turns that last word toward the room. It says the chair belongs to a pair, not a man alone. It says what Anatoly did not have time to finish, we will finish.

The blessing over bread and salt is brief and exact. We touch bread to salt, we share, we are fed. I catch Misha's face in the second row, the line of his mouth never soft and his eyes set to duty as prayer. Katya's face, a small light at the corner of her mouth. Reza, laughter in his eyes and dance in his gait. Yelena touches a kerchief to the edge of one eye and then the other, hands steady, lips moving with a word she keeps for cradle nights. Kostin, I can see, is tracing a slow cross with his thumb, his mouth set as if a missing link is found.

We don't kiss. She gives me her hand, and I give her mine, not fingers alone but palm to palm, pressure that tells a story our people can read.

"*Pakhan and Pakhanessa*," the old brigadier says softly enough to avoid violating the sanctuary with politics, loud enough to ensure the council hears it. This is not power seized. This is a house received with kneeling and with salt.

We turn to the people. All of them. The drivers outside with hot soup. The kitchen women who will not eat until plates are set for those who stood in the nave. The choir boys who will walk home in pairs along streets that will pretend nothing has changed and will be wrong. The Bratva stands for the benediction like parishioners at a Matins that finally warmed their hands. This is the brotherhood as God sees it when candles are lit and lies are hiding.

Sunlight touches the new glass as a blessing. A blade of gold slips through the repaired pane and climbs the nave. It finds the crowns, then the Gospel, then the ring on her hand, then my scar. The old window's saints receive their light through modern lead, and the union holds as if to teach Chicago that restoration is not rust.

I let the moment hold, the hall around the altar like a ship that has taken a blow and found her ballast again. I think of the men who will test us. I think of the women who will hold us. I think of the child who sleeps under her heart like a secret already turning into a charge. I hear Anatoly's last instruction without hearing it. *Don't let them sell the altar.*

She threads her fingers through mine where the red cord still binds and raises our joined hands so every row sees whose hand steadies mine. She looks at the council, then back to me, and inclines her head once, deliberate and calm. We face the room.

The nave holds its breath.

"My rule is not yours to fear," I say. "It is yours to deserve."

30

VALYA

I turn the corner where a sedan used to idle and find it empty. I walk slowly, because a child in my womb turns each step into a count, and because for the first time, the city feels like a room that knows my name. The South End listens to my footsteps. Salt freckles the stoops. Iron rails keep their chill under a passer's palm.

Snow still trims the brownstones like an altar cloth kept for feast days, but daffodils pry up through the city beds and lift their small gold heads. They take the low sun and give it back in little coins of light. My palm finds the curve under my coat. It is early, still a rumor under wool. Warmth spreads, and I smile before I know it. I take in the city's thrum as if it were a hymn learned in winter and sung brighter in spring.

Two longshore stewards lift two fingers in greeting. Another turn brings me to the community center. A boy spots me and calls, "Mama Valya!" before he skips inside. The call runs ahead down the block. Heads turn, smiles open, and greetings rise from doorways like candles catching from one wick to another.

Reza looks up from a copier.

"Welcome home," he says and tries to coax it back to life.

"This machine is beyond forgiveness," I say. "Replace it."

He grins, eyes crinkling, fingers tapping a friendly beat on the copier. "We don't discard the old simply because they age and wobble," he quips, lifting the room with him.

Together, we sort winter coats and job forms, circling the names of mothers who need child care for interviews. It is almost noon when I touch Reza's sleeve and say I need a short break.

I step out toward the corner bakery. Toma is there in the yard, dribbling a ball, his smile intact. He reads my mouth, his nod cheerful. Then he taps his chest twice to sign *with you*. I tap back.

The girl sets out black bread and a tray of poppyseed rolls glazed thin as ice. I look for honey cake and the battered tin of strong black tea. A single loaf waits on the top shelf like a kept promise. Two of our boys warm their hands on paper cups, coats zipped, eyes alert and at ease. There are watchers on this parish corner, but they keep the circle around us now.

I think of Dmitri. He takes the chair and refuses to make it a throne. He asks for the ledgers and reads them line by line. He calls in brigadiers, stevedores, and the man who runs the lot behind the customs shed. The keeper of the *obshchak* comes to a plain table that sets three rules—widows first, no one pays tribute twice, and vows are kept in the open, not only at funerals.

At night, Dmitri walks the docks with Misha. He speaks straight to men who like hard orders, then adds in a low voice that any truck with our mark will carry food and family first until the day of Theophany. Everything else can wait. He calls off guns and calls in debts. It works. Since the Vigil, the river has not given back a name we know.

Sergei is a story told in customs lines and frosted mirrors. He slipped through Logan under a doctored passport built from a dead cousin's file, photo swapped, paperwork greased, and turned up in Hamburg, then nowhere. He will send letters before spring. He cannot hold his tongue when a city refuses him. A man like that mistakes silence for loss.

Aleksandr lives. He sits in a room with a bed, a crucifix, and a window that opens no more than a hand's width. He will leave this coast when the first ships cut the channel. Exile, not execution. That point is mine.

I set terms so mercy doesn't turn into a door left ajar. His accounts are frozen. His phones are gone. The name on his papers is one we issue. One flight, one city, no return, the ban is signed before two elders and the keeper of the *obshchuk*. He checks in each week with a code phrase only we use. If the call fails, the room he left will be the room he sees again. We salt his path with one false detail. If it surfaces, the leak is named.

The elders frown the way men frown when they think mercy is a hole in a fence. I tell them mercy is a lock we choose to use because we intend to sleep and wake in the same house. Dmitri listens, then nods. The decision goes into the book with his mark and mine. We do that now. Both hands for the same pen.

I return to the center, steam from a paper cup warming my fingers. The chalkboard lists homework, soup, and a coat drive. Reza is back at the copier, a smudge of toner on his thumb.

"You have done it." I chuckle.

"A new drum, a careful hand, and it will serve another season." Reza smiles, almost triumphant.

I laugh despite myself. "Order the drum. I will find a careful hand."

I step into the small meeting room. Father Sava waits with a parish magazine that is six months out of date, reading every line as if time were gracious. He rises, sets a sack of rice on the desk, and kisses both my cheeks. On his way out, the old veteran with an old limp taps the radiator, pronounces it sound, and promises chess at six.

An old woman from Dorchester presses a paper icon into my hand, soft as cloth, with edges thinned by coins and shopping lists. "It will hold, *zolotko*," she says. "God likes a stubborn woman." The children don't call me princess now. That word belonged to a city that wanted a pageant. They gather and shout *Mama Valya*.

We are building an empire with screws and soup and a book of names that no longer fear a ledger. I jot three notes for Dmitri on a scrap. *The shelter's old wing needs a new furnace belt. The children need wool mittens, not acrylic. The parish choir needs folders because the spines have split.* I tuck the list into my coat with the knotted ribbon a little girl gave me. The children braid my scarf into ropes and crowns. I tell them a story about a bear who promised to guard a garden and learned to love kale. They boo the bear, then forgive him.

I know the streets from the center to our gate like I know my grandmother's kitchen and refuse a ride back home. This walk is mine. The deli lines its window with jars of pickled tomatoes like small jewels. The barber keeps his chair empty on Wednesdays because his wife lights candles and he sets her table first. A patrol car glides past the corner. The officer lifts two fingers from the wheel, a sign that says present, not hunting.

Under the arch at home, polished brass returns the lamps' light with good manners. The runner holds straight on the stair. The house smells of wax, rosemary, and the faint metal truth of gun oil that no soap erases. Misha passes with a clipboard and two men in new coats. His single nod tells me which rooms now share a code and which doors put on armor. Sasha stands near the north corridor, posture loose, eyes working. Staff ease from their tasks and offer small bows, respect and affection both. I ask after a housemaid's mother who is ninety and keeps forgetting things. I ask the cook about his boy who broke a wrist at the docks, the break clean, the lesson hard. I sent our doctor to the pier flat. Yelena took him after, wrapped him, and watched. The boy sits now by the kitchen door stirring stock with his good hand.

I stop at the chapel. The new glass receives the winter sun. The saint's face has returned, a shade brighter, as if he endured a hard season and learned how to shine. The crowns sleep in their velvet, deep in a good rest. I light a taper for my father and set it beside the one that has burned each night since he lay down. The flame doesn't lean. It stands. I touch brow, chest, shoulder, and shoulder.

Down the stairs, the long hall pulls me toward the fire. Night falls early, the windows holding a blue that tastes clean. The carpet softens steps the way felt under an icon stand does. Voices float from the kitchen, spoons against enamel, talk about spice and deliveries and a cousin who is late again and will be forgiven again because he is the sort who tells a story and makes an old woman laugh until she forgives herself for scolding.

He is where I knew he would be. The library glows, wood warm, spines in foxed reds and browns steady on the shelves. The mantel clock counts like discipline.

Dmitri sits in the chair he pretends is too soft. Exhaustion has not won. He holds our prayer book open on his palm as if it were the first tool he ever learned to use. The other hand holds a glass of tea, throwing steam into the air, a slice of lemon glimmering like a small coin. His vow scars at his wrist and throat rest, pale bars that never lie.

He looks up and doesn't rise in a hurry. He learned not to startle a room that has finally sat down. He sets the tea on the table and keeps a finger in the book to hold the place where we finished last night. The page has a crease in the corner, a small sin my grandmother would forgive because there are worse ways to remember a line.

I cross the rug. I touch the back of his chair, and then, not touching it, I lower myself the way a woman sits at a hearth that belongs to her and to the man who keeps it. He meets my eyes and then opens a blank page. He keeps one finger marking our place and says, "Let us write our own vows now."

31

EPILOGUE

Spring loosens the city by degrees, and the first sign inside our house is not the thaw of the garden but a voice, small and sure, the house has never heard before. My daughter tests her morning, and the corridor answers as if the walls understand rank. I stand in the doorway and count the rise and fall of Valentina's song, Russian softened for a cradle, the tune her grandmother swore could coax a wolf to guard a gate.

She is Natalya, after Valentina's grandmother, her dark hair already certain of itself. Valentina's mouth, full and certain even in sleep, my gray in her eyes when they open, a promise I did not know I needed. A small cross is pinned to her gown, silver bright, the kind of blessing that asks for care.

The nursery is a crossroads of our worlds. Icons look down from the north wall, Nicholas and the Mother with three stars. Fresh roses lift from a glass that belonged to Valentina's mother. A rosary hangs from the frame, beads dull from many hands. Inside the locked cabinet to the left, two handguns sit in leather, magazines on the lower shelf. *Krysha* is not an idea in this room. It is a readiness that doesn't frighten. It steadies. The crib rests between these signs the way a small boat rests between two piers, safe because both exist. On the side table lies our prayer book, the cloth ribbon marked at the last line we chose to add together.

Valentina hums and the baby answers with the smallest sound a person can make. I watch her mouth form the vowels my bones learned in winter and I think of the line on the chapel wall that changed its meaning when the glass broke and we stood anyway. *To honor her heart above ambition.* There was a time when the chair lived in me as an end. Now it lives as a consequence, a tool, a beam among others. I did not lose hunger. I learned its right meaning.

The house has softened around the edges since her birth, not in guard or in rule, only in the way men carry their hands. Katya now stands at the crib with a stethoscope and a clock, the guardian of small hours. Misha walks the side halls with quieter boots. Sasha has learned to turn a corner without announcing it with his jaw. The new nurse from the parish makes tea in a brass pot and leaves it by the samovar with a note that says drink while warm. Respect moves through a building by such small courtesies, and the building remembers.

The priest came last month with oil and salt. He held Natalya in both hands as if presenting a secret to the light. Valentina's veil slipped when she laughed and no one adjusted it because it looked like spring itself had put a hand on her head. He stood as godfather, and Yelena took her place as godmother, steady as ever. Reza stood as witness, not by canon but by trust, the kind of man who shows up before he is asked. The elders formed a clean semicircle and did not shift until the prayer was done.

We keep a new habit. Each morning, one of our former enemies walks the perimeter with one of our oldest men and tells him what the street is whispering. I remember each face the first week, the way contempt tries to hide and cannot. A month later, the contempt is gone, replaced by the professional pride of men who have chosen where to stand. Power did not make that happen. Keeping a promise did.

We told them what the lines would be and we did not move them for convenience. It is a duller story than a coup, and it is why the house breathes.

There are visits to make. I make them now without an entourage meant to impress. Two guards at a distance, one driver in a car that declares nothing, a city map in my head that has replaced routes of flight with routes of service. We stop at the community center where the basketball rims show fresh paint from a long winter and the after-school room smells of paper and wool. A boy who once scuffed my hallway now mops the gym before the girls arrive. He nods, and I see his shoulders lift when I nod back. Respect is a loop. Send it out, and it returns with work done.

We stop at the docks where men who distrust speeches trust a steady hand. I take coffee from a thermos and sit on a crate with the union steward whose nephew we pulled from a pickle he could not win. I don't sell modernization. I tell him the cranes will not sit idle this summer and mean it. He tells me which new foreman counts without stealing. When we stand, his palm rests on the crate in a way that says two spines have agreed to hold the same roof.

At noon, I meet the young harbor master who watched our winter with the eyes of a man who doesn't wish to be famous. We speak the language of schedules and manifests and men. He asks once if Pascha, the Orthodox Easter, will delay unloading. I answer that the Vigil will hold and the cranes will move, both, since love and work don't sit on different benches in our house. He tries the answer, finds he can say yes to it. The city feels less brittle.

There is still a night each month when I put on a dark coat and the street becomes what it was for me at fifteen, a place to learn where fear lives and what it feeds on. We pass the corner where an old debt taught me that humiliation is a currency men spend when they have nothing else in their pockets. I don't stop there. I turn left and enter a basement where four men sit with tea glasses and a ledger. I take out a pen and sign the page that cancels a debt a widow did not incur. I tell the man who created it he has a week to leave my city quietly. He leaves that night. It is not fireworks. It is a vow, cashed.

Valentina keeps her own rounds. The kitchens know her steps. The parish knows her hand on the candle box. She walks the schoolyard behind the center with a stroller and shows the girls how to lace a boot for speed and for steadiness. She sits with the ledgers that track our favors, the ones that carry no dollar sign, and refuses any line that trades dignity for publicity. We argue twice in a week about an invitation that would have put our faces on paper. She wins because she is right.

The first lilies push through the narrow bed along the chapel walk, and the house notices how everyone stands a little taller. On the morning of Natalya's forty days, we bring her to the cathedral nave. She cries once, the small, outraged sound of a sovereign whose bath ran cold.

Valentina lifts her higher, and the priest smiles. He traces the cross on brow, mouth, chest, and tiny hands. He asks for her name. The church answers with us as one voice.

Afterward, in the side room with honey and bread, I watch Valentina laugh with the women who taught her to braid dough. I watch the men make space for the stroller without staring. This is how a rule reshapes a house. Again and again.

Word travels that our winter has ended, and that those who worsened it have fled or been found. The city will always raise another man who calls himself modern. He will arrive in a clean coat and say cost and synergy. He will learn that a roof built on vows doesn't leak for a consultant's plan. If reason fails him, consequence will teach him. I wait for him where the altar meets the door.

I carry the memory of smoke off cathedral stone in every suit pocket. It keeps my spine from bending when an easy bend would buy a soft week. Valentina keeps her grand-mother's scarf folded in her bag. When she ties it for kitchen work, ledgers begin to speak of hospitality as strategy.

Respect has substance. You can measure it when a room stills for a voice that has never lied. You can measure it when a foreman pockets his phone because the person in front of him deserves the whole of his attention. It buys security that money cannot. We have it now. We did not purchase it. We kept faith, and respect accrued.

There are nights when the baby will not sleep and the corridor turns into a pilgrim road. I walk it with her on my shoulder and lend her my step and low murmur instead of song. Valentina laughs from the doorway, hair loose, feet bare on tile that remembers winter and forgives it. Marriage becomes a choreography of such exchanges, unremarkable to those who have loved well, miraculous to those who have not seen it done.

I'm done hunting crowns. It arrives each morning in the same places. In my wife's eyes when her palm rests on our daughter's crown. In the steward's mark beneath a policy he once believed he wouldn't outlast. In the priest's small nod as he crosses the court. In the slight bow of the woman who runs a kitchen that feeds a street and trusts we will keep her doors unharmed.

The vow line returns without effort. *Let her light guide me through darkness.* I once treated darkness as an enemy to conquer. It was only a room waiting for the right candle. After that, the path arranged itself.

By late spring, we test a rule we wrote in snow. We open the chapel to anyone who must lay down a truth too heavy to carry alone. They come. Not to confess to us, but to place a word where it will not be traded. A dock man who drank through Lent and wants another chance. A girl who refuses a ring from a man who thinks hands exist for applause. A mother who needs work that ends at three so she can meet the bus. The house listens. The house answers. We are not saints. We are a shelter. Shelter is enough if it doesn't leak.

The last light of a long evening rests along the cloister the way wine rests in the base of a glass. Valentina stands at the window with Natalya asleep along her forearm, her cheek to our child's soft crown. I come in with river on my coat and the clean bite of spring in the wool.

"Do you remember the first time you stood in the chapel and chose not to speak?" I ask.

She smiles without turning. "I was measuring whether my voice would remain mine."

"It does," I say.

"It is ours," she answers. "The way a song belongs to the two who sing it and to the room that learns the tune."

We sit. She places Natalya in my arms, and the child settles with a small, satisfied sound, like an elder deciding to trust sleep once more. I look at that mouth that is her mother's and the pale lashes that catch the last gold, and I feel the vow pass through me again like hearth warmth, steady as a kept promise.

Weeks pass, and our rule shows itself the way a coastline shows itself to a sailor. Not by speeches, but by a harbor that feels known.

Elders arrive by schedule, books stay clean. Boys who thought a gun was a passport take a broom, a wage, a foreman who expects them at seven and gives them a reason to come. Men who miss fireworks find other rooms. The city doesn't fall silent. It steadies. Victory, when it is not performing, looks ordinary. A day with no headline.

I carry Natalya home and lay her between the icon and rose. Her fingers open and close in sleep. I touch the prayer book where our ribbon holds the old line. Then I find Valentina on the balcony. We stand with the city at our feet. She leans into my shoulder.

I look at her. I give the truth its simplest form.

"I'm not the Pakhan because I rule. I'm the Pakhan because I chose you. And you chose me."

She watches me, the Pakhanessa, with a smile that knows winter and spring. I hold her gaze.

"We did not only make vows," I say. "We became them."

ALSO BY AVA GRAY

CONTEMPORARY ROMANCE
Bratva Christmas Vows Series

The Bratva's Christmas Bump

Bound by the Christmas Vows

THE DUBININ BRATVA Series

Captive Vows

Forgotten Vows

Shattered Vows

A NEW YORK Criminal Empire Series

The Irish Redemption

The Russian Retribution

The Italian Reckoning

The Celtic Resolution

The Criminal Redemption

MAFIA KINGPINS SERIES

His to Own

His to Protect

His to Win

His to Possess

His to Claim

THE VALKOV BRATVA Series

Stolen by the Bratva

Kept by the Bratva

Captured by the Bratva

Captivated by the Bratva

Trapped by the Bratva

FESTIVE FLAMES SERIES

Silver Hills' Christmas Miracle

Holly, Jolly, and Oh So Naughty

The Christmas Eve Delivery

Valentine's with the Silver Fox

HAREM HEARTS SERIES

3 SEAL Daddies for Christmas

Small Town Sparks

Her Protector Daddies

Her Alpha Bosses

The Mafia's Surprise Gift

THE BILLIONAIRE MAFIA Series

Knocked Up by the Mafia

Stolen by the Mafia

Claimed by the Mafia

Arranged by the Mafia

Charmed by the Mafia

ALPHA BILLIONAIRE SERIES

Secret Baby with Brother's Best Friend

Just Pretending

Loving The One I Should Hate

Billionaire and the Barista

Coming Home

Doctor Daddy

Baby Surprise

A Fake Fiancée for Christmas

Hot Mess

Love to Hate You - The Beckett Billionaires

Just Another Chance - The Beckett Billionaires

Valentine's Day Proposal

The Wrong Choice - Difficult Choices

The Right Choice - Difficult Choices

SEALed by a Kiss

The Boss's Unexpected Surprise

Twins for the Playboy

When We Meet Again

The Rules We Break

Secret Baby with my Boss's Brother

Frosty Beginnings

Silver Fox Billionaire

Taken by the Major

Daddy's Unexpected Gift

Off Limits

Boss's Baby Surprise

CEO's Baby Scandal

Scandalous Whispers

PLAYING WITH TROUBLE SERIES:

Chasing What's Mine

Claiming What's Mine

Protecting What's Mine

Saving What's Mine

THE BECKETT BILLIONAIRES SERIES:

Love to Hate You

Just Another Chance

STANDALONE'S:

Ruthless Love

The Best Friend Affair

PARANORMAL ROMANCE

MAPLE LAKE SHIFTERS SERIES:

Omega Vanished

Omega Exiled

Omega Coveted

Omega Bonded

EVERTON FALLS MATED LOVE SERIES:

The Alpha's Mate

The Wolf's Wild Mate

Saving His Mate

Fighting For His Mate

DRAGONS OF LAS VEGAS SERIES:

Thin Ice

Silver Lining

A Spark in the Dark

Fire & Ice

Dragons of Las Vegas Boxed Set (The Complete Series)

STANDALONE'S:

Fiery Kiss

Wild Fate

Printed in Dunstable, United Kingdom

76076103R00170